LIFE SUCKS AFTER YOU DIE

Twice Bitten: Book One

CRYSTAL-RAIN LOVE

ACKNOWLEDGMENTS

Thanks to Christle Gray for all the "You Can Do It"'s.

ONE

Life sucked. To say I was feeling a little pessimistic as I sat at the bar nursing a shot of whatever the bald guy seven stools down had ordered for me was an understatement. I had no life, no man waiting for me at home, and was just barely holding on to my job.

So yep, I was getting drunk. Maybe I'd get so drunk I'd go home with Mr. No-Name at the other end of the bar and forget myself for a few hours. Then I could pass out in his bed and by the time I woke in the morning I'd feel so bad about sleeping with him, I'd forget everything else that sucked about my life.

It was a plan. A bad plan, but a plan nonetheless. Besides, it seemed bad plans were the only ones I made. Why stop now?

I looked down the bar at the man who'd bought my last drink. He was grinning at me with that predatory look in his eye, the one that said he knew I was too far gone to refuse. It was all a done deal for him.

He was tall, probably; it was hard to be definite about someone's height while they were sitting. He had a strip of hair winding around his head, just over his ears, and even that was nearly gone. Why didn't men just shave it off

1

when it started to go? The fact that it bothered me meant I wasn't drunk enough. Wasn't everyone supposed to look good when you were truly plastered?

"Another," I said as I tapped my shot glass on the bar, but the request came out more like "Anuh-na-zer."

The bartender peered at me. He was a big man, tall and broad-shouldered with dark hair cut short and just a shadow of a beard. I thought he was handsome until he shook his head at me. "No, ma'am. You've had enough. I can't serve you anymore."

Jerk.

"I'm fine," I whined. "Jush one more."

The bartender shook his head again. "Your speech is slurred and I'm not even going to tell you what you look like."

"I'm ugly?" I pouted and could feel my eyes burning with waiting tears.

"No, ma'am, you're very pretty. You just look as drunk as you sound, which means I have to stop serving you."

I crooked my finger at him, motioning for him to lean forward. He did, and I caught the scent of his cologne. It was warm and woodsy and made me think of my daddy, God rest his soul. The feeling of loss made me want to get drunk even more.

"You see that guy down there?"

He directed his gaze toward the other end of the bar where the balding guy sat, and nodded.

"He bought me thisss drink. That means I's gotta sleep wiz him."

The bartender's eyes narrowed. "You don't have to sleep with any man just because he buys you a drink."

"But Gina would."

"Who's Gina?"

"Gina. You know, Gina. Fun Gina. Big boobs, lozza hair. Blonde. Ezerybody loves a blonde. I should be blonde. I need some dioxide, and then I'll be blonde and pretty too." I twirled a lock of boring brown hair around my finger.

"You mean peroxide?" His mouth turned up into a cute little smirk.

"Yeah, yeah, oxicide."

Man, I was feeling woozy all of a sudden. Maybe I *was* plastered. I looked down at the man again, and he still didn't do it for me.

"Damn. How muzz do I hafta drink to make that guy look good?"

The bartender laughed, bringing my attention back to him. "I think what you need is a cab ride home, then you can sleep this night off, and whatever problems brought you here."

I shook my head. "Gina's coming."

"Gina is your friend?"

"Yesss, she's s'posed to be here."

"When is she supposed to be here?"

"Ten."

He looked at the round clock hanging over the bar. "That was two hours ago, darlin'. I don't think your friend is coming."

"She's coming. She said it."

"Well, why don't you drink some coffee until she gets here?"

I attempted to nod my head and proceeded to slide off the barstool. Two hands caught me around the waist, and I leaned back against a hard body.

"I got her," a deep voice purred across my cheek. "Bring us over some coffees. Strong."

I felt myself being led away from the bar, supported on the arm of a stranger, a stranger who smelled good, like midnight rain. I inhaled deeply, discovering his scent helped clear my head. Why was I purposely getting drunk? Did I really need to add more mistakes to my long list?

"Here you go," his deep, rich voice said as he helped me to sit in one of the booths near the rear wall of the bar.

I raised my head to look at him and gasped. He had the

bluest eyes I'd ever seen. My gaze stayed glued to his while he rounded the small table to sit opposite me in the booth.

His hair was black, not deep brown, but truly black. So black I could see purplish blue highlights. It was a color which would have made most people look washed out, but he had a deep, bronzed tan, which was a true gold. There was no way that color came out of a bottle. His long hair was pulled back into a low ponytail, showing off his chiseled jaw, his straight nose, and kissable lips, the bottom one slightly fuller than the top.

His black leather jacket covered a black button-down shirt. Both were unbuttoned enough to show the hint of a very muscular chest. He was still lean, but noticeably strong.

He had Bad Boy written all over him.

"Who are you?"

"Rider," he answered. "What's your name?"

I thought about it, thought about giving him some cutesy, fake name like Candy Cane or Taffy Apple, then I was pulled into those eyes of deep sapphire. They told me he wouldn't hurt me, and I believed them. Don't ask me why, because all men have ever done is hurt me, but I knew he wouldn't.

"Danni Keller," I answered, my voice barely above a whisper.

"Why, Danni Keller, are you trying to drink away your sorrows?"

"I heard it works."

Our coffee came, and he took both cups from the waitress, rewarding the brunette with a wink and a smile. She blushed down to her toes and I couldn't blame her. He might look like trouble, but Rider was definitely doable.

"It doesn't work," he said, sliding both cups of hot liquid in front of me. "It just delays the inevitable."

"Aren't you drinking?"

"No," he answered. "I don't drink coffee. You,

however, need it."

I picked up one of the mugs and blew on it. It was still hot enough for steam to rise from the top.

"Hey! This one is mine," the balding man from the bar said, approaching our booth.

"Not this one," Rider said calmly, facing the man. His face showed nothing. No fear, as though he knew he could take the heavier man, and no surprise, like he knew the man would come to confront him.

"She's mine, Rider."

I nearly choked on the coffee I'd sipped. "You two know each other?"

"Unfortunately," Rider said, never taking his gaze off the man standing over him. "If I were you, Barnaby, I'd walk away and pretend you never saw her."

"Why don't you make me take that walk?"

"Gladly," Rider said, rising to a stand. "Stay here, Danni. Don't leave with anyone."

I started to speak, but found my head swam with the effort. I simply nodded and watched the two men walk away, exiting the bar through the back door.

Two men were going to fight over me, and one of them was pretty hot. Wow! Maybe it was childish, but I couldn't help getting a little thrill out of it. Men had never fought over me before. I'd always been the one fighting for them, and losing miserably.

I'd have a better chance if I had the right ammo. I glanced down at my meager chest in disdain. Twenty-eight years old and I had yet to hit puberty. Oh, sure, I'd had heavier women tell me I was so lucky to have such a little body, but men just didn't want to ogle a pair of 34As. There just wasn't enough grippability to them, I guess.

Oh, well. It was a problem which was going to be rectified soon. I had an appointment the following week to have them enlarged. I was going to walk into the doctor's office with the body of a twelve-year-old, and walk out looking like Pamela Anderson's stunt double.

Well, except for the hair. I twirled a strand of the murky brown mess around my index finger, considering bleaching it. Then I remembered seventh grade, when I had tried to bleach my hair, and it had turned out horrible. Bright, orange, *horrible*.

What was wrong with me? I glanced around the bar at all the miserable saps lurking around. A few greasy guys leered at me as if I were a small, frail bird, and they were the great big cats ready to pounce. *Yuck.*

I drained the first cup of coffee I'd been offered, letting the warm brew help clear out the fog which was my mind. Damn Gina. One day I'd learn she would always get me in trouble. She was supposed to be at the bar with me. She said we'd have a few beers, meet some guys, and forget all about Dexter Prince. My boss.

Was it stupid to have a childish fantasy about marrying your boss? Probably. Did the knowledge of that help me stop drooling over the man? Nope.

I'd started working at Prince Advertising straight out of college, actually interned there beforehand, long before the Prince family bought out the original company. Dex had taken over the Kentucky office two years ago and had yet to truly notice me. He went through women like people went through paper towels, but never had he asked me on a date. Or back to his place for casual sex. I'd settle for either. I just wanted a chance.

Surely, that wasn't too desperate. And if it was, so what? I was twenty-eight years old and had only had sexual intercourse with one guy, one exceedingly disappointing guy. I was the only woman I knew of who'd had sex with her geeky lab partner just to say she'd had the experience.

What was taking Rider so long? I looked around the bar, feeling stranger by the minute. Something was wrong. I had that feeling you get on Christmas morning when you wake up and you know Santa has come, but it wasn't a good feeling. It was like I knew somebody was coming, and my body was excited about it, all nervous and jittery, but instead of happiness, I was overcome with a cold, chilling fear.

No more alcohol for me. The stuff was turning me into a spaz.

I took a drink from the second cup of coffee, letting its warmth chase away the chill, but once I swallowed, the cold was back. Damn.

"Excuse me, miss?"

I looked up into eyes the color of an inky midnight. The man looming above me was tall, muscular, and blond. Not a fake blond, but that deep, golden blond that only comes by way of genetics. In the right light, it probably looked as though it were spun of pure gold. I couldn't tell how long it was from this angle because it was pulled back into a low ponytail.

What was it with the guys with the long ponytails? Rider, this guy... even the balding guy had his last remaining hairs pulled back into a ponytail, or a rattail, depending how you looked at it.

I shook my head, clearing my mind. "Yes?"

"The bartender called. He said you needed a ride home."

I looked for the bartender and found him engrossed in conversation with a big-breasted blonde. Figures.

"Miss?"

"Yeah, um, I'm sorry. I didn't know he'd called for a cab."

"Shall we go?"

I turned toward the back door of the club, wondering if Rider was all right. He had, after all, gotten into a confrontation with a man over me.

"Miss?"

"Yeah, um, I need to wait for someone."

"Who? The bartender said you were alone."

"A friend. I... I, uh, just met him. He'll be right back."

The blond arched an eyebrow, then glanced around the bar. "Do you really want to go home with any of these guys, ma'am? I mean, it's none of my business, but I think you're classier than that."

An icy chill ran up my spine and I shivered, wrapping my arms around myself. My blazer didn't seem to help me stay warm.

"Are you cold?"

I nodded, feeling the onset of another shiver. It was nearly June, and I didn't seem to sit directly under any air conditioning vents. Why was I freezing?

The man leaned over the table, looking intensely at my two cups of coffee. He picked up the cup, which still held the liquid, and sniffed it, his eyes widening just the slightest bit before shaking his head.

"Are you waiting on the guy who ordered you these drinks?" he asked, setting the mug back down on the table.

"Yes."

"Let's go," he said, his tone firm. "Those are laced with a date rape drug. It makes you cold and soon you'll be hallucinating. After that…" He shrugged. "You don't want to be anywhere near this guy when the effects start to set in."

My mouth fell open, not wanting to believe what I was hearing. Rider had seemed like such a decent guy… although he did look like a Bad Boy. Apparently, he was a very bad boy. Damn it. Would I ever learn?

"Come on. We need to hurry."

The driver held his hand out to me and I took it, sighing as warmth crept from it to chase away the bitter cold in my fingers. I didn't know what was in that coffee, but the room felt arctic.

"What's your name?" I asked, letting the man lead me toward the front door of the bar.

"Ryan."

He opened the door and let me precede him out. Very gentleman-like. I looked at him again. He was wearing a nice, dark blue silk dress shirt and dark gray slacks. His black shoes were buffed to a sparkling shine, and the overall effect was very nice. A little too nice. I'd never seen a cabbie dress so nicely. He was handsome. Movie-star handsome. Maybe he was just driving until his acting career took off. Of course, if he was an actor-wannabe, he'd have better luck in New York than Kentucky.

I shook my head, shaking the thoughts out with it. Why was I trying to figure the guy's life out? I needed to take care of mine, and that meant getting my butt out of there. Maybe I should see a doctor, seeing as how I'd swallowed down a whole cup of who-knew-what.

"Well, thank you, Ryan, for saving me."

"Thank you," he said, a dark gleam in his eyes. "The pleasure will be all mine."

I started to ask what he was talking about, but my head spun, and then I was on my knees. I tried to focus, but the surrounding buildings kept spinning, dizzying me with their movements.

I felt myself being lifted into the air, felt a terrible coldness wash over my body. It felt like I was enclosed in a block of ice, and my teeth chattered from the bitter cold. I swore I could feel an arctic wind blowing around me.

I was moving. I tried to see where, but I couldn't focus. Everything was a red haze. I was being carried, I realized as my head fell back, carried by Ryan. Had I passed out? My stomach churned, and I knew I was going to be sick.

"I'm gonna puke," I said, feeling myself being lowered to the ground.

Something hard was beneath me, and to my back. I was outside. I could hear the sounds of traffic far away.

"You're going to be fine," Ryan said. "I'm going to take away all your troubles."

I opened my eyes and finally could see, although the image was blurry. Ryan kneeled before me, watching me intensely with red eyes. It looked like two little bonfires were burning in his pupils.

"Your eyes are on fire," I whispered, trying to comprehend what I was seeing. I should have been afraid, terrified. I should have been screaming. Instead, I found myself drawn to him, drawn to the fire inside him. If I could make it there, maybe I could find warmth.

"The hallucinations have begun," he said, his smile slightly menacing, or maybe it just seemed that way. "You will be fine as long as you stay away from Rider."

Ah, of course, I thought. The hallucinations he'd warned me about because Rider had ordered me a couple of spiked coffees. Rider… Wait a minute.

"How do you know his name?"

Ryan smiled, if you could call a gesture with no humor a smile. His lips drew back, revealing two long teeth at the corners of his mouth, like the teeth of a saber-tooth tiger. They were sharp and pointed, curving inward as they continued to grow from his mouth.

"My, Grandma, what big teeth you have," I murmured, mesmerized by what I was seeing.

"Hallucinations," he said, managing to speak with those big teeth.

That was when I started to laugh, a full laugh-your-ass-off laugh. I don't know why I laughed, because it wasn't a funny situation. I was in an alley somewhere, about to be eaten.

No, no, I thought. Hallucinations. It was all in my mind.

"That's right," Ryan said. "It's all in your mind."

"How do you know what I'm thinking?" I asked, trying to close my eyes against his, but I couldn't manage the task.

"Because you are mine," he said. "The fragrance of your blood has called me."

I burst out laughing, unable to control myself. It wasn't until the tears streamed down my face that I realized I wasn't laughing from humor. I was hysterical. Something terrible was about to happen and although my head was screaming for me to run, my body couldn't follow its command. I was too enthralled by the fire in

Ryan's eyes. I knew if it touched me, I would burn to a cinder, but there was nothing I wanted more than to feel that heat.

His face came closer, saliva dripping from those long, strange teeth, and I continued to cry. My brain ordered me to run, fight, do something, but my heart said no. I wanted to be consumed by that inferno, to burn from the inside out.

I felt a sharp pain in my neck, and after that, a blast of indescribable pleasure. It jolted through my body, racing through my veins like hot liquid, shooting out sparks of ecstasy.

It felt so good I cried, cried because somehow I knew it would be the death of me.

I heard a deep growl and felt Ryan being ripped away from my body. Air hit the raw wound he'd left in my neck, burning the tender flesh. I winced in pain, not pain from the wound, but from his departure. The departure of ecstasy he'd sent coursing through my entire body.

I watched as he and another man rolled on the ground. They stood to face off against each other and I could make out Ryan's opponent. It was Rider. He was covered in blood, and I couldn't tell whether or not it was his. His eyes glowed yellow, and some form of energy seemed to cloak him.

I closed my eyes and slumped to the ground, no longer caring about the fight. Rider had drugged me, the effects of which I still seemed to suffer. Ryan had… I don't know what Ryan had done, but I was sure it wasn't very nice.

Let them beat each other to a pulp.

I wanted to go home. I wanted a do-over. If I could just get safely home to my bed, I would forget this night had ever happened. I would never drink again, never count on Gina to actually be there for me. I would work harder, get Dex Prince's attention and keep it. I wouldn't care that my mother had never thought I was pretty, that I was never good enough. I'd forget it all if I could just go home.

"Danni!"

I was jerked upward into a sitting position. I opened my eyes and saw Rider before me, his eyes back to their normal piercing blue color.

"Get away from me." I tried to push at him, but my arms refused to move.

"I can't. Damn it, I told you not to leave with anyone!"

"You drugged me."

"No!" He growled, his eyes darkening. "We don't have time for this. He almost succeeded in killing you. You must choose now, Danni."

"Choose?"

"I can bring you back, but you must choose."

"Bring me back from where?"

"Death. You're already gone. It just hasn't set in yet."

I tried to breathe, but found I couldn't. My body was limp, my mind cloudy. I just wanted to cry.

"Choose, Danni. Choose now. Life or death."

"Life," I whispered, with hardly enough energy to form the word.

He ducked his head, and I felt pressure against my neck, the opposite side from where Ryan had hurt me. I didn't feel any pain. It was as though all of my nerve endings were dead.

He straightened back up, and his lips were a deep red in the moonlight. I felt myself being pulled into a black hole, a hole I knew I'd never escape from if I tumbled inside. I struggled to watch him, but I couldn't keep my eyes open.

Something was against my lips. Warm liquid slid through my open mouth, rolling along my tongue. I instinctively swallowed the coppery-tasting substance, then jerked my head away with what little energy I had left.

"No more drugs," I whispered, my voice shaking in fear. What was he trying to do to me?

"No drugs," he said. "Medicine. Take it and heal."

It was against my mouth again. I weighed my options. I was so weak I could barely move. I had no idea where I was at or how I was getting home. Hell, I might die. I could trust him and drink the stuff, possibly dying, or I could lie down and definitely die.

I decided possibly was better than definitely when it came to dying.

I opened my mouth and let him pour the thick, warm substance into it, swallowing as my mouth filled.

Eventually, he took it away, and I felt myself being picked up. I opened my eyes to see him gazing down at me, holding me in his arms. I struggled against his hold, remembering he had drugged me earlier.

"Stop it, Danni. You have a long, hard couple of days ahead of you. Get some rest."

As if on cue, I closed my eyes and felt sleep take me.

TWO

My mouth was so dry it hurt. A gnawing hunger ripped through my body, bending it like a bow. Too much pain. I struggled to cry out, but couldn't make a sound.

"I've got you," a familiar voice said as hands slid around my waist, pulling me back against a hard wall of flesh.

I tilted my head back, opening my eyes to take in the beautiful, deep blue orbs studying me. I tried again for words, but they wouldn't form. I had no voice.

"Rest," he whispered. "Drink and rest."

There was a dark glass before my lips. I drank from it, having no clue what was in it, but damn, I was thirsty, and craving... something.

"Rest, beautiful," he whispered against my temple, pulling me back so I lay with my back against his chest, his body wrapped around mine, as if to protect me.

I managed to keep my eyes open long enough to realize I was in my bed, alone with a stranger, a man who'd drugged me.

Rider was still there when I woke again, my fingers

digging into the mattress beneath me. He held me tightly from behind, rocking with me as I rode out wave after wave of pain. It tore through me from head to toe, like liquid fire flowing through my veins, charring everything in its path.

Something was in my mouth, I realized, as I tried to scream through the agony, but all I managed were small sounds of pain. It was cloth, and it was soaked. Something coppery seeped into my mouth when I bit down against it. I thought I was tasting my own blood, thought maybe I'd busted my lip or something, then I recalled the glass with the same taste to its contents.

What the hell?

I tried to buck, to throw Rider off of me, but he remained like an unmovable statue behind me, securing me to my bed, holding me prisoner in my own bedroom.

"No, Danni, no. It's the only way you'll make it through this."

Make it through what? I wanted to ask. What had he done to me? And what had I done to deserve it? Most women got drunk and slept with a loser. I allowed myself to get drunk one frigging time, and I was at the mercy of a psycho.

I tried to scream, the action causing me to taste more of what was on the soaked rag—blood. I tried not to swallow, but couldn't do it. To my disgust, I liked the taste of the blood. It fed the hunger roiling in my stomach.

I was going to puke. I was going to puke and choke to death on my own bile, with this gag in my mouth. Or maybe if he saw me gagging, maybe Rider would take the gag off and I could scream for help. Someone in my apartment building would hear me.

I started gagging, helping along the vomit threatening to rise.

"No, Danni," Rider said against my temple as he squeezed his hand along the back of my neck.

I don't know what he did, but I faded fast.

The next time I woke, the sheets were soaked, and I shivered from the feel of my sweat chilling against my skin. I was wrapped in blankets, being rocked in Rider's arms. I didn't know whether to cry, scream, or vomit. Maybe I'd do all three.

"You're halfway there," Rider said, his voice soothing.

"Halfway where?" I asked, and it was as though speaking opened up a door to a pain-inducing hunger.

My body arched away from his, and that was when I noticed my nudity. Maybe most women would have been too overcome with the pain to worry about the nude thing, but most women didn't have my insecurities. Heck, most women had breasts worth baring.

I pulled the wet sheet over my body and tried to escape Rider's hold, but his arms were like steel bands. For such a slender guy, he was strong. Then again, I was only a whopping 120 pounds, held together on a five-foot-three-inch frame. You didn't have to be that big to hold me down.

I'd been out like a light for who knew how long, I was naked, and my body ached. Not good signs. "Is this your first time, or are you a serial rapist?"

"I undressed you because your clothing was sweat-soaked. It's not good for you to lie in wet clothes."

"It's not good for me to lie on a stranger either." I turned my head as far as he'd allow, and saw his bare chest. It was a nice chest, just the right amount of muscle tone to his slim, athletic build.

What the hell? I had probably been sexually assaulted by the guy and I was checking out the goods.

I lowered my eyes slowly, fearing the worst, but he still had pants on. "You're not naked."

A dark eyebrow arched, followed by a grin. "Would you prefer it if I was?"

"No."

I attempted to give him a good, testicle-shrinking glare, but my body chose that moment to convulse.

"Shit. This is the worst of it." He tightened his hold on me, gripping me around the waist and neck, trying to keep me from flopping all over the place like a fish out of water. "Hang in there, Danni. Ride it out."

I wanted to ask if I had any other choice, but I shook too hard to speak, not to mention sharp stabs of pain pierced my body like a thousand knife wounds. The pain tore through me like a chainsaw and I had to look down to make sure I wasn't being literally torn apart.

Rider's hand slid over my mouth just before I opened it to scream, muffling the sound. I felt my fingers sinking into the mattress, and I bit down into Rider's hand, breaking through the skin of his fingers.

He didn't even cry out, just held me tighter as I greedily sucked on his fingers, letting his blood flow over my tongue. I knew what I was doing. I knew it was blood being swallowed down my throat, but I didn't gag. In fact, I wanted more.

"That's a girl, Danni. It'll help ease the pain."

I didn't question him. He was right. I could feel the pain lessening as I slurped the coppery nectar from his fingers, chugging it down until the flow became annoyingly slow. I needed more… more than blood.

I twisted my head around, able to do so now because he'd loosened his grip on me when the convulsions subsided, and licked his neck, tasting the salty sweat glistening there. It was like an appetizer before the main course, which was beating away beneath that bronze skin.

"You want more?"

I nodded.

He offered me a wrist. I shook my head, then angled it toward his neck again, opening my mouth wide.

"No, Danni!" He forced my head away, placing his wrist against my mouth. "Take the wrist."

"I want more," I growled, surprising myself with the

strange sound of my voice. It was nearly as deep as a man's.

"Danni, no."

"Yesss," I hissed, and struggled to break free of his hold.

I wanted the blood pulsating through the veins at his throat. I wanted to rip it out of him while he was inside me, humping away his last moments of life, and I wanted to be riding him like a bull the moment he died.

The thoughts alone should have stopped me. He was a bad guy. He'd kidnapped me, drugged me… who knew what he did to me during the blackouts I kept suffering… but he was a man. And I wanted to kill him. Not by gunshot, or blunt trauma…

I wanted to screw him to death.

"Eliza! Nannette!" Rider yelled as I tried to snap at his throat.

I felt pain in my gums so intense, I feared they were cracking open. Saliva poured from my mouth, thick and gooey.

I heard footsteps running toward us and knew I didn't have much time. Someone was coming to help Rider, someone was going to keep me from killing him. Part of me begged them to hurry, but another part of me, a part dark and newly born, cursed them.

My bedroom door swung open and two women stood in the arch, gasping. One was a tall, pale, willowy blond, dressed in a tight, white T-shirt and faded jeans. The other was a shorter, slender, chocolate-skinned woman with hair shaved down to her scalp. She wore black from neck to toe.

"Her eyes!" They said in unison.

"She doesn't have the teeth yet, there's still time!" Rider yelled, still struggling to keep my mouth away from his neck. "Take her! Hurry!"

The women approached, and I hissed at them, digging my fingers into Rider's thighs, wanting so badly to keep part of myself touching him.

He pushed, and they pulled, until I was effectively snatched away from him.

I rolled to the floor, sandwiched between the two women, and instantly felt a cold wind blow over my body. Maybe it was the cold, maybe it was the fact that I was on full naked display, but I freaked.

I bucked and rolled, trying to shake the women off, but they went along for the ride, relentlessly holding on to me. It terrified me, and the coldness beating against my body seemed to find a way in. I wanted away. I didn't want women touching me.

I wasn't a homophobe, but I liked what I liked. No, that wasn't it. I *needed* a warm male.

I raised my head and sniffed, smelling Rider's scent wafting out from my bathroom, from which the sound of running water also came. I began to drool again, salivating at the thought of riding him to his death.

"Her teeth are about to come in," the black woman yelled, stuffing a wad of cloth into my mouth, unfortunately before I could snap her fingers off. "I don't think your bite canceled his out!"

"There's still time!" I heard Rider yell from the bathroom. "Bring her in!"

The blonde grabbed my wrists, the black woman gripped my ankles. Together, they raised my body entirely off the floor. Strong bitches.

I writhed between their hands, but they managed to carry me into the steamy bathroom. I saw Rider next to the tub, testing the water inside.

"Toss her in," he instructed the women.

"She's already gone," the black woman said. She seemed to be the only one of the two who spoke. "Just let her go."

"There's still time," Rider barked. "I'm not going to let her turn into a succubus while she's still got a fighting chance."

Suck-your-what? I thought as I was lowered into the tub none too gently. The hot water swallowed me, chasing away the icy cold which consumed me only seconds before. I didn't bother trying to right myself when my head slipped under; it felt too good being consumed by the heat of the water.

A hand reached down, grabbing me by the arm, raising me until I sat up above the water line. I spit out water, rested my head against the back of the tub, and glared at the three strangers hovering over me.

Who were they and what had they been doing to me? Did I even want to know?

Rider sat on the tub's edge, looking down at me warily. "Still want to eat me alive?"

"Don't flatter yourself, psycho," I said, after pulling the cloth out of my mouth. "Who are you? Who are they?"

"I already introduced myself at the bar. These are friends."

"You're not my friends, and you need to leave right now." I sucked in my breath and opened my mouth, ready to let it out in one loud scream.

Rider's hand clamped over my mouth before I could make a peep. I bit it, injuring his palm, but it didn't weaken him. He held on tight.

"We're trying to help you, Danni."

I struggled against him, fighting with teeth and nails, but he barked an order to his friends and I found myself gagged again. Gagged with a pair of my own sweat socks, one balled inside my mouth, and the other over that, tied around the back of my head. At least they were clean. I'd swallowed blood earlier, but I don't think I could've handled foot funk.

Sometime during the struggle, I became aware of my nudity again. I grabbed a towel from the bar above me, covering myself the best I could in the water. That was when I noticed the redness of my skin. Although I probably was blushing right down to my toes, I don't think the bright redness was caused by that.

I was being boiled like a lobster. Were they cannibals? Was I going to be boiled alive and eaten?

I panicked and tried to make a run for it, but Rider's strong arms held me down before I could even rise to a stand.

The women came forward, but he told them to stay back. "This isn't succubus. She's just scared. I don't think she's letting herself accept what's happening."

"Does she *know* what's happening?" The blonde asked.

Aha! She did speak. Maybe she'd tell me what in the world was going on. Besides the fact that I'd been abducted by psychos. That much, I'd figured out already.

Rider looked at me, considering, then told the women to leave, stopping the black one with a glare when she started to protest. "She's not a succubus, Nannette. She didn't get the teeth. I'll be fine alone with her."

"If it's her true—"

"It's not. I stopped it."

"Her body will keep trying, Rider. The beast will try to claw its way out."

"I'll keep her hot and with regular infusions of blood I'll redirect her change. Now, go. I know what I'm doing."

The women left, Nannette giving Rider a good eye roll first.

He turned back to me, placing the back of his hand against my forehead. He seemed to think for a moment, then twisted the plug at the bottom of the tub, letting the water seep out slowly. I thought he was going to take me out of the bath, but instead he turned on the tap, letting more hot water pour into the tub.

"This should keep the water a steady temperature," he said. "You shouldn't need to be in here too much longer. I think you'll be good enough soon that warm blankets will do the trick."

What was he babbling about? I tried to ask, but all that escaped around the socks in my mouth were muffled sounds.

He looked at me, seeming to study me. "Do you understand what's happening to your body?"

I tried to talk, but of course, made little progress.

"A nod or shake of the head will do, Danni."

I thought of all the things I wanted to call him and tried to convey them through my eyes. Then I noticed the mirror on the shower door next to me was fogged up. Seeing as how I didn't have a pad and pencil nearby…

I touched the mirror with my index finger and wrote: WHY DRUG ME?

Rider looked at the words, a frown forming across his face. "You said something about drugs earlier too. Where did you get the notion I drugged you?"

I looked at him in disbelief, but realized he really did look confused.

I wrote: RYAN

"Selander Ryan," he said, shaking his head angrily. "That's why you left with him. He told you I'd spiked your coffee with something. That son of a… Danni, I didn't drug you. I saved you. Don't you remember?"

I shook my head, more to clear it, than to give an answer, but he took it as one.

"Selander Ryan attacked you, nearly killed you. I got him away from you before he could finish the job, and then I asked you if you wanted life or death. You chose life, and that's what I gave you."

I tried to speak and gagged on the socks.

"If I take off the gag, do you promise not to scream? I swear I'm not going to hurt you. Neither are Eliza or Nannette."

I nodded my head. I could always change my mind later, once the socks were out of my mouth.

He took away the gag, tossing the socks to the floor. "There you go. Now, what did you want to say?'

"Why have you abducted me? Why do I keep fading in and out of consciousness, waking in pain? Why are the

22

three of you holding me a prisoner in my own home? Why are you trying to boil me alive?"

Humor lent a sparkle to his deep blue eyes. "Boiling you alive? Are you even uncomfortable?"

I thought about it. Before being dumped in the bathtub I'd been freezing, aching, but the hot water had stopped that, even soothed my gums, which had felt as though they were about to split open.

And although my skin was bright red, I didn't feel the slightest bit of discomfort. The scalding hot water wasn't hurting me.

"How is it possible that this water isn't causing me pain?"

"Your body craves heat. The hotter the better. Do you remember what you were doing before we put you in here?"

I thought about it and felt myself blushing. I'd had a fantasy about killing him… by having sex with him. I'd practically thrown myself at him.

"You were changing over into a succubus. A succubus gains heat from testosterone. They seek it in men, and not only do they try to suck that warmth out of men, but they suck out man's life force as well. Estrogen will chill a succubus. That's why I brought Eliza and Nannette with me, in case Ryan's bite succeeded in turning you into a succubus."

I tried to wrap my mind around what he was saying, but the drugged theory I was working on made more sense. "You're trying to tell me some succubus thing attacked me and I'm turning into one, like something out of a horror movie."

"You were attacked by an incubus, and I know this is hard to accept after being told all your life that there's no such thing as the bogeyman or vampires and all that, but it's true."

"I don't believe you."

"Think, Danni. What do you think Ryan was doing

when he was gnawing at your neck?"

I thought back to that moment, my mind a little fuzzy on the details. I remembered the good-looking blond kneeling before me, lowering his mouth to my neck... and then pain, followed by pleasure. "We were necking?"

Rider laughed. "That's one word for it, I guess." He shook his head and used his hand to clear a large circle of fog from the mirrored door. "Do hickeys usually look like that?"

I looked at my reflection and gasped. The skin at my neck was a mottled mess. "I look like I've been mauled by a dog!"

"Close enough. The incubus makes its victim feel ecstasy when it attacks, so they aren't really aware they're being killed. Or, in some cases, they know, but they don't do anything to stop it because that would also mean stopping the pleasure."

"No, none of this makes sen—" My body arched in pain, and I tried to dig my fingers into something, but they only found water and the hard surface of the tub. Agony engulfing me, I cried out. "Rider! Help me, make it stop!"

He grabbed me out of the tub, wrapping me in a dry towel, and we collapsed on the white-tiled floor, my back to his chest. "I've got you, Danni. It's going to be all right."

I started to scream as a sharp, stabbing pain ripped through my mid-section, but Rider placed his wrist in my mouth, blood already welling above its surface. I wrapped my lips around his wrist, greedily gulping down the blood. It was all reflex, my body knowing what it needed to end the horrific pain it was being forced to endure.

Rider rocked me while I fed from his wrist, whispering soothing words. "I know it hurts, Danni, but you've made it through most of it. And this, what's happening right now, is a good pain, this means you're not turning into a succubus."

I couldn't begin to comprehend how the pain I was

going through could be labeled as good. I just closed my eyes, continuing to drink down his healing blood, letting it ease my pain.

The last tremors of pain ran their course, leaving me exhausted and limp. I pulled my mouth away from Rider's wrist, resting my head on the cool tile floor.

"You're doing great, Danni. You've almost completed the change."

"What change?" I murmured, barely having the energy to speak.

"You're becoming one of us. You're becoming a vampire."

THREE

The next time I woke, I was back in my bed, a fresh set of sheets under and over me. I was lying on my side, facing the bathroom door, not wrapped up in a man-cocoon. I raised my hand to my neck, running my fingertips over the skin and found it as smooth as a baby's bottom.

It had all been a dream, a strange, scary, frankly disturbing nightmare of a dream! Glancing at the alarm clock on my nightstand, I realized I had about an hour and a half before I was due at work.

I flung the sheet off my body and sat up, panicking instantly. I was buck naked yet, I never slept in the nude. Turning to my right, I choked back a scream. My nightmare abductor was sleeping in my bed, all nice and cozy between my sheets.

Had all the weird stuff I recalled really happened? Had I—*gulp*—drank blood? I couldn't have. It was all just a dream. I'd gotten drunk at a seedy bar and brought a guy home. That wasn't so bad. Well, it wasn't a good thing, but it beat out drinking human juice.

I shoved Rider hard enough to roll him out of the bed. He let out a little *oomph* as he hit the floor, then he rose to stand in all his naked glory. "Well, good morning, feisty.

You know, most of our kind prefer to sleep until sundown."

I didn't pay any attention to his words, embarrassed, and at the same time, enthralled by the long, happy part of him which had popped out to say hello. Unsure what to do, what the proper etiquette was after a drunken one-night stand, I did the only thing that came to mind. I reached into my nightstand drawer, making sure I was wrapped securely in one of the bedsheets, and grabbed a pair of scissors, wielding them like a weapon.

"You get out now!"

"Danni, I—"

"Don't you just stand there waving that… *thing* at me, talking to me like you belong in my bedroom! Shame on you, getting a girl drunk and taking advantage. Now you go before I decide to just…" I gestured toward his package, which I couldn't help but notice was rather impressive, "… cut that thing off!"

Rider folded his arms across his chest, grinning from ear to ear, obviously not embarrassed by his own nudity, nor concerned with my threat. No real surprise there. For one thing, I'd need bigger scissors to accomplish what I'd threatened to do.

"Will you please at least put some clothes on?"

His grin widened while he reached for the pants resting on my other nightstand. "You got my pants wet when I pulled you out of the bathtub. I just didn't want to get into your bed all wet. I tried to make this experience as comfortable for you as possible."

He stepped into the black pants, pulling them upward to cover himself. He obviously was going to go commando. He gave me another cocky smile before taking his black button-down shirt from the bedpost and slid his arms through the sleeves.

"Are you more comfortable now?" he asked, threading the buttons through their holes.

"Hard to be comfortable after waking up naked with a

stranger," I answered, tightening my grip on the scissors. "The bathtub was real?"

"It was all real," he said as all traces of humor marking his face turned into concern. "I redirected your change, brought you over as a vampire."

"Vampires aren't real."

"Yes, they are. You and I are living proof."

"Vampires are the animated dead. They can't *live*."

Rider rolled his eyes. "Obviously, we can, and there's nothing dead about us."

I backed away slowly, like he was a wild animal and I didn't want to spook him. It wasn't a good idea to spook the crazies. "You're nuts. I am not a vampire and neither are you. I just had too much to drink and picked up the wrong guy, now I'd appreciate it if you'd leave before I call the cops."

"Danni, you need my help to adjust to your new way of life. Trust me, it's easier when you have a mentor."

"Get out!"

He seemed to think it over, reluctant to leave. "Fine, but let me at least get Nannette or Eliza back over here to explain—"

"Get out, get out, get out!" I screamed at him, angry tears threatening to fall from my eyes. "I've had a really bad night—"

"Two nights."

Back the hell up. "What?"

"Two nights. The incubus attacked you late Tuesday night. I found your keys and personal information in your wallet and brought you back here before sunup Wednesday."

"You're telling me…"

"It's Friday morning. The change takes a while."

I shook my head, trying to rearrange all the chaos inside until it made some sort of logical sense. If I hadn't simply gotten drunk and picked up a guy, brought him home and preceded to have the strangest, most realistic nightmare ever…

"Tell me what happened."

"Danni, you know what happened."

I shook my head again, not wanting to believe it. "The things I remember can't be memories. They have to be pieces of a really bad nightmare."

"I'm afraid not. You were attacked by an incubus and you said you wanted to live, so I didn't leave you to die."

"No." I refused to accept what he was telling me. "I had too much to drink. I brought you home with me and we slept together. My shame, mixed with the alcohol, caused me to have this really intense nightmare. I'm still having it. I just need to wake up."

There. That was my excuse, and I was sticking to it.

"We did not have sex, Danni, and I brought you home, not the other way around. For two days and nights I've watched over you, helping you to get through the change. You're a vampire now and you have to accept it."

"I can't accept something this crazy."

"Danni, you asked me to save you. Now, let me help you through the transition."

"Just get out, Rider, if that's even your real name. I don't believe you. I think you're just some sick perv who gets off on messing with women's minds."

"And how would I make you remember all the things you've seen and done these last few days?" He tilted his head to the side.

I just raised an eyebrow at him.

"You still think I drugged you? "

"It's the only thing that makes sense. Now, I'm only going to ask you to leave one more time before I start screaming my head off."

"Fine, I'll go, but you're making the situation you're in much more difficult." He made a sound, something along the lines of a ticked-off grunt, and turned to leave, grabbing his leather jacket off the floor.

He paused in the doorway, turning back to face me. "I

can't leave in good conscience without warning you of a few critical things."

I opened my mouth to order him to leave, but he must've seen it coming because he raised a hand to halt me.

"Just shut up and listen to me, ice princess, then I'll be more than glad to walk out of this apartment and leave you to fend for yourself."

I let my mouth fall open, tightening my hands into fists, but didn't comment on his rudeness. I wanted him gone as soon as possible so I could get on with my life and forget all about him and the things I'd done, things I still wanted to believe were all fragments of a drug-induced nightmare. "Make it short and quick."

"Fine." He reached into his jacket pocket, extracting a white plastic bottle, and tossed it on my bed. "Use this lotion to protect you from the sun any time you must be in it, and I say must because you should avoid as much of it as possible. Staying out of it altogether is the best protection."

"Oh, let me guess. I'll burn to a cinder." I didn't bother hiding my irritation. This was insane, but to my growing annoyance, he was actually scaring me with the nonsense.

"Not right away, but we are allergic to the sun, and burn very easily. It drains our power, and yes, it can be deadly the longer we are exposed. Nannette's contact info is on the label. She can get you more when you need it. She's a nurse over at the university hospital. If you're ever truly injured, more than you can heal yourself, contact her. She'll meet you at the underworld hospital ward."

"Underworld hospital ward? What is that, where all the vampires, witches and werewolves go?"

"Yes," he answered, his handsome face completely expressionless.

I looked at him, concerned he truly did believe this psychobabble he was spewing, and shivered. Man, I really knew how to pick a guy.

"You also need to understand how fragile we are. We are faster, stronger than the mortals, but our blood is extremely thin. We bleed out easily. Even a minor cut could turn deadly for us if not handled properly. If you are cut in any way, you bandage the injury immediately and go to sleep as soon as you can. Our bodies heal during sleep. Our saliva has healing properties as well."

I raised my fingers to my neck, running them over the smooth skin. It had been mottled the last time I was awake.

"When you changed completely, your new vampire healing properties kicked in, healing your wound."

I shook my head slowly, refusing to accept the things he was saying. "I let you speak. I listened to this madness. Now, go."

His beautiful blue eyes darkened into something cold and bitter as he withdrew a business card from his pocket. He walked to my desk and placed the card there. "Call Eliza if you have any questions or problems. She's a counselor for the newly changed."

He picked up something off of my desk and I cringed with embarrassment, identifying the item as one of the brochures I'd taken from the plastic surgeon's office. The cover featured a large before and after shot of a pair of augmented breasts. It was one thing knowing I intended to get my boobs done, but having a man looking at the brochure, wondering what was going through his mind… It wasn't comfortable in the least.

The grin he bore when turning to face me was smart-assed and deserving of a kick to the groin.

"We can't have surgeries, too much blood loss," he said, seeming to enjoy himself. "The porno boobs will have to stay in the brochure."

I could almost feel my blood boiling beneath my skin, could definitely feel my face flushing, but whether with embarrassment or anger I couldn't discern.

"Get out!" The last word came out as a bone-jarring

scream, and he had the nerve to laugh at me, turning nonchalantly toward the door.

"Maybe I'll see you around in the underworld, Danni," he called back to me after leaving me alone in my bedroom. "And please don't be an idiot and go hunting for sustenance from normal people. Call Eliza first, or better yet, come to me. My number is programmed into your cell, and you'll always be able to find me."

With that parting remark, I heard the front door to my apartment close behind him. I instantly felt scared. What had I just gone through? What did I need to do?

Did I call the police? The gynecologist? He said we hadn't slept together, but could I believe him?

I didn't want to go to the police. What would I even tell them—and what if we truly hadn't had sex? What if they arrested the guy for something he didn't do? Those deep blue eyes of his had looked so sincere when he'd said we didn't do anything. Then again, they'd looked sincere when he'd said we were both vampires. The man was delusional, and as for me…

Someone drugged me. That would be my defense until the day I died, I decided then and there. No way was I believing any of my "memories" had any basis in reality.

The phone rang, the shrill sound of the ringer screaming through the room, causing me to jump. I took the few steps over to my nightstand and picked up the cordless receiver, growling when I recognized the name on the caller ID. I wasn't really in the mood for a call, especially not for a call from Gina. If she'd showed at the bar like she was supposed to, maybe none of this would have happened.

"Hey Danni-kins," Gina squealed into the phone, "you're finally well enough to answer! I'm so sorry about not showing up at the bar, and if I'd known you were going to come down with such an awful little bug—"

"A bug?"

"Yeah, that's what you call a virus isn't it? Anyway, it

should be almost over now, shouldn't it?"

"How did you know about my… bug?"

"Your doctor faxed in your excuse. Didn't they tell you that? Oh, it doesn't matter. When are you coming back to work?"

I sat on my bed, thinking about that, thankful I still had a job. Nannette must have faxed over a note, excusing me from work while I was going through the… change. No. She covered while Rider was keeping me prisoner. I was not a flipping vampire. I just wasn't. I couldn't be.

"I'll be there today," I answered. I'd been held captive in my home for too long. I wanted back somewhere where everything was normal, where no reminders of Rider lurked.

"Today? Wow, that is a fast recovery. Of course, your friend, Rider, said you'd be fine soon when he answered your phone. I fully expect you to spill all about him when you get in. He sounded absolutely delicious."

He tastes delicious too, I thought, and for a moment, I could taste his intoxicating blood rolling over my tongue. Gross. What was wrong with me? I had to have imagined drinking his blood. No way in Hades would I actually have done that.

"Rider answered my phone?" If he was a real psycho with plans to hurt me, he wouldn't have wanted anyone knowing he was with me, would he? I was growing more confused by the minute.

"Yes. You're going to have to tell me where this mysterious man popped up from when you get here. I'll tell everyone you're coming back today. See ya!"

She hung up before I could say anything more. That was fine with me. Gina was my friend, in the we-speak-to-one-another-at-the-office kind of way, but you kind of have to be in a certain mood to fully appreciate her. I so wasn't in that mood today.

I showered quickly, washed and conditioned my hair. I was already running late, so a quick blow-dry and brush-through would have to suffice. My hair just passed my shoulders and had a nice, gentle wave to it so I could leave it down without it looking a total mess.

My last day at work had been less than stellar. I'd had two clients walk out after hearing my pitches, apparently not sharing my sense of humor. Needless to say, Dex Prince hadn't been pleased with me.

When he'd stopped by my cubicle later that day I'd been sure it was to fire me. Instead, he'd delivered the final blow to my already threadbare self-esteem.

"When I took over this company, I was told how brilliant you were, but frankly, I haven't seen that brilliance," he'd said, his voice completely devoid of emotion, all matter-of-fact. "We don't do the same advertising your former employer did. The cutesy, funny stuff has its place, but that's not all we do. Sex sells, Danni. Most of our clients are looking for sophisticated, sexually stimulating ads, not this fluff." He stressed his words by throwing two unsigned contracts on my desk—contracts which would have been signed if I hadn't sent the prospective clients running out the door. "In fact, these two clients specifically stated they wanted something sexy. I need better from you, Danni. If you don't know how to do sexy, I suggest you find someone who does and take notes."

After that statement, it hadn't been very hard for Gina to convince me I needed a few drinks. At the time of her suggestion, it'd seemed like a wonderful idea. Of course, I hadn't thought a few drinks would get me up close with Mr. Tall, Dark and Psychotic, but I couldn't dwell on that. One problem at a time. Dex Prince wanted sexy. I spent twenty minutes artfully applying makeup—foundation, concealer, powder, lip liner, lipstick, shadow, eyeliner and blush—so that it looked as though I wasn't wearing any, then stood before my closet, deciding on what to wear. Sexy, sexy, sexy….

Aha! I grabbed the little black skirt my mother had

bought me the year before. "For when you lose those extra pounds," she'd stated, handing me the pink-tissue wrapped gift box containing the skirt. Oh, yeah. She was a real confidence booster.

I grabbed a snug-fitting rib knit top and tossed the two articles of clothing on my bed before walking over to my dresser. I reached in for underwear, then paused. If I was going to be sexy, I couldn't do it halfway. I perused through my underwear drawer, looking to see what I might have to fit with the whole sexy theme. The bra was easy to choose—lacy and gel-filled. You know, a bra with built in boobs for those of us lacking those most necessary parts.

As far as the rest… I sifted through pair after pair of granny panties, realizing that for the most part, I had the underwear drawer of a saggy-boobed senior citizen. No wonder I hadn't gotten laid since college. Maybe my own subconscious fear of watching a man go limp as the sight of me in my undies made him think he was doing his dear old nana kept me from taking that particular adventure.

I had a couple of thongs I'd purchased on impulse, but I'd bought them planning to adhere to the three-minute rule, the three-minute rule being that a man had to be readily available to take them off me within three minutes. I didn't care if they seemed to be the panties of choice for most men's nothing sexy about walking around all day digging up your butt because you have a permanent wedgie.

I finally found a pair of bikinis, white to match the bra, and slipped them on, deciding I would need to visit a lingerie department in the near future. The bra came next, and I did my best to studiously ignore the fact that I didn't fill out the cups. It was hard exuding an air of sexiness when you thought you had the body of a prepubescent child, and I was going with the whole "Think it, be it" theory. If I thought I was sexy, I would be sexy, and hopefully some of that sexiness would spill over into my work and keep my butt employed.

I finished dressing, did my best not to pick myself apart in front of the mirror, and grabbed my purse. Although I hadn't brought my purse into the bar with me, I'd had my wallet.

I found the blazer I'd worn that night hanging on the coat rack next to my front door. My wallet was inside, none of its contents missing. Another point in Rider's favor.

I thought again about whether I should report him to the authorities, but in all reality, what would I say? He drugged me—evidence of which I did not have—at a bar, saw me home, then cared for me, even making sure my employer knew my whereabouts? I just didn't see the boys in blue rushing over.

Of course he could have done stuff to me while I was unconscious, but part of me didn't think so. However, that part of me *wanted* to think so, because the alternative was… No. I wasn't even going to entertain the thought of the things Rider said as being true. The man was a nutcase, and I was fortunate he hadn't hurt me. That was that. I wouldn't even think about it anymore.

Making up my mind to act as if I'd never set foot into The Midnight Rider, I swung my purse over my shoulder, grabbed my keys, and left my apartment. There were only two things I needed to concern myself with: keeping my job, and snagging my boss.

I walked out of my building, my eyes immediately zeroing in on where my car sat parked in the small lot. Rider hadn't stolen that either. I winced, remembering my vow to never think of him, or anything related to him, again. On the tail of that thought came the memory of him standing before me, naked. There was an image I wasn't so sure I wanted to forget, even if it was for the best.

My face and hands started stinging, stopping me in my tracks. I looked down at my hands, blinking hard. My eyes burned badly enough to form tears.

There were no bumps or welts, but my skin was so hot,

like the flesh was burning. I could imagine it blistering up, eventually peeling back from the muscle to fall at my feet like so many ashes. I turned around and ran for my apartment, for the bottle of lotion Rider had left behind, but I wasn't admitting to anything. I was just being precautious. Everyone should take care of their skin. That I'd suddenly taken an interest in caring for mine didn't mean I was a vampire.

FOUR

My first day back at work after Dex tells me I have to "think sexy" and I get stuck with hemorrhoid cream and baby wash ads. I could try until I died from exertion, but there just wasn't anything sexy about hemorrhoid cream, and as for baby wash… well, making a sexy ad with babies just went against my morals. Babies are meant to be nothing but cute.

It was while I leaned back in my desk chair contemplating witty slogans for the hemorrhoid cream that I suddenly found myself under attack by my overly eager friend, Gina.

"Who's this Rider guy? What's he look like? What's he do?" The questions shot out of Gina's mouth like rapid fire as she plopped her bottom down on the top of my desk.

"There's nothing to tell," I answered coolly.

"Oh, come on. You're not mad that I didn't show up, are ya? Barry from security asked me out before I left. You know he's a fox."

A rodent was more fitting if we were describing Barry by way of animal but I kept my thought to myself.

"Besides, you apparently found a new friend, the best

kind of friend, or have you known this Rider guy long and just didn't say anything?"

I just looked at her. The last thing I needed was to rehash my night—oh, that's right, my nights—plural—with Rider. Not while I was sitting in my cubicle at work wondering why I had to slather some specially made lotion all over my exposed skin just to be able to walk to my car without burning to a crisp or why my darkest pair of sunglasses hadn't done diddly squat to stop my eyes from burning.

I wasn't a vampire; that was just screwy, but something was definitely wrong with me.

"Danni, are you listening to me?"

"No," I answered truthfully, realizing Gina had been talking to me for a while, and I had been zoned out, thinking about Rider, and all the weird little bits and pieces I remembered—or thought I remembered—from the past two days and nights.

"Come on, Danni-kins, tell me about him. It's exciting. You hardly ever have guy news."

See. That right there was why I considered Gina my friend in the we-speak-at-the-office way, not the I'd-help-you-hide-the-body-if-you-killed-your-cheating-boyfriend way.

Besides, when she showed an interest in anyone else's guy, it was because she was interested in him herself. Why was she so interested in Rider after having just spoken with him over the phone? Who knew? But I couldn't imagine anything he could have said to enrapture a woman over a phone line. Nobody was that sexy, not even his tall, dark, and gorgeous self.

"I'd rather not talk about Rider, or the bar, or anything else, really. Dex isn't happy with me after losing two potential clients and I've just missed two days of work. I have to focus on working today."

"Is that why you broke out the hoochie skirt? You're trying to get back into Dex's good graces."

"It's not a hoochie skirt!" I exclaimed. Short, yes, but not hoochie.

"Please, Danni, if anyone knows about hoochie skirts, it's me. You look great. You should show off those legs more."

And there was the reason I associated with Gina. Although she was a man-eater, she didn't get catty like most other women of her type. Of course, with long, silky blonde hair, legs that went on forever and breasts the size of volleyballs, why should she envy anyone?

"Well, whatever your reason is—Dex or the mysterious Rider… You look great." She hopped off my desk, turning to leave. "Oh, and F.Y.I. — it wouldn't hurt to accidentally drop something the next time you pass Dex, that way you have to bend waaay over—"

"Go, Gina." I couldn't stop myself from laughing as she walked away, grinning coyly. Even with all her faults, she was good company when you needed a laugh. And I had definitely needed a laugh.

"Danni, can I see you please?"

The buttery voice of my dreams floated over the cubicle wall, enveloping me in nervous energy. I always felt like an awkward middle schooler when he gave me his direct attention. Just hearing him say my name was enough to make me too nervous to eat lunch.

Dex came into view as I stood from my desk, and what a view he was. Dark blond hair, combed away from his face, the gentle waves held back by some kind of mousse or gel. It was shorter in front, but the back touched down to his collar. He had a thing for silk button-down shirts, preferably white, and dress slacks in black or gray. I didn't care what he wore; he'd look great in anything.

"Feeling better?" He asked as I stepped out of my cubicle.

"Yes, thank you."

"Ladies first." He swept his arm out, gesturing for me to precede him.

I walked toward his office, which sat at the end of the hall, fully aware his eyes were on my ass. I could feel the weight of his gaze on me so heavily I almost stumbled from nervousness. Falling on your face wasn't sexy so from there on I was careful to avoid tripping.

Halfway to his office, I recalled Gina's advice. Tacky as it was, I couldn't help but wonder…. Unfortunately, I didn't have anything to drop, except for my panties and maybe it's just me, but I think that would have been a bit too forward.

I paused at his door, and waited as he came around me to open it, gesturing with his hand for me to enter his office first.

His office was fairly big, with an impressive mahogany desk sitting dead center. The walls were a grayish-blue, pleasant and inviting, and went well with the dark gray carpet. Pictures of seascapes adorned the walls, along with diplomas and award certificates. I'd often dreamed of a large family photo adorning these walls—Me, Dex, our two beautiful children, and the family dog. Some kind of fluffy poo or doodle dog. They seemed to be all the rage with the rich and high class.

Behind the desk was a black leather chair so massive it seemed more like a throne. He didn't take the chair, but instead half-sat on the corner of the desk.

I sat in one of the cushy black leather chairs before the desk, choosing the one farthest from him. As much as I wanted him, I didn't like being too close. Get me too close to him and my knees would start to shake worse than Beyoncé's booty.

I crossed my legs, and his eyes followed the movement. Sitting there beneath his gaze while he hovered over me, I kind of felt like a small mouse being circled by an owl, but in a good way, if that's possible.

"There's something different about your appearance today," he said, his gaze rolling over me.

I started to push my chest out, then remembered I

didn't have one, so I just sat there under his scrutiny, hoping my posture was good enough. I normally didn't wear skirts to work; I normally didn't wear skirts, period. I was a jeans and slacks girl, and my tops tended to run on the big side. No sense wearing something tight on top just to draw more attention to the fact there wasn't much curve to cling to. My hair was usually combed back and secured by bands or combs. A more professional look.

"You look very… nice," he finally said, and I released a breath which had somehow gotten stuck the moment he'd started to study me.

"Thank you, sir."

"Dex."

"Dex. Thank you, Dex."

And then we just sat there, staring at each other. Him, with a predatory gleam to his eyes, and me, fighting the urge to start gnawing on my fingernails, and I didn't even have a nail-biting habit. It just all of a sudden seemed like a good thing to start up.

"So…" he began, and I nearly jerked, having grown used to the anxiety-feeding silence, "I brought you in here to discuss last Tuesday…"

A ball of dread started to uncoil in my belly, filling my stomach with acid. The last time we'd discussed how I lost us two clients last Tuesday had been on Tuesday… and I'd run out to the nearest bar, afraid my job security was hanging by a thread. "I'm sorry about the clients," I started, but was interrupted before I could continue groveling.

"And I'm sorry for the things I said to you after that incident."

I looked at him, stunned silent, and judging by his humorous expression, realized I must have been gawking.

"Don't look so surprised, Danni. I can admit when I am wrong, and I was definitely wrong. I'd just had a bad fight with someone that morning," he said, waving his hand in a dismissive gesture, "and I'm afraid I wasn't in a very professional state of mind, taking my anger out on the wrong person. You are very good at your job, and I realize your material tends to run more to the comical and cute. Those particular clients should have been given to someone else."

"I can be sexy!" I blurted out, and could feel the heat suffusing my face, growing fiercer as Dex burst out into laughter.

"I'm aware of that," he said, reining in his obvious amusement. "Your work, though, is geared more toward the comical."

"I can *do* sexy," I said forcibly, rising from my seat to stand in front of him. He wasn't going to just cut me down and then sweep everything he'd said aside without giving me a chance to prove myself and redeem my pride, no matter how perfectly gorgeous he was.

"Danni, it's—"

"Don't. Don't stick me with all the crappy hemorrhoid cream and baby product ads. Give me something more. I can do it. You want suave, sophisticated and sexy? I can do it."

He looked at me, those beautiful baby blues sparkling with laughter. One of our most often discussed topics around the office water cooler was whether those baby blues were real, or the product of colored contacts.

"Tell you what," he said, reaching behind him for a file. "I like this fire I'm seeing in you. You want a shot at something bigger, try this." He handed me the file. "You have a week. If you let me down on this…"

"I won't."

"Good." He stood before me, putting us only a breath apart. "You know, you really do look really, *really* good today."

"Um, thank you, sir, er, Dex." I felt wobbly all the way down to my toes.

His response was a simple nod, and he slipped around the back of his desk.

Taking that as my cue the little impromptu meeting was over, I turned to leave, walking on shaky legs. I'd spent what felt like forever waiting to be noticed by Dex Prince, and it seemed as though it was finally happening.

"Oh, Danni," he called as I opened the door to leave. I turned to find him leaning back in that throne of a chair, his feet propped on the desk, crossed at the ankle. "How is that crappy hemorrhoid cream ad coming?"

I smiled, a self-deprecating gesture. "To be honest, I'm going to have to go with my trademark comical-ness on that one."

"Well, I could hardly think you might find a suave, sophisticated, let alone sexy, way to advertise an ointment for hemorrhoids. In fact, if you did, I'd be more than a bit worried."

I smiled, lapping up how good he looked, stretched back in his chair, all warm and inviting.

"Out of curiosity, what have you got so far?"

"I was kind of going with the slogan, 'We'll cover your ass', but I've still got time for fresh ideas to pop up."

I left the office with the sound of Dex's rich laughter trailing behind me.

Back at my desk, nestled away behind the walls of my cubicle, I tried to calm the giddy excitement coursing through my system. I had work to do.

Opening the file folder Dex had given me in his office, I shuffled through the papers inside, learning what my assignment was, and what the client wanted, the client being a new company by the name of Nocturnal, Inc. Interesting name, I thought, reading the bio on them. There wasn't much about the company, but I at least had a clear idea of their products. They manufactured cosmetics, clothing, jewelry, and fragrances, geared toward the younger crowd—late teens to lower thirties. My particular job was to develop an ad for their new fragrance, Midnight Passions. It sounded like the name of a romance novel.

I picked up the nifty little scratch and sniff fragrance

strip they'd included and took a whiff. I, myself, didn't care for perfume, but this one was nice. Not too heavy, but not light. It seemed to wash over me, drawing me in with its spicy, sensual scent, promising a night of passion I'd never forget. I shook my head, surprised by my reaction to the scent. I must've still been reeling from my conversation with Dex. My imagination was running awry.

I set to work, brainstorming for ideas how to best advertise the fragrance—placing the hemorrhoid ointment and baby wash ads on the back burner. The client wanted print ads and commercials, and a slogan, of course.

I thought back to the moment I'd inhaled the scent myself and a slogan immediately popped into my head: *Can you handle the passion?* I thought about it, weighing the strength of the words, not one hundred percent sure I liked it, but it was a start.

I was contemplating ideas for the print ad when my phone rang, jostling me out of the deep thinking mode I'd entered. Glancing at the little clock on the bottom of my computer screen while reaching for the phone, I realized I'd spent twenty minutes in a trance-like state, working on the project.

"Danni Keller," I announced, holding the receiver to my ear while I opened a file on my computer for the Nocturnal, Inc. project, wanting to get the slogan idea saved before it escaped my memory. "Hello?" I added after a long pause.

Heavy breathing was the only response I got for several seconds. I was about to hang the phone up and star sixty-nine the perv when he finally spoke. "Danni…" He drew my name out, so it sounded like *Dan-neeeeeeeee….*

"Yes? Can I help you?" I tried to place the voice, but couldn't.

"You should have never left with him."

Icy cold fear traveled the length of my spine, and my suddenly clammy hand gripped the receiver tighter. "Who is this?"

The caller hung up, leaving an ominous dial tone sounding in my ear. I held the receiver in my hand, frozen in a state of shock. Who was that? I immediately searched my memory for the sound of voices of all the men I'd had recent contact with.

My first thought had been Rider, but his voice was warm and rich, a voice that seemed to stroke your skin when used. The voice I'd heard over the phone was abrasive, and not as deep. That ruled out Dex's silky smooth baritone, but then again, why would he even have reason to be on the list?

With Rider and Dex, my two most recent male contacts, out of the way, I sorted through those who remained, which turned out to be coworkers. Any of my coworkers would have my extension readily available, which made them prime suspects, but if it was one of them, they hadn't called from inside. The caller ID read *unavailable*.

"Hey!"

I nearly jumped out of my skin as Gina's perky voice sailed over the cubicle wall. Realizing I still held the phone in my white-knuckled grip, and its annoying dial tone was echoing around my small workspace, I tried to relax my nerves enough so I could place the receiver back in its base.

"I'm sorry. Were you on a call? With Rider?"

"No, no call. I was just hanging up." I placed the receiver in its base and quickly withdrew my hand, as though the phone had just turned into an asp and was about to strike. "Have you gotten any strange calls?"

"Strange, how?"

"Like… threatening."

"Did someone just threaten you over the phone?" Gina's eyes widened, her happy expression transforming into concern.

"No," I said, shaking my head. "It was just that the tone used was kind of scary."

"What kind of tone? What did they say?" She perched on the side of my desk, giving me her full attention.

"It was a man with this creepy voice, kind of like the male version of that little woman from Poltergeist's voice."

"That is creepy," Gina said, adding a little shiver for effect. "What did he say?"

"He said I never should have left with him."

"With him, the guy?"

"No, another guy."

"What guy?"

"I don't know."

"Well, that should be easy to figure out. Who's the last guy you left somewhere with?" Her eyes widened again, her mouth forming a little O before she spoke. "Rider! Didn't you leave the bar with him?"

I thought about it, and even though Rider had been my first guess, I didn't want to immediately assume the caller had meant him. I'd initially left with another man anyway.

"Actually, I left the bar with another man after Rider told me not to leave with anyone."

"But you ended up with Rider."

"He took me home. I don't know what happened to the other guy."

"Two guys in one night? Impressive."

I looked at her hard, letting my eyes relay my irritation.

"I'm sorry, I know—not the time. Maybe it was a joke, or one of those guys is jealous of the other. You said he didn't actually threaten you, right?"

"Right."

"Then let's go to lunch, get your mind off the call. It was probably some creep just messing with your head."

I didn't want to eat, but I didn't want to sit right there by the very phone I'd been reached on. Sitting so close to it made me feel vulnerable somehow, like a sitting duck just waiting to get plucked off. A scary thought when you had no idea which direction the shooter would strike from.

"Okay," I murmured, signing off my computer.

Gina waited patiently as I locked the Nocturnal, Inc. file in my desk drawer and grabbed my purse, which now contained the bottle of lotion Rider had left, just in case I started to feel like an ant under a magnifying glass on a sunny day again. There were no instructions on the label stating how often the stuff needed to be reapplied.

The first rays of sunlight hitting my skin as we left the building didn't carry as big a bite as they had that morning, but I was still uncomfortable, and tired.

"So, I heard you had a private meeting with Dex earlier. Everything go all right?"

"Yes," I answered, extracting my darkest pair of shades from my purse and placing them over my watery eyes before they formed a trail of tears. "He gave me the Nocturnal, Inc. file."

"Never heard of Nocturnal, Inc."

"It's a new company. The product they're advertising is a fragrance, a really nice one."

"Dex gave you a fragrance ad after what he said last Tuesday?"

If I didn't know Gina, I'd have thought she was being bitchy due to the disbelief in her tone, but I did know her, and she was just shocked by Dex's turnaround. I couldn't hate her for that. I was surprised too.

"I told him I could do sexy."

"It's the skirt," Gina said with a sly grin.

"What does my skirt have to do with him giving me a fragrance ad?"

"Because, you ditz, you look hot! It is so the skirt… and the hair."

I simply shook my head at her grinning face as we continued our walk to the little cafe down the street.

Gina ordered a salad and a diet cola. I ordered a glass of ice water and dry toast.

"Are you sure you're all right?" she asked, looking at my plate once our order was delivered to the small table we shared outside the cafe. I'd made sure we chose one with a full umbrella to block out the sun, and felt mildly better. "That's not much of a lunch."

I could have pointed out that a small plate of salad wasn't much of a lunch either, but I chose to play nice. "I'm not hungry."

My stomach was burning, actually. Whether from nerve-induced acid or the need to vomit, I wasn't sure. I just didn't feel good at all. In fact, all I wanted to do was curl up into a ball and go to sleep, and on some deeper subconscious level, I thought sleep would make everything better. It was almost as though the daylight was calling to me, signaling to me that it was time to rest. I instinctively knew I'd feel better after night fall. And with that thought, Rider's words whispered through my mind:

You know, most of our kind prefer to sleep until sundown.

No! I wasn't going to believe for a moment that I was turning—had turned—into some sort of creepy crawly creature of the night thing who sucked blood out of people's necks. Maybe I'd been given something to make me imagine my skin was so hot under the sun, and that the sun was pulling me toward sleep. Maybe I'd imagined the whole phone call too.

But, as I released a vigorous yawn, I couldn't help entertaining the thought that all this weird stuff was real. It *felt* real. The burn of the sun, the desire to sleep until sundown, the weight of a stare on my face. Wait… *What?*

I searched the surrounding tables, trying to find the source of the gaze I felt boring into me, while fighting the urge to succumb to panic. Finding myself the subject of a stalker's gaze wasn't the best thing that could happen within the same hour of receiving a vaguely threatening phone call from an anonymous, possible psycho.

Looking toward the direction I felt the gaze originating from, I found the source. A man with deep black hair sat at a table on the other side of the terrace. Thanks to the open newspaper he held before him, appearing to be reading, all I could see were his hands and the upper part of his head.

I saw enough to realize he had ultra-dark sunglasses on, purplish blue highlights in his hair, and hands I remembered….

I rose from my seat a little too fast, nearly knocking my chair backward.

"Danni?" Gina paused with her fork halfway to her mouth, giving me a look which said Oh-dear-I-think-my-friend-is-a-wee-bit-unstable. "What are you doing, honey? You look like you just saw a ghost."

More like a vampire, I thought, but fortunately had the self-control not to say the words out loud. It was bad enough I thought I was going crazy, but when your friends and family started believing it too, the straitjackets were brought out. Personally, I don't think that particular cut would work for me.

Gina turned to see who I was staring at, but I was already on the move, so I didn't know if she made the connection, nor did I care. The man had already invaded my home. Now he was stalking me on the street, and possibly had something to do with that phone call.

I had questions, and he'd better have answers.

I dodged a server seconds before we would have collided, and marched right up to the back table where my new *friend* sat, knowing he was grinning at me the whole time from behind that newspaper, delighting in the annoyance on my face.

Another server cut me off before I reached the table. I was stalled long enough for the server to deliver drinks to his waiting customers, then he moved out of the way, allowing me a straight path to the table… where nobody sat.

No! I glanced around frantically, looking for that tall, athletic body, those purplish streaks of hair, but he'd vanished in mere seconds.

"Danni!" I turned to see Gina approaching me, her eyes holding a hint of worry. "What is it? What are you doing? You nearly ran over that poor server a moment ago."

"I'm sorry," I mumbled absentmindedly even though I knew it was the server I needed to apologize to, not Gina, "but he was here."

"Who was here?"

I walked the remaining two steps to the table he'd just vacated and picked up the newspaper he'd left behind. Scrawled across the pages in red ink were the words: *We Need To Talk*.

"Rider. Rider was here."

FIVE

"Rider? Really? Where'd he go?" Gina seemed to jerk her head around in every possible direction at once, reminding me of a psychotic chicken my grandfather had owned when I was a little girl.

I tried to ignore her as I turned my own head left and right, searching for the mysterious stranger who had practically kidnapped me a few nights ago and now was stalking me on the street. He was gone, vanished in an instant. I thought of all the vampire movies I'd seen featuring vampires as creatures with extraordinary speed, then shook off the thought. I supposed next I'd hypothesize that he had simply turned into a bat and flown away. Good grief. The man's insanity was rubbing off on me.

"I don't know where he went," I muttered, finally giving my overexcited friend an answer. I rubbed the back of my neck, where even my long hair couldn't protect it from the scalding heat of the sun. "Let's pay the check and go back to work. I don't feel all that great."

"I wanted to meet your mysterious man," Gina said with a pout. "He sounded amazing over the phone. Are you sure he was here?"

"Definitely," I answered, making my way back to our table to grab the check.

"Ooh, so you pick him up at a bar, get a creepy call later and now you see him but he disappears when you approach… Danni, you didn't pick up a wacko, did you?"

You have no idea, I thought to myself, as I withdrew tip money from my purse and placed it on the table. "Let's just get back to the office." *Please*, I added silently, *before my neck turns into one big blister.*

By the time I walked back into Prince Advertising, my neck was burning so badly I couldn't tell if the tears streaming from my eyes were from the fact they too were burning, or simply a response to the pain of having my skin fry.

No amount of Tylenol or cool paper towels seemed to abate the pain, so I grabbed the Nocturnal Inc. file and left work early.

The drive home was agonizingly slow, or maybe it just seemed that way because I was burning to death. You see, when your skin is literally frying every second spent feeling the pain seems like an hour, and unfortunately for me, even the so-called safety of my Ford Taurus's interior did diddly squat to offer me any relief. The end result was I spent the longest twenty minutes of my life driving from my place of work to my apartment, all the while fighting the urge to scream.

I had barely brought my car to a screeching stop outside my apartment building before I was on the run, sprinting as fast as I could in the strappy sandals I'd regretfully chosen to wear my first day back to work post-Rider-episode. I found out quickly that strappy sandals weren't designed for full-on running as my knees and palms connected with pavement. The new pain ricocheting through my body was the last straw. I started wailing like a day old baby as I ungracefully picked myself up and ran—make that hobbled really quickly—inside my building.

There was a package outside my door, which was odd

considering my mail was never left directly by my apartment, but I was too concerned by the amount of blood gushing from my palms and knees to care about the package.

I opened the door as quickly as I could, a feat which would have been easier if I hadn't been looking through a heavy film of tears while trying to fit my key to its lock, and kicked the package inside before slamming the door shut and hobbling to the bathroom.

My first order of business was cleaning my scrapes, but the more blood I mopped up, the more came pouring out of the seemingly harmless scratches I'd received after biting the pavement outside. Giving up, I wrapped large lengths of gauze around each knee and bandaged my hands as securely as I could. It didn't take very long before I saw dots of crimson leaking through the bandages.

"What the hell?" I growled, throwing my damaged hands up in the air. "All I did was trip on concrete, not fall off a frigging building!"

Giving up on the scrapes, I grabbed a fresh washrag and wet it, laying the cool cloth on the back of my neck where the skin still burned. I cried out in agony as a searing pain roared to life against the contact of cloth. Pulling the rag away, I gagged upon the realization of what I was holding in my hand. A strip of my flesh stuck to the rag while fresh blood dripped from the back of my neck.

I don't know how long I vomited afterward, but by the time I finished my entire body ached from the strength of the retching. And I was still bleeding.

We bleed out easily. Even a minor cut could turn deadly for us if not handled properly. If you are cut in any way, you bandage the injury immediately and go to sleep as soon as you can. Our bodies heal during sleep.

I heard Rider's voice so clearly in my mind I turned, expecting to see him kneeling behind me, those beyond blue eyes looking straight into mine, but I was all alone, bleeding to death on my cold bathroom floor.

"I'll be damned if I'm found dead on the bathroom floor like Elvis," I muttered as I picked myself up, grabbed the last of the gauze I could find in my medicine cabinet and set to work wrapping every damaged part of my body with it. Once that task was completed, I grabbed the bottle of sleeping pills I'd come across and dry-swallowed a few before hobbling to my bed, no idea if they would work or not. I fell across it face first and closed my eyes, willing myself to sleep, not sure if I would wake back up again, judging by the blood I could still feel seeping out of my wounds.

The dream began the second I hit the mattress. How did I know so soon that it was a dream? Easy. I was gorgeous, absolutely flawless. I wore a long gown made of some kind of gauzy gold material, but it wasn't see-through or trashy. It was classy, very elegant. Very not like anything I could actually get away with wearing. My short legs looked a mile long and the biggest shocker of all was the fact my tiny little breasts were actually somewhat visible. Usually, when I attempted to wear something long and slinky, they disappeared.

My hair was swept up in a fancy chignon, glistening with highlights I didn't have in reality. My makeup wasn't heavy, but it was obviously more than I normally wore. At first I thought it was the makeup making me look so great, but upon closer inspection I realized what really made me look incredible was the confidence radiating from me as I climbed the marble stairs to… wherever I was.

The structure I entered was huge and dark. A golden rug lined the torch-lit hallway I traveled down as I walked deeper inside the building, having no idea where I was going, but I felt as though wherever this place was, I belonged there.

"This can be your home," a smooth, seductive voice said from somewhere up ahead. A chill ran through my body as something about the voice niggled at my memory. My instincts were telling me to turn and flee, but still I continued walking down the long hall, closer to where the voice had come from. "That's right, Danni. Inside you, you know you belong with us."

"I don't belong anywhere," I—that is, the dream version of me—replied, approaching a gold door, a *pure* gold door. I must have been in some sort of palace or castle. The décor was definitely fit for a king.

"You don't belong anywhere in the world you knew before. In this world you belong with us. You can be our queen."

"I don't trust you," I said, placing my hand on the doorknob.

"You belong to me, not the intruder."

"Who are you?"

"Your mate."

The door swung open to reveal a room glistening with diamonds, rubies, and other assorted treasures. A large canopied bed sat in the middle, adorned with red velvet blankets and scarves, and a very attractive shirtless man who was not quite a stranger.

"Selander Ryan."

"I prefer just Ryan," he said, his thin mouth curving into a sexy grin as he lay propped up on an elbow in the big inviting bed.

"Why am I dreaming of you? You attacked me."

"Rider attacked you. I was trying to keep that from happening."

"You attacked me. I saw your teeth, the fire in your eyes. You left me for dead."

"Rider ripped me away from you. I had to defend myself. It was never my intention to allow your death."

"Then what was your intention?"

"To make you mine. You would have loved it."

"I don't think so. My life has been hell since that night."

"You no longer have life. Rider sucked it out of you. You're a walking corpse now, or haven't you figured that out yet?"

"I don't want to see either of you again."

"I doubt that, not after you know what it's like to be with an incubus."

All at once, hundreds of images assaulted me, filling my mind with a view of what my life would have been if I'd been changed into a succubus. Orgies, baths taken in blood, power. I saw myself making men beg to touch me, holding their hearts in my hand before crushing them mercilessly. Although the images were horrendous, the most gruesome part of the whole ordeal was how I felt imagining these things. I loved it. Especially when the images turned into a porno starring me and Selander Ryan. We did things I didn't know were possible, and although there was pain, it was wonderful, addictive. I felt my heart hitch, adrenaline pumping way too fast, yet I couldn't tell him to stop.

Can I survive the passion burning inside me? I thought and must have said the words out loud because Selander chuckled against my neck moments before rearing back to allow his long, curved fangs to emerge from his gums. He looked at me and all the desire I'd seen in his eyes seconds before vanished, replaced by burning rage as a wicked smile formed on his beautiful face. That was the moment I realized, dream or not, Selander Ryan was planning on killing me. I did the only thing I could think of. I screamed for Rider.

I hit the floor with a thud and quickly scrambled away. It took a moment or two for me to realize I'd woke up and was scrambling around on my bedroom floor, not the golden carpeted floor of the palace Selander Ryan had attacked me in. I was cold and sweaty, but my wounds weren't bleeding,

I ignored the ringing telephone as I carefully unwrapped the bandages I'd placed on my knees and hands, blinking rapidly as I saw the smooth, unmarred flesh being revealed under them. "How?" I tried to comprehend what had happened, not wanting to believe in the supernatural hooey Rider had fed me after what I still wanted to believe was a truly regrettable drunken one-night-stand.

The phone continued to ring, the shrill sound reverberating around my bedroom. "Who in the world is calling me now?" I muttered, glancing at the clock to see it was one o'clock in the morning. Although it only seemed I'd slept a short while, I'd been out for several hours. Growing irritated by the never ending ringing of the phone I picked myself up off the floor and grabbed the receiver out of its base.

"What happened?" I heard Rider's voice before I'd even had the chance to say hello. "Danni? Danni!"

"I'm here. How'd you know something happened?"

"I heard you call me. You were afraid of something. What happened?"

"How could you have heard me? I was dreaming."

"I sired you. We shared blood."

I shook my head, feeling the onset of a terrible headache. "I don't know what you did to me—"

"You know exactly what I did to you and you know what you are. The sooner you accept it the safer you'll be."

"What's that supposed to mean?"

"Just tell me what happened. You were terrified."

"I had a nightmare."

"Was Selander Ryan in it?"

"Yes." I held the phone away from my ear as a loud string of curses filtered through it.

"Danni, I feared this. You're in danger. You have to stay with me."

"I don't think so."

"Danni! You were marked by an incubus and I stole you! An incubus doesn't take that sort of thing lightly. He'll try to kill you, which is exactly what happened, isn't it? He lured you into a dream and tried to kill you."

"It was a nightmare, nothing more."

"You know better than that, Danni, quit acting like an airhead!"

"An airhead?"

"I'm not trying to make you mad, I'm trying to make you see—"

"You're trying to con me. Both of you attacked me that night and both of you are psychos. Stay away from me!"

"Danni, I never intended to change you into a vampire! I was trying to save you, but I had no choice once Selander attacked you!"

"Enough! This is insane!"

"Well, you wouldn't be going through this now if you'd just listened to me at the bar, but no, you had to do exactly what I told you not to do and you left with someone, the very someone I knew was tracking you!"

"What? Selander was stalking me?"

"Yes."

"And you knew this but didn't tell me?"

"What was I supposed to do, tell you an incubus was waiting to either kill you or turn you into a succubus? I've turned you into a vampire and you don't even believe that when you're walking proof! You should have listened to me then and you should listen to me now! You're in danger, Danni."

"Yeah, I'm in danger of falling for this insanity," I snapped before slamming the phone down and turning the ringer off. I'd had enough nonsense for one night. I might have been delusional, maybe even a trace deranged, but I wasn't a vampire. Vampires, succubi, and all the other creepy crawlies from horror lore did not exist. The only thing I was walking proof of was that you shouldn't bring strange men home.

I was going to have to see a doctor in the morning, possibly the gynecologist as well. Then again, I'd waited too long. If I had been raped, the evidence would be long gone. A regular doctor could find drugs in my system though, and they had to still be in my system since I was obviously still having delusions. I'd imagined my skin coming right off my neck, my perfectly flawless knees and palms skinned and bleeding profusely.

Of course, there was blood on the bandages, so I could have scraped myself up running into the apartment in those ridiculous sandals, but my skin coming off my neck because the sun had burned it off... That just wasn't possible. "No way possible," I murmured, reassuring myself as I walked into the bathroom, taking in the blood staining my sink and floor tiles. "Not possible," I said out loud again, my voice shakier than before. I peered into the wastebasket where I'd thrown away the chunk of flesh I'd pulled from my neck and quickly turned away before I gagged. It was still there. Proof of... no. No! If I admitted Rider was telling the truth, then that would mean I was a... a... I couldn't be. I had a reflection in the mirror. I was pale as I'd always been, but I wasn't white as a sheet and I hadn't drunk anyone's blood unless I counted Rider.

I grabbed a bottle of bleach from the laundry room and began cleaning my bathroom, removing all traces of what had happened to me that day. Out of sight, out of mind I'd always heard, but later, after the room was restored to order, I found I couldn't escape what had happened.

I kept seeing Selander Ryan attacking me, and shame burned through me as I recalled how I'd wanted it. I hadn't cared about dying as long as I could feel the passion his bite put inside me. I remembered Rider, the way I noticed his hard abs even as I lay against his half nude body knowing it wasn't right. What was wrong with me? Was I so desperate for male attention that I would welcome it from two deranged lunatics?

I couldn't be a vampire. I was already a flat-chested, mediocre, middle-class loser. Life couldn't get any better if I was mutated into some sort of supernatural freak of nature. "Why me?" I asked aloud between sobs as I sank to the floor, pulling my knees up to my chest. It wasn't fair. My sister got everything she'd ever wanted. She was blonde, blue-eyed and drop dead gorgeous with all-natural D-cup boobs on a tall, slender frame. She'd been homecoming queen and prom queen, valedictorian and head cheerleader. She didn't even have to work. Her rich, sophisticated fiancé spoiled her rotten.

All I'd wanted was to prove I could be somebody too. I could get a rich, sophisticated man to *ooh* and *ah* over me just as well as she could. Dex Prince was supposed to be my knight in shining armor, my chance to prove I was worthy of someone like him, despite my less than spectacular body, which now I couldn't even have molded into something better thanks to Rider!

I thought back to the night I'd met Rider inside the bar, the way his strong arms had caught me as I slid off the bar stool, the way his deep blue eyes gazed right into my soul, the purplish-blue highlights in his long black hair, those lips... Rider was definitely what my sister would consider a bad boy fuck buddy. She would purr like a kitten if she saw him, I thought with a sly grin. But he would only hold her interest until she had a taste of him. That's the way she was.

I could dangle him in front of her and make her jealous for a moment, but that wouldn't be good enough. I'd lived in her shadow for twenty-eight years and I was sick of it. I needed a relationship she'd covet for the rest of her perfect little life. I needed husband material, someone rich, powerful and gorgeous. I needed Dex Prince.

The question was how was I going to snag him when I had two weirdos trying to make me as insane as they were? Mind over matter, I told myself. If I refused to give in to what I had to admit seemed like a plausible idea of what was going on with me, then I could overcome it. I'd live in denial. It's not as if most of the world didn't already do that anyway.

I peeled off my clothes and pulled on a nightshirt, glancing at the bed accusingly as I walked past it. There was no way I was going back to sleep after the nightmare

I'd had. I was actually pretty wide awake. I briefly wondered if that had anything to do with the whole vampires sleep during the day theory but quickly pushed the idle thought away. If I had any chance of retaining my sanity, I was going to have to stay in permanent denial mode.

The light on my answering machine blinked furiously, taunting me to push the button which would dispel its secrets. "I might as well hear what he has to say," I muttered, thankful Rider wasn't talking to me inside my mind like vamps did in horror movies. I'd have really gone nuts. I pushed the play button, telling myself I could simply fast forward through the message if I didn't like what I heard. Unfortunately, the first message was one my mother had apparently left earlier in the day. I groaned while listening, not sure which person I'd rather hear from least.

Danni, this is Mother. Your sister and I will be out your way next week picking out some things for the wedding. Your grandmother Clarice is going to be with us and wants to see you. We'll just stop in whenever, it's not as though you ever have dates or anything important to do with your evenings. Try to make your little apartment look a little presentable please. Toodles, darling, and try not to work so hard. Find a man to do it for you!

Her shrill giggle was enough to make me wince by itself, but combined with the knowledge my grandmother would be coming to visit made me scream on the inside. Wherever my grandmother went, her tiny little rat-dog followed, and along with him came his gas problem which my grandmother referred to as "his condition" in a hushed whisper as though she were afraid the little toe-biter would be embarrassed if we discussed it aloud. It would be nice if she gave that much consideration to others' feelings, but she didn't which meant I'd be spraying room deodorizer like crazy while her nasty little mongrel tried to kill us all with his fumes.

Danni, it's Rider. I know you're angry and overwhelmed with all of this. I don't blame you, but I am not the bad guy you think I am. I was only trying to help you and, as the man who changed you into this new way of living, I want to protect you. I know what it's like to be alone, Danni. Don't hide from us. If you don't want to trust me, then trust Eliza. There are things you need to know. It's better to have someone guide you through rather than learning from mistakes. Trust me, I know. Just… take care of yourself and whatever you do, stay away from Selander Ryan. Once you fully accept yourself as a vampire, his mark will be useless. Until then, be careful. I'm here if you need me.

The answering machine clicked and beeped, awaiting my command. I deleted the messages, part of me regretting losing access to Rider's voice. "I'm so pathetic," I muttered to myself, wiping away a tear from my cheek, not remembering how or why it had even fallen. "He's bad news, Danni girl. You're too old for fuck buddies, especially ones with fangs. You have a husband to snag."

With that thought in mind, I left my bedroom, catching sight of the package I'd kicked inside the door earlier as I reached the living room. Curiosity outweighing my need for sustenance, I cut off my trek to the kitchen and headed toward the package instead. It was a small box wrapped in brown paper, with no address, only my name scrawled in bold cursive letters. I opened it to find a pair of extremely dark black sunglasses and a small white card which read *"These should keep those big beautiful eyes tear-free."* It was signed, R.

"For a nutcase, he sure is considerate," I commented, having to laugh a little at the insanity of my predicament. "Only you, Danni. Only you could attract two incredibly hot guys who would be perfect if not for the fact they're supposedly creatures and not men at all."

I grabbed a can of coffee beans in the kitchen and brewed a pot, letting the pleasant aroma comfort me as a million thoughts ran around in my head. Little things like what I was going to wear and what shade of lipstick would look good on me were mixed in with the more pertinent issues, like how was I going to impress Dex Prince while avoiding a mental breakdown?

I went through the motions of preparing my cup of coffee robotically as I pondered the questions in my mind. By the time I'd sat down to take my first sip of the warm liquid I still didn't have any answers, but I came to one stunning conclusion as I noticed the flavor of the liquid in my mug and vaguely recalled having drained off the blood from a package of steaks in the refrigerator to use in place of creamer.

"Aw, hell. Who am I kidding? I am a frigging vampire."

SIX

"I'm a vampire." I said the words out loud, feeling slightly silly and half fearing men in white lab coats were going to come for me any minute. It was too crazy even if it was real. "Real," I murmured, still in a state similar to shock. I was too calm to be in shock, too accepting. That scared me more than anything.

I looked down at my mug of bloodied coffee and wondered how it was possible the realization of what I'd flavored it with didn't make me nauseous. I drained the mug and my stomach growled in response, longing for more. Unfortunately, I had the feeling what little blood I could drain off the meat in my fridge wasn't going to abate my hunger. What I was hungry for, I didn't even want to think about how I was supposed to get.

Rider had said there was an underworld hospital. Maybe there was an underworld McDonald's, where instead of Big Mac's and fries, you could order a pint of O-negative. The thought made me laugh, but laughter soon gave way to tears as I remembered this was real. I was a monster, a creature of the night, a... I really didn't know what I was, but I knew it wasn't good.

And I was all alone.

I scooted away from the table, and the sound of the chair legs scraping across the floor sounded shrill in the silence of my apartment, further enunciating just how very alone I was. Oddly enough, it would have been better had I contracted an STD or some strange jungle disease. Then I could at least turn to a friend for solace. Who did you go to when you came down with a case of vampirism? Anyone I told would think I was insane or on the off chance they would actually believe me, they'd run screaming for their lives, fearing me, the bloodthirsty beast.

Of course, none of that really mattered since I didn't actually have any friends, unless I counted Gina and she wasn't exactly my BFF. It wasn't until that moment I realized just how pathetically alone I was. Why did I have to wait until I was dead—or undead—to realize what a miserable sap I was?

I know what it's like to be alone, Danni. Don't hide from us.

I forced the memory of Rider's message out of my mind, choosing loneliness over his company. He was the one who had done this to me, turned me into this weirdo-undead-walking-corpse. Yuck. The thought of myself being the walking dead sent a shudder through my body. "All right, first off… I'm not dead."

Walking toward my bedroom, I decided I needed to do some research. Rider wasn't even close to pale, and I didn't have the urge to morph into a bat and fly away into the night. Obviously, some details I recalled from vampire stories were untrue. What I needed to do if I was going to survive this… eternity?—was find out just what exactly Rider had turned me into.

I plopped down at my desk and booted up my laptop, googling *Vampire*. Obviously I was going to run across countless mentions of books, movies, you name it, but somewhere in the vast expanse of knowledge that could be found floating around on the Internet had to be something true, something that could tell me just what type of being I had become.

As I had expected, I had to filter through a plethora of websites devoted to various movies based on vampires, and there were tons of books, mostly horror and paranormal romance. Nothing helpful like, say, *The Idiot's Guide To Vampires*. Well, actually, there was an idiot's guide to vampires, but it wasn't an actual survival manual. It was all about the myth of the vampire. Same with *Vampires For Dummies*.

I glanced at the card Rider had given me. Eliza's name and telephone number were right there, sitting on my desk. All I had to do was pick up the phone and dial in order to get the answers to my burning questions.

"Uh-uh. No way."

I pushed away from the desk and walked to my dresser to pick out clothes. I wasn't running to one of Rider's lady friends for help. They were just as untrustworthy as him.

I'd deal with this thing on my own. I'd done everything else on my own since my daddy died anyway. I could be un-dead all by myself.

What was the worst that could happen?

By Sunday, I was ravenous. I paced my small apartment like a caged beast, terrified of what I might do if I left. I could sense that blood was out there, just waiting to be sucked out of the veins of unsuspecting citizens. I licked my lips, thinking about it. Then I cried.

It hurt so bad. Hunger tore at my insides, trying to claw its way out, begging me to feed it. How could I? I'd drained all the blood off of the meat in my refrigerator. I'd even eaten chunks of the meat raw, but it barely abated the thirst inside me.

Rider kept trying to talk to me in my head. Apparently, vampires could do that after all. The sound of his voice in my head drove me crazy. I didn't want to hear him, but how could I escape what was in my own mind? I couldn't sleep because of the hunger and the fear of running into Selander Ryan in the dream world. All I could do was pace back and forth… back and forth… and slowly starve to death.

Another current of blazing, white-hot pain ripped through my stomach and I grabbed my keys. It was night, safe for me to prowl. Unsafe for the poor fools walking out there alone.

I couldn't focus well enough through the pain to attempt driving, so I walked down the city streets, silently arguing with myself. It was wrong to kill, an unforgivable sin, but each time a stranger passed me on the sidewalk I heard the sound of their heart beating, blood gushing through their veins. Every heartbeat brought me closer to murder.

I found myself downtown in an area most single women wouldn't dare walk through at any time of day, but I didn't let that thought stop me. I'd reached the realization that it was time to kill or be killed, and, well, if I was going to have to kill someone, I'd rather it be someone who probably wouldn't be missed.

"Hey, baby! Won't you come on in and party?"

I turned my head to see a man swaggering out the door of a bar. He grabbed his crotch and made lip-smacking noises at me. I seriously doubted anyone would miss him.

I smiled coyly at him, hoping he'd see it in the spill of moonlight I'd just walked through, and turned down a dark alley. He stumbled in after me. I waited, leaning against the wall, doing my best to appear nonchalant while my body screamed for sustenance.

I argued with myself, the still-human part of me begging me not to do this, but my vampire side had to do what it had to do.

The drunk stepped closer to me, a disgusting smile spreading across his chubby cheeks as he grappled with his fly. In that split second, I came to my senses. What the hell was I doing? Was I seriously about to kill a man in an alley? I opened my mouth to tell the guy to shove off, but then he made a very stupid mistake.

He unzipped his pants, revealing himself, and after I just looked at him, said, "Well, it's not going to suck itself."

Oh, hell no. Uh-uh. This drunken waste of skin was not suggesting I actually go down on his little two-inch dick in some dirty alley. Anger engulfed me and the hunger escalated to an uncontainable degree.

"You want me to *suck* you?"

"Oh, yeah." His slimy little tongue darted out to lick his lips.

"Okay," I agreed, and pushed off the wall. "I'll suck you."

I grabbed him by the shoulders before I lost my nerve and bit into his sweaty neck. There was a slight pressure in my gums and then I tasted the sweet, tangy nectar I'd been longing for. The man groaned, and it excited me. I tightened my claw-like fingers into his shoulders and forced him to the ground, straddling him. To a passerby, it probably looked like we were going at it in the alley, which was fine with me. All I cared about was draining him dry and stopping the hunger burning through my system.

"Danni, stop! He's had enough!"

I registered Rider's voice barking loudly in my head, but didn't pull away. The man's blood had a stronger hold on me than Rider's commanding tone.

"Let him go now, Danni! Do it!"

Not gonna happen. I slurped greedily, felt the warmth of the blood as it slid down my throat, fueling my body. My aches and pains started to diminish, energy buzzed inside me. I was drinking liquid power, and I had no intention of stopping.

Until I was forcefully made to.

I was ripped away from the sweaty pig's throat none too gently and held away by the scruff of my neck, just like a mutt. Rider stared down into my eyes. His own held a feral gleam. No wonder he'd sounded so loud and clear. He'd been right there with me.

"Let me go." My voice came out deep and raspy, calm despite the panic I felt rising inside me. There was still blood inside the man, and Rider was going to allow all that precious liquid to spill out in the alley!

I kicked out and Rider grunted as my foot connected with his leg, but he only tightened his hold. When his eyes closed, I feared seeing what would be there when they opened, but to my surprise, there was no anger, no murderous intent. He opened his eyes to look at me with sheer pity.

"You should have come to me, Danni."

He squeezed the back of my neck and everything faded away.

The scent of fresh spring rain enveloped me as I opened my eyes to stare up at a white ceiling. I turned my head to see I rested in a bed of soft, blood red silk. The walls were a dark gray and unadorned. I heard a soft rustle coming from the opposite direction and turned my head to the right.

A chubby dishwater blonde in a tight red dress sat on a stool before a bar. Her head was thrown back, allowing a man to suck greedily at her throat. No, not just a man. Rider. His hand was splayed across her stomach, his other arm supporting the woman from behind.

A white-hot streak of ire scorched through my chest as he pulled back, licked the woman's throat to seal the gash he'd made and then licked the last remnants of blood from his lips. He pressed a button on a small black box sitting atop the bar and said, "Come get Billie."

His body tensed, then he turned to look at me, his eyes dazed and content. "You're awake."

"Don't let that stop your fun," I snapped, unable to

bite back my anger, anger I didn't know why I felt. Anger which intensified when Rider grinned at me.

"Danni Keller, are you jealous?"

"Where you're concerned? Hell no." I squirmed under his I-know-better-than-that look and rose to a sitting position. My head spun with the action and I had to blink to bring the room back into focus.

When I could see clearly, I observed my surroundings. I was in a massive bed. To my right, a black and chrome bar lined the wall. A painting of a beautiful, dark-haired woman hung above it. To the side of the bed, a chaise and a chair, both in red leather, sat empty. To my left sat a dresser and a door I assumed led to a bathroom. One light fixture hanging in the center of the ceiling illuminated the entire room with a pale glow.

"What's this? Your bachelor pad?"

A door opened directly before me, on the opposite side of the room, and a burly black man dressed completely in black entered and scooped up the unconscious woman whose mouth was turned up in a drunken smile. Without a word, he carried her out, closing the door behind him.

"This is my home," Rider answered, placing his hand over his stomach. "I live over the bar."

"The bar?" Suddenly it hit me and I felt like slapping myself in the forehead and letting out a Homer Simpson-worthy *Doh*! "*Rider*. You own The Midnight Rider."

"Yes."

"So, what? You draw unsuspecting women here, get them drunk and prey upon them?"

Rider's nostrils flared and his eyes darkened. I felt my heart—apparently vampirism didn't cause it to cease beating—hitch in my chest and I cringed, expecting violence.

Rider closed his eyes and let out a heavy breath, visibly calming himself before speaking. "I don't prey on innocents."

He opened his eyes and once again, they were a beautiful deep blue, untouched by fury. "A lot of other predators, human and not, do tend to stalk their prey in bars though. It's part of the reason I chose to purchase this type of establishment. It keeps me nearby when someone needs my help."

I laughed. "Like the help you gave me?"

"I told you not to leave with anyone, but while I was fighting one enemy, another strolled in and you just walked off with him. Damn it, Danni, I can protect you from predators, but I can't protect you from yourself."

"What's that supposed to mean?"

"It means you're hard-headed and stubborn, a trait which has already nearly killed you once. You have to listen to me when I tell you things."

"I don't have to do anything you say." I swung my legs off the bed and reached for my ankle boots on the floor, frowning when I realized I was wearing a black long-sleeved shirt, not the blue T-shirt I'd had on when I'd left my apartment earlier. And I could tell I was no longer wearing a bra. "You undressed me again."

"Your shirt was covered in blood, so I exchanged it for one of mine. If you'd prefer to wear the ruined one, I could probably still retrieve it from the garbage bin for you."

"Don't be a smart-ass." I let out a sigh of relief as I noted the fact my jeans were still on, and pushed aside the shame of what I'd done earlier. I'd attacked a man in an alley like a wild animal, hurt him badly enough to have drenched my shirt and bra in his blood.

I pushed my feet into the boots and stood.

"Where do you think you're going?" Rider asked as I walked past him toward the door.

"Anywhere but here."

"Danni, you know you killed that man, right?"

I came to a dead stop as the blood in my veins froze. Tears fell from my eyes as I turned toward Rider, my head shaking from side to side. "No."

"Yes." He held my gaze as his eyes changed from angry to reflecting pure pity. "I can't hold you here, but I can help you not to make the same mistake which will haunt you for the rest of your life, and believe me, sweetheart, it's a long, *long* life. Too damn long for that kind of regret."

"No." Another tear fell as I remembered fangs erupting from my gums as I sank my teeth into the man's neck. He was a disgusting pig, but I shouldn't have murdered him! "No, I couldn't have, I…"

"I'm sorry, Danni. I should have made you come to me before your hunger got too strong for you to take. I just didn't want to dominate you like that."

Rider stepped closer and tried to wrap his arms around me, but I twisted away from his grasp and walked over to the bar, gripping it to keep myself upright when my legs turned to Jell-O.

"You should have made me come to you? What you should have done was left me to die after Selander Ryan attacked me! You should have never turned me into this!"

"Danni."

"I killed a man. I'm a monster!"

"You're not a monster." Rider's hands grasped my shoulders and spun me around. "A monster wouldn't feel remorse for killing a man. You were hungry, so hungry you couldn't control yourself."

"And that makes it all right?" I stared up at his face, unable to comprehend how he could think that could possibly make it all right. Then I remembered he was a blood-sucking monster too. "Of course you do. You kill people all the time."

"No, I do not."

"Oh, yeah? What about the woman you just had carted away?" My stomach roiled at the thought of the woman being murdered while I'd just watched it happen, actually feeling jealous because Rider had desired her.

"Billie is fine." Rider released his hold on my shoulders

and stepped back. "She's a donor. I pay her and my other donors good money to supply me with fresh, living blood and I never take more than they can spare."

I shuddered. "You make me sick. You make it sound like you're actually doing these *donors* a favor, when you're sucking out their life blood!"

"Considering the fact that my donors were all prostitutes before I hired them, I am doing them a favor. Selling blood to vampires for money is a hell of a lot safer than selling one's body to any random stranger." He turned away, muttering a curse. "Damn it, Danni. You don't have to like me, but you do have to trust me. I'm not this evil creature you think I am and I'd never hurt you."

"And why should I believe that?"

He looked at me, held my gaze for a long moment before turning it to the floor, not uttering a word.

"Exactly," I said and crossed the floor to sit at the foot of the bed. I let out a groan of frustration and fell backward, hopelessness filling my chest. "How are you supposed to help me? How are you going to keep me from killing again?"

The mattress dipped, and I glanced up to see Rider leaning toward me, unbuttoning the billowy, dark red shirt he wore. Instinct kicked in and I jumped up, but he quickly snagged my wrist.

"Relax, Danni. I'm not attacking you. I'm going to feed you." He pushed the collar of his shirt aside and beneath his skin, I could see the flutter of his heartbeat in his throat.

I licked my lips as the hunger flared back to life inside me and he pulled me down so that I straddled his lap on top of the bed. A hunger of another sort shot through me, sparking little fires through my body, but I fought against it. He was a vampire, a blood-sucking vampire, not the type of man I could see myself checking out china patterns with any time in the future.

"Drink, Danni. Quench your thirst with me so you

don't accidentally kill again." He cupped his hand around the base of my skull and pushed my head toward his throat until my mouth met sweet, salty skin.

My tongue darted out to take a little taste and the hunger in my belly roared. The pressure in my gums grew until they cracked and my canines lengthened into deadly fangs. I scraped them along Rider's skin and he groaned.

"Do it, Danni. Take all you need."

I plunged my fangs into his flesh and felt a jolt as his blood hit my tongue. It was far stronger than what I'd taken from the man in the alley. I heard a growl, but couldn't tell who it came from as I was consumed by the heady rush Rider's blood sent spiraling through me.

He ground his pelvis against mine and I felt the hardened length of him through my jeans. One of his hands slid up the back of my—his—shirt as the other held my head tight against his throat. His fingers gently caressed the skin between my shoulder blades, whispering a trail over my spinal column, and I shivered. It felt so good I forgot to remember I wanted someone else.

As his blood filled my mouth, I slid my hands into his unbuttoned shirt, let them roam over his hard, muscular chest. He smelled like rain, tasted like the richest dessert, and felt like steel. He felt so good I didn't object when he slid his hands to my collar and started opening buttons.

"You smell like midnight after a rainstorm," I whispered as I withdrew my fangs from his skin and licked over the two small holes I'd left, closing the wounds before lapping up the blood trickling down his skin. I didn't want to waste one precious drop.

"You smell like a dream," he whispered in response before rolling so that I was pinned beneath him on the bed. He raised my arms so my hands were by either side of my head and parted the open shirt I wore. "I'm so glad you didn't have enough time to alter these before I changed you."

Realizing my meager chest was on full display was like a

bucket of ice cold water thrown in my face. I jerked upward so quickly, I banged my forehead into Rider's, sending him crashing backward off the bed.

I ignored his surprised curse and the pain in my head to quickly button my shirt and jump up from the bed.

"Danni! What are you doing?" He was standing again, reaching for me.

I did the first thing I could think of. I shoved him with all my strength, which seemed like a lot after drinking from him, and he landed against the wall, his eyes open wide in surprise.

"What the hell is wrong with you?"

"I'm not your cheap whore!" I yelled. "Nice try seducing me, but it won't work."

"Seducing you?" He barked out a laugh. "You're the one who seduced me. You have a damn succubus's bite! If I wasn't a stronger vampire, I'd probably be humping against your leg right now. No wonder it was so easy for you to kill that man in the alley. He died while coming."

I gasped in disgust. "That's sick. How dare you—"

"I changed you into a vampire, but you still have a little succubus in your system, in your bite. No wonder Selander Ryan is haunting your dreams."

A chill snaked down my spine at the reminder of why I hadn't slept since Friday. "I'm not like him. I'm not one of those beasts. I didn't kill that man by… by…"

"Screwing him to death?"

"Right."

"You might as well have." Rider buttoned his shirt, relieving me of the too-hot-to-handle-just-then view of his perfect chest. "When you bite, you send an orgasmic current through your prey. No man will fight you off when you take too much. They'll ignore their survival instincts rather than shut off the current. That's going to make it damned hard for you not to kill until you've learned to control your hunger."

"I didn't take too much from you." I rose my chin

defiantly. I didn't care what he said, I wasn't a demonic turbo-slut. "I obviously held back."

"I'm a powerful vampire, and your sire. If I wasn't…" He looked toward the bed and shuddered. "You still sent the current through me, and for the record, you didn't hold back. You simply took all you could. You'd already feasted on a man before I brought you here and I'd just filled up on Billie. I had plenty to spare, so I didn't need to stop you."

He stepped before me and held my chin in his large hand. "You're in danger, Danni. Selander Ryan knows you're alive, and he is still after you. He'll come to you again in your dreams."

"Why? What does he care that you made me a vampire?"

"He'd marked you as his, but I stole you away. Incubi don't take that very well. Especially Ryan." Something dark flitted through his eyes and I could tell there was something he wasn't telling me. Hell, I'm sure there was a lot he wasn't telling me. Like what his real interest in me was.

"So let him kill me."

"What?" His eyes grew wide. "Are you insane?"

"No." I shrugged my shoulders, going for nonchalant. "I'm such a stubborn pain-in-the-ass, why not let him kill me and get me out of the way? Why should you care if I live or die?"

Rider frowned, narrowing his eyes on mine as though trying to read the thoughts behind them. "You don't strike me as the suicidal type. What are you trying at?"

"The real reason you pretend to care about me," I confessed. "What do you have to gain from me staying alive?"

"Is it so hard to believe that someone could care about you?"

I chuckled, unable to stop it from erupting. "Someone like you, a sexy, arrogant vampire who has women willing to sell their own blood? I find it impossible that you'd give a damn about an ordinary woman like me. What's your real motive?"

He shook his head and moved a lock of my hair, securing it behind my ear. "Why do you do that, Danni?"

"Do what?"

"Think so low of yourself. How can you be so blind to the fact you are so fucking beautiful?"

As far as compliments went, the statement he'd just made combined with the deep, resolute, throaty growl of his voice was one hell of a good one. His eyes held the same sincerity I'd witnessed downstairs in the bar that night he'd ushered me into a booth and ordered me to drink coffee and sober up. It reached inside me, wrapped itself around my heart, but I couldn't allow it to take hold. There was something so powerful about him, so awesome to behold… He couldn't possibly consider me worthy. He obviously had a vendetta against Selander Ryan and I was something he could use against the incubus. He was evil, a monster who'd stolen my normal life and given me one where I'd be subjected to killing in order to live. I couldn't trust a word he said, or that stupid quickened beat in my heart when he looked at me so intently.

His firmly spoken words didn't make me swoon at his feet, didn't turn my legs to Jell-O. They pissed me off.

"If I'm so fucking beautiful, then why am I always so fucking alone?" I shoved past him and ran out the door, down the staircase to burst through the door leading to a long hallway which took me to the door leading to the bar.

I received a few frowns as I pushed past the people mingling inside the bar, but didn't care. I found the exit and ran to it like my life depended on it. What the hell was I doing? My life was not going to be changed by this crazy thing that had happened to me. I would not let an arrogant vampire and a sneaky incubus take away what little sense of normalcy I could still hold on to. I damn sure wasn't going to let them creep inside my head or heart and make a home there.

You're not alone, Danni.

Rider's voice filtered through my mind, along with a powerful compulsion to return to him. He sounded sad… hurt that I'd left him. No! It was a trick, a mind-game he was playing with me. A game he would not win.

Despite the urge to turn around and walk back up those stairs to where I sensed him waiting, I turned away from the bar and ran all the way home.

SEVEN

Morning came far too soon. After leaving The Midnight Rider, I was wide awake, and that, combined with the fear of Selander Ryan finding me in a dream, kept me from getting any rest. Unfortunately, the moment the sun rose, lethargy crept in.

I realized it was a part of being a vampire and cursed myself for having a day job, a day job I had no intention of quitting. What else would I do? Work the midnight shift at an all-night diner? Become one of Rider's barmaids? Uh-uh. No way.

I popped a bottle full of No-Doz, figuring they probably wouldn't work but giving it a try anyway, and opened my closet. While I'd been out Sunday night—killing a man—Dex had left a message on my machine. Nocturnal Inc. was speeding up their deadline. They were going to come to the office today. Wonderful.

I pulled out a short, slinky black dress, figuring even if I totally bombed at the presentation, I could at least *look* sexy. I stepped into one of my many pairs of granny panties and a beige gel-filled bra before rubbing the lotion Rider had given me all over my body. For the first time in my life, I looked forward to winter, when I could wear long-sleeved shirts and cover up the majority of my skin.

I put on the little black dress and turned in front of the mirror, half thankful and half sad vampires could still see their own reflection. Thankful because I could make sure my bra straps weren't showing, sad because I could still pick myself apart mercilessly.

I let out a sigh and headed toward the bathroom to brush my hair. On a whim, I paused by my desk and picked up the Nocturnal Inc. file I'd brought home with me and removed the small sample of perfume. I applied it to my throat and gasped as the scent of it hit my nose.

Images of couples kissing and... *more than kissing...* filtered through my mind. My breath quickened, and I realized I wasn't just watching them, I was feeling them. Their every thought, emotion, and physical sensation washed over me, suffocating me with its intensity. The rush that came with the images was so heady with raw unrestrained passion, so powerful I was once again struck with the question of would I survive it, and just like that, a full-blown campaign hit me like a sledgehammer.

I could barely keep my eyes open by the time I reached the office, but somehow I'd managed to make it there without falling asleep at the wheel of my car. I zipped past Gina in the hall, too rushed to bother with a greeting, and she gave me a "Go, girl" look of approval as she took in my slinky little dress, black heels and upswept chignon, which featured a few loose tendrils for effect.

I ignored the dropped jaws of my co-workers as I made it to my cubicle, knowing if I took too long to analyze why they were looking at me, I'd find a way to convince myself I looked stupid and blow the presentation due to lack of confidence, my biggest enemy.

"Danni! Thank goodness you're—"

I jerked around to see Dex standing outside my cubicle, his mouth hanging open as his eyes traveled my body from chest to foot, and back up again.

"Here," he finished, then shook his head, blinked his eyes, and cleared his throat. "Nocturnal Inc. has arrived and, um, they're, uh, waiting in the conference room. Is that a new dress?"

A nervous giggle escaped me and I groaned inwardly. *That's the way to get him, Danni. Act like a silly schoolgirl.* "This? No, um, I haven't worn it, but it's, um, not, uh, new. I mean, uh, I guess it is since I, uh, haven't ever taken it out of, uh, my closet, but uh, um…"

I smoothed my hands over my hips, stared at my feet and wished the ground would open up and swallow me whole. Dex Prince was staring at me like I was some decadent dessert he'd just ordered and I was stammering and sputtering like a bumbling moron.

"Looks good," he said and flashed me the sexiest smile I'd ever seen when I glanced up. He nodded toward the portfolio in my hand. "Are you ready?"

"Ready for whatever you have to offer." The words shot out of my mouth before my brain caught up to my hormones. I froze as Dex's eyebrow arched and cleared my throat. "I mean, yes, I'm ready to blow Nocturnal Inc. out of their socks and start on the next assignment you have for me."

Dex's eyes narrowed as he bit his lip, and at that moment I would have given my immortal life to bite that same lip between my own teeth, especially when it turned up into another sexy-as-sin smile. "I like this new confidence, Danni. Let's get in the conference room so you can show me what you've got."

I closed my eyes against the image provoked by the double entendre and brushed past him, doing my best to not visibly tremble as the slight contact with him sent shivers through my body.

I stumbled, and he quickly righted me, keeping his warm hand on the small of my back as we traveled the length of the hallway. It didn't take more than a minute to reach the conference room, but with the heat of his hand burning into my back and the weight of a dozen or so knowing looks on us, it felt like longer. Come the next morning, the office would be abuzz with gossip and I'd be labeled as the office slut, riding Dex Prince straight to a new promotion. I could have done a happy dance, because despite what they thought, I knew what I was and what I wasn't. I wouldn't sleep my way into a new promotion, but I would do whatever it took to get Dex to realize we'd be great together. Now that he seemed to notice me, it was just a matter of time. The first major step was blowing away Nocturnal, Inc.

I squared my shoulders and took a deep breath as Dex opened the door to the conference room. Showtime. Pitches and presentations before clients were the worst parts of my job. Actually, they were the only bad parts. I loved advertising. It gave me the creative power I craved and a way to do something big yet stay behind the scenes. If only someone else could do the selling to the clients.

I took another calming breath as I entered the room. I wasn't going to let nerves ruin this pitch. I wasn't just pitching a campaign to a company. I was pitching myself to Dex Prince, and dammit, I couldn't lose. Not when my only other option was a vampire who was probably using me to get back at an incubus.

"I hope you haven't been waiting long," I said as I walked to the head of the long table and laid my portfolio on top. I smoothed the skirt of my dress as Dex took his seat to my right and rose my eyes to give eye contact and a smile to each of the Nocturnal, Inc. representatives sitting around the table. "I'm Danni—"

My smile faltered and my heart skidded to a stop as my gaze met with Selander Ryan, who was to my left, leaning back casually in his chair, a lascivious grin etched across his face. He wore an expensive looking suit of steel blue with an open collared white silk dress shirt, no tie and his long blond hair was unrestrained, left to drape over his shoulders. His accessories were a large, silver ring and a gleam in his dark eyes that promised he was up to no good.

"This is Danni Keller," Dex cut in, snagging my attention. His eyes showed his wariness as he finished. "Danni is a very clever associate here at Prince Advertising. I'm sure you will love her campaign idea. Right, Danni?"

Shit. I was already screwing up in front of him. Damn it. I swallowed past the fear lodged in my throat and nodded my head affirmatively. Selander Ryan might be up to no good, but surely the man wouldn't kill me in front of a witness, especially not on the third floor of a large business building full of people who'd seen him and his business partners come in. "That's right, Dex, and thank you for the introduction."

I faked a bright and confident smile as I studied Selander Ryan's business partners. The man on his left side was incredibly handsome, his face all hard angles, his brown hair long and curly. The deep brown eyes aimed at me were full of heated interest. Incubus. I was positive of it.

The woman to Selander's right, my immediate left, eyed me with contempt. Her skin was pale, arctic pale and her eyes were like two crystal blue orbs, so light I could almost see through the color. The effect gave me a chill. The long white-blonde ponytail perched atop her head was pulled back so severely from her chiseled face, I winced, imagining how painful it would be for her to blink. No wonder she looked so bitchy. Both of Ryan's assistants wore business suits, and just by the cut alone and the crispness of the material, I knew they'd dropped a pretty penny on the attire.

Across the table, next to Dex, was another man, this one extremely broad-shouldered and heavyset. He wore a suit, a blue pinstripe number, but I could tell it didn't cost anywhere near what the others had spent for their business clothes. His dark, bushy brows hung low over his round brown eyes as he sized me up. He had to be the hired muscle, I surmised as I noticed the big golden rings decorating each one of his chubby fingers. Great. If the incubi didn't suck out my life essence, Mr. Muscles would beat me to a pulp. It was a win-win situation all the way around.

Dex cleared his throat, drawing my attention to the fact my mind had wandered again. I took a deep breath and pushed everything but the presentation out of my mind. I had to focus on my job. My incubi and vampire troubles could be dealt with later.

"First, I'd like to say how grateful I am to have been given this project. I find the Nocturnal, Inc. project to be incredibly satisfying. The fragrance is delicious, a dessert for the senses. From the moment I smelled the sample, I was transported to a place…" I shivered, allowing them to see the effect the perfume had on me. "The scent is absolutely captivating and I want to capture that in our campaign. My sketches are a little rough since this meeting wasn't supposed to be so soon, but I'm confident what I do have is strong enough to get my idea across."

I opened the file folder and withdrew the sketches that had hit me full force that morning. I hadn't had time to add color, but as I looked at the graphite and charcoal drawings, I knew they'd get the point across.

I hung the sketches on the board behind me, my fingertips tingling as I touched each one. It was as if I'd transferred the images from my head directly to the paper and somehow included the passion and raw energy with them. They were vibrant and alive, even without color.

"Midnight Passions is going to be the sexiest fragrance on the market," I announced as I stepped away from the display board and turned around to address Selander Ryan and his minions. The looks in their eyes were feral as they studied the sketches. I glanced at Dex to see what he thought and nearly stumbled as I saw the heat blazing in his baby blues.

"The sketches behind me represent the print ads we will run in major magazines and on billboards in high-traffic areas." I turned sideways so I could show each sketch as I referred to it. The first sketch featured a topless mermaid, her breasts barely concealed by the sculpted torso of her human lover. The man held her half in and half out of the water as various exotic flowers and plants bloomed around them. The mermaid looked directly out of the shot, appearing to hold the viewer's gaze with a hungry gleam in her eye as she held the man's earlobe between her teeth, her fingernails digging into his shoulders. "This is the fantasy piece. Fantasy is big now and mermaids have always been seen as beautiful, sexy creatures. This captures what the female buyers of the fragrance want to feel like when wearing your scent. Alluring. Exotic. Better than real."

I allowed them a moment to take it in before moving to the next sketch. One by one, I moved through the sketches, pointing out the specific selling features of each and how they directly tied in with the feel of the fragrance. Each featured a couple in a state of near-sex, all of them featuring at least one person whose gaze seemed to come right through the page to meet the prospective customer's, begging them to sample the fragrance for themselves and taste the passion it evoked.

"And this is the sketch which will be the basis for the commercial advertisements." I gestured toward the largest sketch, the one that had left me sweating after completion. Six people, three males and three females, wrapped around each other, clothes ripped and shredded. One woman clawed at her neck as her male suitor licked the glistening skin. Another woman pinned a man to a chaise, her tongue tracing the seam of her lips as she looked directly at what would be the camera, her eyes full of hunger. The other couple appeared to climb each other, flames licking their bodies as they struggled to breathe through the rush the fragrance caused. Beads of sweat glistened along all of their brows as they pulled at their clothes, trying to escape the suffering heat. Beneath the sketch, in blazing letters, was the slogan. "Can you survive the passion?" I took a deep breath, fanning myself as I pulled my gaze away from the sketch and faced my audience. "That's the slogan, the catchphrase we will use on everything. That's the one thought that will fill your prospective customer's mind every time they see, hear about, or smell your product. Their eyes will fill with the same hunger as the people in these sketches as they line up at the cash registers to find out for themselves."

Dex loosened his tie and reached for the glass of ice water in front of him, downing it in two big gulps before standing. "Well, thank you, Danni, for that… passionate presentation. I'd say you definitely captured the essence of the product. Wouldn't you agree, Mr. Ryan?"

I held my breath as Selander Ryan leaned forward, his eyes gleaming as they raked over me. I trembled, whether from fear of his proximity or his response, I couldn't say. "I am thoroughly impressed, Prince. In fact, I wouldn't mind stealing Miss Keller away from you. I could use her… *passionate fire* in my line of business."

I bet you'd like that, you soul sucking son of a bitch.

He grinned slyly and I got the sinking feeling in the pit of my gut that he knew what I'd just thought. The incubus with him grinned, his smoldering eyes absorbing me with interest. The woman leered at me, her eyes still cold as ice, and that's when it hit me. She was a succubus, the thing Ryan had tried to turn me into. No wonder she seemed icy cold to me. She was. My succubus side couldn't stand her, and I'm sure she felt the same about me.

Dex's hand rested along the small of my back as he pulled me to his side, providing much needed warmth. "I'm afraid we aren't willing to spare our Danni. She's very special to us here."

Irritation flared behind Selander's eyes, causing my heart to lurch somewhere near my throat, but he blinked and hid the emotion behind a cool, businessman façade. "I can understand your possessiveness about such... *talent*." He looked at me, the corner of his mouth barely tipped upward at the corner. "If I had such a treasure in my possession, I assure you I would never let it go."

The air left my lungs at the thinly veiled threat and my knees weakened. I leaned into Dex to keep from falling. "If there aren't any questions, I'd be glad to get to work on the commercial while you iron out the contract. That is, if you're satisfied with the campaign." I licked my lips and swallowed hard, fighting back a scream. I had to get out of there. I could feel pressure in my skull, sense Rider trying to push his way in. If my fear grew any stronger, I wouldn't be surprised to find him crashing into the office to rescue me from danger. Especially if he knew I was so close to his arch enemy.

"I am extremely pleased with the campaign and one hundred percent sold." Selander Ryan grinned impishly before turning his gaze to Dex. "I like your employee's enthusiasm with the project. Let's sign the contract so she can move forward with the ads."

"Excellent." Dex beamed with satisfaction as he walked me out of the office. "Are you all right?" he whispered, leaning in close as I sucked in a big gulp of air.

"Fine," I lied. The entire floor was spinning. "I think my nerves are just a little jangled. I wasn't expecting to give the presentation so soon."

"Well, you knocked it out of the park." A brilliant smile lit up his handsome face, sucking more air from my lungs. "I had no idea you had such... *hot* ideas stewing in that pretty little head of yours. You're a little devil in disguise, Danni Keller."

More like a succubi-slash-vamp, but close enough.

"I don't think I like the way that big, blond Fabio wannabe had his eye on you. You're my special talent." He frowned as he swept a tendril of hair behind my ear, his fingertips tickling the skin along my neck and sending a spark down my spine. "Get a drink of water, take a break if you need it, and I'll come check in with you after I get this contract signed and escort our newest clients out."

He bit his juicy lip, grinning predatorily as he turned around and vanished back into his office, leaving me breathless, leaning against the wall. Take a break and get a drink of water. Right. What I needed to settle my stomach was a nice, tall glass of blood. I doubted I could find it in the break room.

One thing I knew for sure though, I didn't want to be standing outside Dex's office when Selander Ryan and his minions came out. And I didn't want him to snatch me when I left work. I had to call Rider and tell him what had happened. If I didn't, it was only a matter of time before Ryan captured me and turned me into his hell-slut. Or killed me. Neither option exactly worked for me.

I walked to my desk on wobbly legs, ignoring the speculative glances from my co-workers and the hushed whispers as they wondered how the presentation had gone. I lifted the phone to my ear and set the receiver back into the base without dialing. This wasn't the type of conversation I wanted to have amid my nosy co-workers. I could talk to Rider in my mind, but I feared lowering the barrier I'd somehow managed to put up against his intrusion. Who knew how many times I could take it down before it wouldn't stick any longer?

Grabbing the cell phone out of my purse, I walked down the hall and entered the solitude of the stairwell. Too weak to stand, I slid down the wall until I crumpled onto the floor, my legs folded under me to provide some sense of modesty. Rider had programmed his direct number into my phone sometime the first night we'd met, the night he and Selander had changed my life into a freakfest.

"What's happened?" Rider's voice was all business as he answered on the first ring.

I ignored the little unwanted jump my heart did and leaned my head back against the wall, closing my eyes against the burn. "Selander Ryan is in my office building. He knows where I work."

"Get out of there."

"I can't. This is my job, Rider. I can't just leave in the middle of the workday without a good reason."

"Your life depending on it isn't a good reason?"

I felt his anger brush against me like a blast of heat sweeping over my body. "I can't tell my boss his new client is an incubus or that I'm a… a…"

"Vampire-succubus hybrid."

"Yeah. I'd like to stay out of the loony bin."

"And I'd like you to stay out of the morgue." I felt him probing in my mind and I squeezed my eyes tighter, focusing my energy on keeping him out. "Danni, let me in."

"No. Just… Don't let Selander Ryan get me. My boss is going to escort him out after they sign off on the contract we just acquired with him. I'll stay out of his way so he can't nab me. I need you here when I leave though, in case he's waiting for me."

"Fine. But I need you to quit blocking me out of your mind. I need to know if he gets near you while you're at work. He might not wait to get you alone."

Now there was a comforting thought. I sighed, defeated. "On one condition. Don't crash in here, guns blazing, unless it is absolutely necessary."

"I won't, and I don't carry a gun."

"You know what I mean."

I felt his smile, though he was miles away. "I promise."

"All right then." I pushed the END button on the cell and took a deep breath, letting it out slowly as I mentally let go of whatever it was I held in my mind to keep Rider out.

I felt him move in right away, settling in to watch over me. It was disturbing, yet strangely comforting at the same time. I was protected in case Selander Ryan tried to kill me at the end of the workday. Now all I had to worry about was hiding the vampire in my brain from Dex and somehow keeping my job when the man after my soul now knew where I worked.

EIGHT

I collected myself as best I could and left the stairwell. The conference room we'd held the meeting in was visible from my cubicle and the blinds were open, showing no one inside. Either Dex had moved the group to his office to sign the contracts or they'd worked out the details quickly and Selander Ryan was on the loose. The thought of him being loose in the building capable of popping up at me at any time turned my legs into a wobbling mess and I fell more than sat in my desk chair as my phone rang.

Keeping my head on a steady pivot, scanning the floor for Selander Ryan and his henchmen, I picked up the phone on autopilot. "Prince Advertising. Danni Keller speaking."

My stomach filled with nausea as I was met with silence, reminding me of the call I'd received the previous Friday. "Hello? This is Danni Keller. How may I help you?"

I'd scanned the entire floor and saw nothing and no one out of place. Dex's door was closed, so I assumed Selander and his people, creatures, whatever they were classified as, were in there. I could only deal with one threat at a time, so I hung up the phone.

"You're going to die," the same voice from Friday said, loud enough to be heard just before I'd settled the receiver into the cradle. I pulled my hand away from the phone, afraid to even touch it as the threat sank in.

Danni. Are you all right?

I'm fine, I thought, unsure if I could actually even get the message across to Rider using only my mind like he could do with me. I knew he could feel what I felt, so I took a deep breath and tried to calm myself. The other option would be to call him and I didn't want to pick up the phone after it had just been used to deliver a death threat and cell phones weren't supposed to be used on the office floor. If I went into the stairwell again, I'd miss it when Selander Ryan left Dex's office and I didn't want to lose track of him while he was in the building.

What happened? You had a spike of fear.

I groaned. I didn't feel like carrying on a full conversation with Rider in my head. I didn't even know if I could. I didn't know if I should tell him about the calls either, not until I ruled him out as a suspect.

What calls? Rider's voice came through firm and angry. Sonofabitch.

Quit eavesdropping! I tried to throw up a mental wall again, not sure how I'd done it before. While I needed his protection, I didn't want him in my head reading my every thought. I closed my eyes and focused on pushing him out, concentrating so hard on the effort I let out a grunt.

"Danni, are you all right?" I heard Gina ask and opened one eye to see her standing next to my cubicle, watching me from over the wall. "Oooh, did you eat the breakfast tacos from that truck down the street?" she asked, leaning in closer since she'd lowered her voice. "Do you need to go to the bathroom? I can cover for you if Dex comes by. I have Pepto if you need it."

I opened my other eye and blew out a breath. "I'm fine, Gina. Just really… focused on something."

"Oh, good. I thought you were about to mess

yourself," she said, sliding into my cubicle to perch on my desk. Clearly, the comment I'd made about focusing on something went right over her head, and she didn't think she was intruding. "That man in Dex's office is pure sex. Please tell me you got his name and noticed whether he was wearing a wedding band."

"Stay away from him," I blurted, not bothering to think how badly that would sound.

Gina moved back as if struck. "Wow, Danni. If you called dibs already, all you had to do was say so."

"No!" I grabbed Gina's arm as she made to leave. "It's not that, not at all." Images from my dream flashed through my mind and I pushed them out as quickly as I could before I melted into a puddle of lust right there in the office. I recalled the look in Selander's eyes as he'd prepared to sink his teeth into me a second time, and that seemed to do the trick and bring me back to reality. "I just don't think he's a man you want to fool around with. He seemed like an arrogant creep."

"Seriously?" Gina laughed. "Honey, he sure looks like the type of man I want to fool with, and so what if he's arrogant? With a face and body like that, he can afford to be. That hair was amazing. I could run my fingers through it for days. And nights," she added with a wink.

"You'd be dead before dawn," I muttered, remembering what Selander had done to me in the alley.

"What?"

I shook my head, realizing Gina hadn't heard what I'd said, and it was best I didn't repeat it. Whether it was true or not, it sounded crazy and she wouldn't believe me. She, like most everyone else in the world, didn't know vampires and incubi were real, and if I tried to tell her she'd think I was insane and friendly with me or not, she'd tell the whole office. Forget snagging Dex Prince for a husband, I'd be out of a job. Hell, I'd never get another job in my field. "I just think it's a bad idea. He doesn't seem like a good guy. I don't want to see you get hurt."

"I never get hurt," she replied. "Good guys go stale after a while. That sexy man of my dreams could give me some much needed excitement."

I sighed in defeat as she sashayed away and glanced up at Dex's door. It was still closed. I'd never paid attention to how long it took to sign contracts before since it wasn't part of my job, so I had no idea if the amount of time he'd been in Dex's office was a good sign or a bad sign. What if they were killing Dex? I shook my head, almost laughed. Incubus or not, he'd have to kill everyone on the floor to get away with it. I hoped. I was letting my fears get the best of me and I was going to be a nervous wreck when he finally emerged from the office if I didn't do something to keep myself together.

I booted up my computer and pulled up everything I had on Nocturnal, Inc. The owner's information hadn't been in my file so I Googled the company and sure enough, S. Ryan was listed as the owner. I searched for a business location and could only come up with a post office box in New York. He was certainly a long way from New York now and despite how well Prince Advertising had been doing, we were a small company compared to the advertising giants in New York. Selander had definitely chosen Prince Advertising to get to me, which proved Rider was correct about him stalking me. I'd thought he only meant in my dreams, but he could get to me in the light of day as well. Until that moment, I'd felt safe in the daylight as long as I stayed awake. I'd foolishly thought of Selander Ryan and his kind as creatures of the night, but like myself and Rider, they could clearly move about in the daytime. I wondered if the sun burned the hell out of their skin too and hoped it did.

My phone rang, and this time I checked the caller ID before automatically answering. It was another unknown number. My stomach churned. If I wasn't a vampire and thought it would help, I'd take Gina up on her offer of Pepto-Bismol. The predators in my life were giving me all kinds of stomach distress.

I looked around and noted a few irritated glances as I allowed the phone to ring, so I turned the volume down and waited to let the call to go to voicemail. Voicemail picked up and shortly after, the red light blinked, letting me know the caller had left a message. A very short message. I was pretty sure it would be a simple, straight-forward threat on my life, so I was in no rush to listen to it. I turned my ringer back up and hoped I didn't hear from the psycho caller again. Unless he knew some very impressive tricks, I could rule out Selander Ryan as the caller. I doubt he'd call and threaten someone while signing contracts.

The air around me seemed to shift, and I looked over to see Dex, Selander, and Selander's creepy crew standing outside of Dex's office. Although he was shaking Dex's hand and saying something to him, Selander turned his head and immediately zeroed in on me. There was no way he should instantly know where I sat in the vast sea of cubicles scattered over the third floor of the office building, but he looked straight at me without hesitation. That fact scared me more than the predatory gleam in his eye when he smiled at me, delivering an unspoken threat. He knew who I was and where to find me. If he couldn't get me in my dreams, he'd kill me on the street, in my office, or maybe in the privacy of my own home.

Gina walked up to Dex, seductively swaying her hips, and handed him a file. She said something to him before turning and speaking to Selander, no doubt introducing herself while batting her lashes. I froze, watching her, a scream of warning wanting to break free, but I couldn't yell a warning across the office floor. It wouldn't do anything to deter her, and I'd only look crazy.

My phone rang. I glanced at the caller ID, not wanting to take my eyes off Selander Ryan while he was near me, but also not willing to take another threatening call at the moment. My nerves were shot enough. According to the caller ID, it was an internal call, so I picked up. "Yeah?" I asked, skipping my normal professional greeting, my focus on the incubi and succubus currently too close for comfort to me.

"Danni Keller?"

"Yes?"

"Ms. Keller, this is the front desk. You have a visitor in the lobby."

I frowned, and it felt like the bottom of my stomach dropped out. Had my creepy caller graduated to making personal calls so quickly? "What visitor?"

"A Rider Knight."

Rider Knight? I nearly smiled, and would have if I wasn't about to piss myself in fear. The name was a bit close to Knight Rider, and I was tempted to tease the vampire with David Hasselhoff jokes, but at the moment I was preoccupied with making sure I lived long enough to deliver those jokes someday. "I'll be right down."

I hung up the phone and considered my options. I could take the stairs three floors down or take the elevator. I imagined getting captured in the stairwell and opted for the elevator. Gina was still talking to Selander, buying me time, so I quickly moved to the elevator and stepped in. I glanced toward Dex's office as I stepped in to see him and Selander Ryan both staring at me. Great.

As the doors closed, I realized I could be caught in the elevator as easily as the stairwell. I still had to make it down three floors. I pushed the button for the lobby and prayed for the best. I held my breath the entire ride down, pretty sure I'd leave a puddle on the floor if the doors opened before I reached my destination. Fortunately, the elevator doors didn't open until I reached the lobby and stepped out to see Rider standing near the front desk being drooled over by the two women manning it. He wore dark jeans, a dark blue button-down shirt with the top three buttons undone, and one hell of a scowl.

I jerked my head to the left, gesturing for him to follow

me to the sitting area off the lobby before we started talking, pretty sure our discussion would include subjects I didn't need the front desk staff to overhear.

"Why are you here now?" I asked, keeping my voice low as we faced off, neither of us choosing to sit.

"Because you told me Selander Ryan was here and then blocked me again. I told you I needed access."

"You took advantage of your access," I told him. "I don't need you in my head listening to every single thought I have. That's a major invasion of privacy."

"I don't listen to anything more than you share freely. If you bothered to let me or Eliza help you, we could teach you how to control what you share. I'm here in daylight, missing out on sleep, to protect you. You could be nicer."

He was right, and I felt a pang of guilt over my snippiness, but I wasn't willing to absolve him of his part in my new sucky way of life so instead I focused on his attire, particularly the wrinkles I could see in his shirt and worn jeans. "You could dress better before coming to my place of business."

"Like I've said before, most of our kind sleep during the day, not that I've been doing that very well since meeting you. My apologies if I didn't put on my best attire after being awakened by your distress and then rushing over here when you shut me out. Both our lives would be better if you'd get a damn night job." His brow furrowed as he leaned in, smelling me. "What the hell are you wearing?"

I looked down at myself. "A dress. What's wrong with it?"

"Not the dress. The scent."

"Oh." I'd forgotten I'd used the Midnight Passions sample that morning. "It's the fragrance for the account I'm on. I was given the Nocturnal Inc. account last Friday. They wanted commercials and print ads for their new fragrance, Midnight Passions. Turns out Nocturnal Inc. is Selander Ryan's company which I found out when they moved their deadline up and I pitched the concepts to them in the conference room."

"Them?"

"He has two men and a woman with him. I'm pretty sure one man is an incubus too, and the woman is a succubus. He's got a big thug with him who doesn't give off the same vibe, so I don't know if he's just a hired goon or something else entirely."

"Probably a shifter," Rider said, before muttering a curse.

"A shifter?" I blinked. "Wait. You mean like a shapeshifter? Like a werewolf?"

"I told you there were shifters."

"No, you—" I remembered making an offhand comment about there being shifters and witches too, when he'd told me I was a vampire and I hadn't believed him. "I thought you were joking. You were serious?"

"As serious as those demonic pheromones you're wearing."

I touched my neck, covering the place I'd wiped the perfume on with my hand. "What are you talking about?"

"Incubi and Succubi come from Hell, Danni. They attract victims with their pheromones and poison them with the essence they secrete from their teeth. It's why mortal men and women can't say no after they've been bitten by one and will allow themselves to be fucked to death for lack of a better way of putting it. Selander and his demon buddies must have used their pheromones in a fragrance. People will flock to buy it, instantly entranced by the scent."

I remembered the way images of sex had flooded my mind when I'd smelled the fragrance for the first time and instantly felt terrible. "And I just gave them the world's greatest ads to use to sell the stuff."

Rider looked at me and frowned before tipping my chin up. "You didn't do anything wrong. The pheromones will make people feel horny as hell, but they're only dangerous when they really come from one of the demons. It's the essence that's dangerous."

"Which I have. I'm a demon."

"No." He shook his head. "I redirected your change. You're a vampire."

"I'm a hybrid. You said so yourself. You said I had a succubus's bite."

"Yeah, well, nobody's perfect."

I laughed, but it was only a short burst of laughter because the moment I'd allowed myself the release, my eyes watered and a tear escaped.

"Hey." Rider wiped the errant tear away with his thumb before smiling down at me. "Don't cry, Danni. It's going to be fine. You don't have the blackened heart of a succubus, and I won't let anyone turn you into something dark and evil. You know you only have to call my name and I'll be here."

The elevator dinged, and the air shifted. The hand Rider had been caressing my cheek with dropped to my waist as he pulled me close to him and his entire body tensed, a tiger preparing to pounce, as Selander Ryan, his associates, and Dex exited the elevator and approached us.

"Rider," Selander said, greeting Rider with a friendly smile that didn't match the murderous glare in his eyes.

"Ryan." Rider's hand tightened around my hip, telling Selander I was under his protection without having to speak a word. They stared each other down, two deadly animals daring the other to strike first, as Dex looked between the two of them, clearly confused. I realized he must wonder how the men knew each other and how I was involved, possibly even thinking I'd had inside knowledge of Nocturnal Inc., which would have made my victorious sales pitch a lot less impressive.

"You two know each other?" I asked, nudging Rider when he frowned down at me.

"Rider and I go way back," Selander answered for him before focusing on me. "Thank you for the wonderful creative ideas, Ms. Keller. I look forward to working with you again soon." He winked at me and left, his villainous trio following him in silence. Each one of them looked at me as a cat would eye a cornered mouse before going in for the kill, and I involuntarily shivered. Rider squeezed my side in response, letting me know he was still there protecting me.

After they left, I looked back at Dex and noticed he seemed to be focused on Rider's hand around my waist, and he didn't seem happy about it. His nostrils flared, and he visually took a deep, calming breath before lifting his gaze to look Rider in the eye. He forced a polite smile and extended his hand. "I don't believe we've met. I'm Dex Prince, Prince Advertising."

Rider looked at the offered hand long enough that I thought he was going to leave Dex hanging, insulting him. I nudged him in the ribs, and he removed his hand from my waist to shake hands with Dex. "Rider Knight."

Dex grinned. "That reminds me of Knight Rider. Your mother must have been a big Hasselhoff fan."

"I was named after my father." Rider squeezed Dex's hand tighter until Dex's jaw clenched. I elbowed him as hard as I could without being obvious, and he let go. The two men sized each other up, the tension between them sucking the rest of the air out of the room before finally, Dex turned to me.

"I'll see you in my office when you're back from break. We have things to discuss." He slid his gaze down my body and judging by the way Rider tensed next to me, he achieved the exact response he wanted. Smiling, he nodded at us and walked away.

"Do you have to be such a jerk?" I asked, spinning on Rider the moment Dex disappeared behind the closed elevator doors.

"Me?" Rider made an innocent face. "I shook the man's hand."

"You tried to break it."

"Tried?" Rider laughed. "If I wanted to break his hand, his bones would be dust now. He was trying to mark his territory."

"So were you," I advised. "What was with that hand on my waist crap?"

"I'm sorry. I thought you wanted me to protect you from Ryan."

"To protect me from Ryan, yes. I didn't want you to get into a pissing contest with my boss."

"A man can't get into a pissing contest with himself. It takes a minimum of two parties. I wonder if you'll call him a jerk too when you join him in his office."

"You started it."

"When my employees have private discussions with people I don't know, I don't walk up and offer my hand to them. He didn't like the fact I was touching you and wanted me to stop. He also tried to intimidate me with an overly firm handshake, only he didn't count on the fact I'm a lot stronger than he is. He started it."

"So the fact that he has manners and you don't makes him the instigator in this childish display of testosterone?"

"If I didn't have manners, he'd be bleeding." Rider studied me, letting his gaze roam over my body like Dex's had. "You seem awfully upset about a man who's just your boss. Is he the reason you stuffed your bra this morning?"

My mouth dropped open as my face heated with the warmth of indignation. "I did not stuff my bra," I growled at him from between clenched teeth, casting a quick glance toward the front desk to make sure we weren't being listened to.

Rider raised an eyebrow, amusement lighting his eyes. "Sweetheart, I've seen you naked."

The warmth of indignation flooding my face morphed into the fiery burn of anger. "Don't remind me. I didn't stuff my bra. If you must know, I'm wearing a gel bra. A lot of women wear them. It's not the same as stuffing a bra."

A grin spread across his face, my anger clearly amusing him. "Yes, well, I don't sense Ryan in the immediate area anymore and I know that despite your talk of manners I'm not going to get a thank you for getting up during the day to come protect your precious ass so I'll be on my way. What time do you get off work?"

"Four-thirty."

"I'll be here in the lobby to escort you. Don't stand me up and don't think you've gotten out of telling me about those calls you were wondering whether you should tell me about. We will be having a discussion about those." He stepped away, headed for the glass doors at the front of the building.

"Rider!" I called as he reached the doors, guilt sinking in. He wasn't wrong about me being unappreciative. I'd been scared to death of Ryan earlier and he'd come to me to make sure I stayed safe.

"Yeah?" Rider asked, pausing at the door to turn toward me.

"Thank you," I said. "I mean it. Thank you."

"I'll always come when you call, beautiful." He winked and pushed through the door. I turned toward the elevator and paused, taking in the dropped jaws of the two women manning the front desk. One fanned herself as the other waggled her eyebrows and gave me a thumbs up.

I groaned and stepped into the elevator.

"Get your personal business all tidied up?" Dex asked as I entered his office to find him typing on his computer.

"Yes. I'm sorry. I know it was a little early to take a break," I apologized as I took a seat in one of the chairs in front of his desk.

"It's fine. I try not to be one of those anal bosses who micromanages every minute of my employees' time." He tapped a key on the keyboard and stood, smiling at me.

"We're all adults here, right?"

"Right." I smiled back, relieved he didn't seem upset, as he crossed the room to close his door and the blinds before stepping over to sit on the edge of the desk.

"You did great today, Danni. I'm very impressed."

"Thank you." I struggled for something else to say, but nerves got the best of me, so I sat there itching to twist the hem of my skirt in my hands.

"So impressed, I think I should treat you to a celebratory dinner."

"Seriously?" He chuckled and heat flooded my face. Could I be any less cool? "I mean, that's so nice, and I was just doing my job. It wasn't a big deal."

"Nocturnal, Inc. signed on to do all their advertising with us, provided you are the person on their account. Mr. Ryan was very taken by you. I think everyone in that room with a pulse was taken by your presentation. I know I was nearly… overwhelmed by it."

I touched my neck and wondered if he had been overwhelmed by me or by the pheromones I'd dabbed on my neck that morning. Did I put them out myself? Rider had said I was a vampire-succubus hybrid. Was Dex suddenly interested in me because some demonic pheromone had attracted him to me? I looked up into those gorgeous eyes, lost in the sea of baby blue, and squashed down the wave of disappointment. Did it really matter what had attracted him to me as long as I got him in the end? I wanted a husband I could show off to my mother and sister with pride and he fit the bill. I'd take him however I could get him. "I'm pleased you were satisfied with the presentation."

"Very pleased. I can't wait to see what else you have to show me." His gaze roamed over my body again, and I felt heat pooling between my thighs as an excited flutter filled my chest. "So, shall we celebrate tonight at Adore?"

Holy bejeezus. Adore was the most expensive restaurant in the city, and the hottest date spot in probably the entire state. If a man wanted to seriously impress a woman, he took her to Adore. Hell, a man caught in the sack with another woman could win his way back into his wife's good graces by taking her there. It wasn't the type of place you just took anyone out to.

"Adore? Isn't that a little expensive for a work dinner?"

"We're celebrating," he said, flashing a million-watt smile, "and I think you're worth the investment. I understand if your boyfriend is the jealous type—"

"Rider's not my boyfriend!" I blurted and instantly noticed the light in Dex's eyes diminish. I realized part of his attraction was that he thought I was taken and getting me away from Rider, an alpha male he'd assumed to be my mate, was a turn-on for him. Damn men and their games, but if it helped me land him, I was more than willing to play. "I mean, we're not exclusive, and if he minds, that's his problem. I'm my own woman. I do what I want when and where I want and with whom."

The predatory gleam in Dex's eyes reappeared as he took my hand and helped me up from my seat. "I'll pick you up tonight around seven-thirty," he said, his lips close to my ear and his hand dangerously close to my derriere as he walked me out of the office.

"Looking forward to it," I said, before stepping away. I walked back to my desk, fully aware of the many speculative looks trained on me and the whispers behind my back of the nosy and possibly even the jealous, but none of that bothered me. I had a date with Dexter Prince. Before that, I had to be escorted home by Rider, who might not want to leave me alone after finding out about the strange calls I'd been receiving. Finding out about the date might definitely make him dig his heels in and demand to watch over me. Shit.

NINE

I logged off my computer at four-thirty, grabbed my purse, and turned to see Dex casually standing outside my cubicle, his arm draped over the wall. "Oh, hi Dex." I glanced at my desk, checking to see if I'd left a file. "Is there something I need to get to you before I leave?"

"No, you've done a perfect job today," he answered with a smile. "I thought I'd escort you out to your vehicle." He leaned in, lowering his voice. "I wouldn't want you to be attacked in such a nice dress."

I knew the comment was supposed to be flirtatious but after receiving threatening calls, not to mention having been attacked in an alley the previous week, it sent a shiver down my spine and reminded me of my vampire guardian who I had no doubt was exactly where he'd said he'd be — in the lobby, waiting for me.

"Thank you, but I'm actually meeting someone in the lobby. I… got a ride to work today," I said, figuring that sounded better than telling him my vampire bodyguard would be escorting me in case our new client who happened to be an incubus was waiting to kill me because he was pissed off I'd been changed into a vampire.

"I can give you a lift home."

"He's already here, but I appreciate the offer."

"He? The Rider guy?"

"Yeah," I said, not sure how I could avoid the answer.

"The not serious boyfriend?" Dex rocked on his heels, hands in pockets. I saw an indentation in his cheek from where he clenched his teeth and realized that while some jealousy seemed to be a good thing with him, he didn't like the thought that another man could win against him, and at the moment Rider was beating him out on the opportunity to take me home.

"That's the one," I answered. "I would definitely take you up on your offer if he wasn't already here. I'm sure you have things to get done before tonight anyway. Seven-thirty isn't that far from now. I better get home so I can get ready."

He smiled, and his shoulders relaxed, appeased by my response, or just the reminder that he was the one taking me to Adore. If two men were competing for a woman and one took her to Adore, he clearly had the advantage. "Allow me to escort you down to the lobby, then. It's on my way."

I took a deep breath and stepped out of the cubicle. I knew somehow that it was a test even if I didn't know what the test was exactly. I also knew Rider would not be happy, which was why I felt stomach acid bubbling the entire ride down the elevator. I wondered if Tums worked on vampires.

The elevator doors opened and Dex did the whole ladies first thing, sweeping his arm out like a gentleman, not giving a single damn about the others in the elevator who would be spinning the gossip mill into overdrive around the water cooler the next day. I didn't particularly care at the moment either. I had bigger problems to worry about, which was made abundantly clear as I took in the tense set to Rider's shoulders as Dex stepped out of the elevator and walked very close to me, a hand at the small of my back.

"See you tonight," he said, his lips tickling my ear before delivering a look of challenge to Rider and making his exit.

I stopped before Rider and felt myself shrink. I couldn't see his eyes behind the ultra-dark sunglasses he wore, but I knew they were blazing with anger. "What's tonight?" he asked.

"You heard that? He whispered."

"Of course I heard it. Can't you hear whispers from across the room?"

I shook my head. "Am I supposed to?"

"You really need to accept what you are and give in to your abilities," he said as he guided me toward the door, his hand in the spot Dex's had recently vacated. I couldn't help thinking it was his way of reclaiming what he thought was his, even if it seemed crazy. I'd never had men fight over me before. Now I was to believe I had two incredibly good-looking alpha males vying for my affection? Maybe when I lost my normal human life, I lost a bit of my sanity too. "Put on the sunglasses I gave you. It's bright as hell out today."

I did as told, not because I barked on command, but because he was right and the sunglasses he'd given me were a hundred times better than the ones I'd had before. "Thanks for these."

"No problem. It took me decades to find ones strong enough to really work for us and I'd hate for anyone to go through the eye burn I suffered for so long before discovering those."

Decades? I stopped, realizing I'd given no thought to how old Rider was. I'd put him in his early thirties and never thought more of it, but he was a vampire, so he'd look the same no matter how many years had passed. "Exactly how old are you?"

"Old enough," he answered, gripping my elbow and prodding me along toward the parking lot. "Let's get out of the sun before we push the limits of the sunscreen."

"I'm never going to age, am I?" I asked.

"No." He opened the passenger side door of my Taurus and gestured for me to get in.

"We're taking my car?"

"I got dropped off. I figured it best I travel with you in case Selander Ryan tries a daylight attack." I got in and Rider crossed over to slide into the driver's seat and held his hand out for my keys. I passed them over without argument. Normally I'd be affronted by a man automatically thinking he would be the one to drive my car, but for the first time since I'd been attacked and changed into a vampire-succubus hybrid, it was really dawning on me what it all meant. "You all right over there?" Rider asked, starting the car and pulling out of my spot.

"Vampires don't age," I said, saying the words out loud more for myself than for him. As a woman in a world ruled by men who judged women for their beauty, it should thrill me I wouldn't age. It'd be like getting the benefits of plastic surgery without the risks and high price tag, but for some reason I felt sad.

"I'd think someone as concerned with her appearance as you would be happy about that."

"I'm not a snob," I snapped at him as he pulled out of the parking lot and headed toward my apartment.

"Never said you were. I said you were concerned with your appearance, which you are. Think of all the plastic surgery money you'll save as you get older."

"I never intended on getting a facelift or anything that would slow down the aging process."

"Says the woman who had a breast augmentation brochure in her room."

"So what?" I snapped. "What if I was going to get a boob job? What's so wrong with that and why is it any of your business, anyway?"

"I just don't see why you'd want to change a body that's perfect just the way it is!" he snapped back, genuine anger in his tone.

I opened my mouth to reply, but ended up shutting it. What could I say to that? It wasn't every day a man yelled at me that my body was perfect. As far as I could recall, I'd never had such a thing happen before. No shocker there. "It's not perfect," I finally mumbled as I folded my arms beneath my small bosom and stared out the passenger side window.

"I already said it was and I'm not going to again, so if you're fishing for compliments, the river's run dry."

"Wow." I turned my head to face him. "What the hell crawled up your ass?"

"A pain-in-the-ass woman I keep trying to protect even though she never appreciates it," he answered, turning the wheel to take a hard right. "I don't have to be here, you know. I didn't have to save you that night. You left the bar on your own, despite me telling you not to. I could have just let Selander Ryan kill you, turn you, do whatever his demon ass wanted to do!"

"So why didn't you?"

He glanced at me. I couldn't see what was in his eyes, but I could feel it and it packed a wallop. He didn't answer me though, opting instead to press his foot down harder on the gas pedal. He didn't let up until we came to a stop in my parking space outside my apartment building. The car had barely come to a stop before he was holding my door open, making a grand sweeping gesture with his arm. I'd never seen anyone turn such a gentlemanly act into something so hostile. I stepped out of the car and held my hand out for my keys. He slammed my door closed and turned to lead the way to my building, keys still in hand.

"You brought me home. I'll be fine now," I said, picking up my pace to keep up with him.

"I haven't safely delivered you home yet," he said, striding through the entrance to my building before removing his shades. "We have things to discuss." He reached my apartment and unlocked the door as if he owned the place.

"Why don't you just move in?" I asked as I crossed the threshold and he closed the door behind us. "You seem to own the keys n—"

He pulled me against his body and covered my mouth with his own, his tongue delving inside and erasing all rational thought from my mind. My back hit a wall and his hands cupped my bottom as he pressed his groin against me and I dug my fingers into his shoulders. I had no idea what was happening or why, but I knew I didn't want whatever it was to end, so I planned on holding on for dear life.

A low growl rumbled from his throat before he pulled away, his dark blue eyes smoldering, and turned away. He threw my keys across the room, where they hit the wall and bounced off, falling to the floor below. "You frustrate the hell out of me!"

I smoothed my dress, removed my sunglasses, and tried to collect myself as he stood behind my couch, his back to me, his hands on his hips and his head lowered. He'd crossed the room so quickly I'd barely seen him do it. "You don't exactly give me a calm, relaxed feeling yourself."

When he turned around, he was grinning, but it was gone in a flash. "Tell me about the calls you didn't plan on telling me about."

And just like that, he was back in bodyguard mode and I supposed whatever had happened wasn't going to be discussed. Maybe that was for the best because my heart was beating way too fast in response to his kiss, considering I had plans with another man that evening. "I got a call last Friday from an unknown number, some guy with a creepy voice telling me 'You shouldn't have left with him' and then earlier today I got another call and after I'd given up on the guy saying anything I hung up but heard him telling me I was going to die before I disconnected."

"And you didn't want to tell me about this because…?"

"I didn't know who to trust. I thought it could be Selander but the second call came while he was in the office signing contracts with Dex, and well, the first thing he said to me was 'You shouldn't have left with him' so for all I knew it could have been you. You told me not to leave the bar with anyone."

"You think I would call and harass you?" His voice gave away nothing but the set of his body and the heat in his eyes more than told me he was pissed.

"Don't look at me like that. I just met you last Tuesday and I was attacked right after. The next thing I knew it was Friday morning, and I was waking up naked next to you, also naked, in my bed and listening to you tell me I was a vampire. You might be able to feel my emotions and talk to me in my head, but I don't really know you."

"Clearly." He fumed for a minute before heaving out a frustrated sigh. "What did the voice sound like? You're sure it was a man?"

"Definite," I answered and thought about how to describe the creep, then I remembered the call I'd let go to voicemail. "There was another call from an unknown caller not that much longer after I'd hung up on the guy, but I didn't want to hear his creepy voice, so I let it go to voicemail."

"That's your way of protecting yourself? Just ignore the bad guys and hope they go away?"

"You don't have to be a jerk about it," I said, crossing over to the side table next to my couch and hitting the speaker button on the telephone I kept there. "Do you want to hear the voicemail or not?"

He stepped over and waited as I dialed in remotely to my business line and selected the prompts to retrieve my messages.

"Danni," the creepy voice said. "Danni, Danni, Danni. Bitches who hang up get strung up. I'm watching you. I'll get you… soon."

"You really weren't going to tell me about that?" Rider asked as I erased the message, knowing I'd never want to listen to it again. "You actually thought that rodent's voice could be mine?"

"You could have been disguising your voice."

"I don't think I could even get my voice to sound like that," he said, offended, "But I know who could. That sounded like Barnaby."

"The man at the bar?" I asked, recalling the man Rider had stepped out with before leaving me alone inside. "I thought you killed him."

"I'm not a bloodthirsty killer, Danni. I simply had a little chat with him and let him know you were off limits. Barnaby and I have an understanding, or at least we did."

I folded my arms. "What kind of understanding?"

"Barnaby is a hunter, from a long line of hunters. One of his forefathers was a good friend of mine and down the family line they've all agreed that my friends and I are off limits. They'd never touch a vampire in my area unless I sanctioned it or it was in self-defense. Succubi and incubi, however, are a different story. He was there at the bar that night because of you."

"Because of me?" I recalled that night, how upset I'd been and how I'd tried to get drunk enough to make what would have been an even worse mistake than I originally had thought. "I was trying to get drunk enough to make him look good enough to sleep with and he was there to kill me?"

"You wanted to sleep with Barnaby?" Rider's voice practically bounced off the walls as he looked at me with a look of disgust that would have probably been humorous if the fact he was openly judging me wasn't so offensive.

"Of course I didn't *want* to sleep with that gerbil-looking troll. Why else do you think I was trying so hard to get drunk? Can we get back to the important part of what I said? He was there to kill me? I wasn't even a succubus or a vampire. I was just a freaking person."

"He wasn't there to kill you. He was tracking Selander Ryan, and you were bait. He knew Ryan was in the area and you had the blood type incubi go for."

"How? How could he possibly have known that?"

"He's been at his job a long enough time and was trained very well. You have a sweetness to your blood that attracts incubi and it's what makes it possible for you to be turned into one. Incubi can sense blood types, just like we can."

"We can?"

Rider raised an eyebrow. "Did you not sense that man in the alley's blood? Can you not sense mine now?" He loosened another button on his shirt so he could open the neck wide enough for me to see the pulse in his throat.

My eyes zeroed in on it and I involuntarily licked my lips as the strength of the blood I sensed there called out to me. I hadn't realized it before, but he was right. I could sense it in people. I recalled how hungry I'd been Sunday and how everyone I'd crossed had been like a moving bag of blood.

"Need a hit?"

I snapped out of the trance to find him watching me, concerned. "No," I answered, shaking my head. "I'm fine."

"You haven't had any since last night. Have you?" His tone darkened, giving me the feeling I'd be in very deep trouble if I said yes.

"I got enough last night." I looked down at the floor as images from the previous night flooded my mind. The man had started undressing me and if it hadn't been for my body insecurities, I would have no doubt slept with him. I'd left him, madder than hell, but called on him the moment I found myself in trouble the very next day.

"It's best you don't wait until you get too hungry."

"I said I'm fine."

"I really don't mind—"

"I'm fine!" I snapped, raising my gaze from the floor to

look him in the eye. "I'm not going to kill anyone else. I'm not going to allow myself to get that hungry."

"What are you going to do when you need to feed?" he asked calmly, unperturbed by my outburst.

I thought about it, not sure what I would do. Rider was the easy source, but there was no denying how badly I'd wanted him the night before. Hell, I'd wanted him not that long ago when he'd kissed me, but I didn't know him, and I wasn't sure I wanted to. Maybe he came to my rescue, but I wouldn't have needed him to if he hadn't turned me into a bloodsucker in the first place. Yeah, Selander Ryan had attacked me first, but Rider had left me alone. Part of me wasn't willing to just forget that and cut him any slack. "You're not the only vampire in the world," I finally said. "You can't possibly be feeding them all, so I'll survive however the others do. I can find my own donors, or just drink off of scummy people no one will believe when they try to tell people they were attacked by a vampire. You said yourself no man will fight me off after I've bitten him, so I shouldn't have any trouble."

"What happens when the man you've seduced with your bite doesn't take no for an answer? You might have to kill your donors, Danni, unless you plan on sleeping with all of them, and I just don't see you liking yourself very much if you do."

"So that's your angle?" I stepped away from him. "You want me to feed from you, to sleep with you?"

"Don't go there, Danni." He stared down at me with eyes dark as night, nostrils flaring. "Am I attracted to you? Hell yes. Would I take advantage of you? Hell no. I've slept next to you naked while you were in and out of your damn mind. I took the hit of that succubus bite of yours last night, and I still stopped the minute you did. You weren't exactly fighting me off before that moment and you can deny it all you want, but you wanted me as bad as I wanted you. Still, the second you changed your mind, I stopped. There are a lot of questionable things I've done in my life, but I have never taken advantage of a woman. Hell, I've lost count of how many hookers I've kept off the streets so other men wouldn't hurt them."

I stepped back, wilted under the weight of his anger, and felt tears forming in my eyes as I turned away.

"Damn it, Danni. Don't cry."

"I'm not crying!" I yelled, wiping at the tears that had escaped. I sniffed in an effort to suck back every ounce of crybaby emotion I felt and turned back to face him. The anger that had engulfed him a moment before had morphed into pity, and that made *me* angry. "It isn't my fault I have a succubus bite. It isn't my fault my blood is sweet or whatever. It isn't my fault Selander Ryan attacked me and it isn't my fault the two of you turned me into whatever the hell I am now! Sorry if I'm not appreciative enough and that I question the motives of a man I barely know, especially one who just pushed me against the wall earlier and nearly kissed me straight out of my underwear!"

Rider grinned, settling on the edge of my couch as he folded his arms. "Straight out of your underwear, huh?"

"Oh shut up, you cocky bastard."

This brought on a full laugh. "All right. I'll play nice, and you're right. You really don't know me well enough to give me your blind trust, even though you could. I really do just want to keep you safe. I'm sorry this happened to you. I only turned you to save your life and I want to make the transition as easy as possible for you. I don't want you to feed from me to control or seduce you. With the power of your bite, I don't think it's safe for you to drink from human men. They'll try to assault you and force you to hurt them, most likely kill them. You can live off of bagged blood, but it has to be heated and honestly isn't that appetizing, but it does the job. I'll speak with Nannette about getting you a blood account set up. If you ever need blood and can't get to a bag of it, please come to me. There's not another vampire in the area I trust enough, and I think I'm the only one in the city powerful enough to resist the pull of your bite, and it's not easy, even for me."

I thought about it. Bagged blood didn't seem that appetizing, particularly since I could see it, which would make what I was doing much more real, but if it kept me from being sexually assaulted and forced to kill random guys, I'd take it. The alternatives would be drink from women which was absolutely revolting thanks to whatever Selander Ryan had done to me when he'd attacked me and made estrogen my arch enemy, or drink from Rider, the man I was dangerously attracted to but not the right man for me. "Fine. That sounds reasonable."

"Good. Now that's out of the way, I'll take care of Barnaby and stay watchful for Selander Ryan, but we need to discuss the other safety issue."

"What other safety issue?"

"Why will you be seeing your boss tonight?"

I rolled my eyes. "You're not my boyfriend, Rider."

He laughed. "I haven't been a *boyfriend* to anyone in more years than I can remember."

"And you may have sired me, but you're not my father."

"I should hope not, not after the way you checked me out in your bedroom when I was naked."

"I did not check you out!"

"Whatever you have to tell yourself, sweetheart."

"My point is you don't have a say in what I do or who I do it with." I rolled my eyes. "Dex Prince isn't a security issue. He's a date."

"He's your boss."

"He's my boss, and he's taking me out on a date."

"Scandalous," he said, trying to be humorous, but I didn't see a trace of amusement in his eyes. "Dex. *Dex.* Man, men's names sure have gotten pussified over the last couple of decades."

"His name is perfectly manly, thank you very much, and it's not like I'm sleeping my way to a promotion or something. He asked me out and I said yes. Co-workers date all the time," I said as I pondered over his word choice. It wasn't the first time he'd used decades as a measure of time. "How old are you?"

"Old enough to know this Dex guy is a primo douchewad."

"Jealous?"

"I don't need to be. He's human. Even if you fall for his bullshit, he has a limited amount of years before he wrinkles up like a prune, loses everything you find attractive about him because it sure isn't his personality and he doesn't strike me as the most brilliant man in the world, and before you know it, he's dead and I'll still be here, looking all young and sexy and shit."

I laughed. "Wow. You really are jealous… and juvenile. I need to get ready."

"What's stopping you?"

"You!"

"Aw, can't draw yourself away from me?"

"Actually, that's easy to do," I said, lying through my teeth as I walked away from him, knowing damn well if he closed the distance between us and laid another of those kisses on me, I'd be putty. I needed to get ready and Rider didn't appear ready to leave soon, so I entered my bedroom and rooted through my closet. I didn't have many fancy clothes since I didn't often go to fancy places, but I had a dress I'd worn to a cousin's wedding that would work. It was black, sleeveless, and form-fitting. It fell to the knee and had a draped neck in the front that helped hide the meager state of my chest. I laid it out on my bed and moved to the dresser to find better underwear than what I had on in case things progressed to the point they'd be seen.

"What a waste of sexy panties," Rider said as I pulled free a pair of red lace bikinis I'd gotten on sale years ago and never wore because there was no point wearing something so nice.

I looked over to see him leaning against the doorframe and narrowed my eyes at him. "He might get lucky."

"I doubt it," he said. "Where's Prince Charming taking you?"

"Adore."

Rider laughed heartily.

"I'll have you know Adore is *the* place to dine in the city. It's expensive and classy, and not just anyone dines there."

"I'm aware of this. You don't find it funny that a man is taking a woman there on a first date? Seems to me he's trying to compensate for something. I'm betting he has a really little—"

"Seriously, Rider? Grow up. Geez, you're proof men never mature no matter how many years you give them to, and what do you mean you doubt he'll get lucky? If he wasn't interested in me, he wouldn't have asked me out and I certainly see no reason why I wouldn't allow him to get lucky. He's a very attractive, successful man."

"Any man with a pulse and taste would be interested in you, sweetheart, but I already figured he'd asked you out to eat, since that's what humans do."

"Yeah, and?" I glanced at the clock and wished Rider would move along and quit trying to get under my skin.

"What have you eaten since you turned?"

I shrugged. "Not much. Some meat, rare. I haven't really been hungry for food."

"You ever stop to think there's a reason for that?"

"Uh, because I've been more thirsty for blood than hungry for snacks," I answered, then frowned. "Wait. We can eat, can't we?"

"Of course we can. We have teeth and stomachs."

"So, what's the problem?"

"I have no problem. You, however, are going to have one hell of a problem after you eat all that human food. You can order the rarest steak on the menu but there's going to be sides, and even the meat will have seasoning.

It's going to do a number on your newly turned vampire tummy."

I studied him. He'd never said anything to me before about food having an ill effect on me, and I'd eaten meat I'd had in my kitchen with no problem at all. "You'd say anything to try to wreck this date. You really are a piece of work."

"Whatever, princess. Don't say I didn't warn you when you find yourself in the bathroom wanting to die."

"Get out!"

Rider laughed as he pushed himself off the doorframe and turned to leave. "Ryan's still out there. I'll have some guys watching you. Call if you need anything."

I followed him through the living room. "You can be a real jerk. Stay away from the restaurant and don't you dare try to worm your way into my head while I'm on my date."

"I'd rather impale myself," he said, opening the door to leave. "Be careful, and good luck. You're going to need it."

"Jerk!" I slammed the door closed behind him and stormed into my bedroom. Glancing at my clock, I saw I had enough time for a quick shower before getting dressed and doing my hair and makeup. Dex would arrive in under two hours and I was not going to let an immature vampire ruin my shot at perfect husband material, not even one whose kiss still made me tingle long after his lips left mine.

TEN

Dex picked me up in a silver Audi R8 that looked like it cost more money than I would make in the next ten years. He gave me a single red rose and opened my door for me, even asked if I wanted to listen to music or not instead of just turning it on. He was a perfect gentleman who happened to be very successful and was beyond what I would consider financially stable so there was no reason whatsoever why I would have Rider on my mind, yet he was still wedged in there pretty good when we rolled up to the restaurant.

My door was opened by a tall, light-skinned valet with dark eyes and a kind smile and although it was just valet service, the way the man took my hand and helped me out as if I were someone important made me feel like royalty, especially when Dex rounded the front of the luxury car to offer me his arm. He wore a dark suit with a champagne colored dress shirt underneath. I figured it probably cost three times the amount I'd spent on the dress I was wearing and hoped he didn't notice.

"Ah, Mr. Prince," the host greeted Dex as we stepped inside the lavishly decorated restaurant, recognizing him instantly. "I have a table waiting for you and your beautiful companion right this way."

"You come here often?" I asked as the maître d grabbed two menus and led us through the most beautiful dining area I'd ever seen. There were a few long tables for groups, but the majority of tables were round and just big enough for two to four people, covered in silky white tablecloths that draped to the floor. Peach and white bouquets surrounded glass votives with peach candles in the middle of every table. Above us, crystal chandeliers gave more illumination, casting light and shadow upon the white marble statues of who I assumed to be Greek gods and goddesses and large romantic paintings.

"It's the best restaurant in the area," Dex answered, smiling.

I smiled back, hoping it didn't look as fake as it felt. I couldn't see a single man frequently dining by himself at such an expensive restaurant, no matter how designer his suit was or how flashy his car. He came to the restaurant often enough to be recognized, and I had no doubt there was a woman on his arm every visit, women far more attractive and definitely more sophisticated and experienced than me. Wife material.

"Here we are." The maître d directed us to a small round table in a dark, candlelit corner and pulled out my chair for me, the first time I'd had that happen. My dining out experiences up to that moment had consisted of nothing fancier than Texas Roadhouse and Cheesecake Factory. The only seating consideration those hosts gave was whether you preferred a sticky booth or a table next to a harried mother with five screaming children with snot running out of their noses and jam hands. "Your usual champagne?" the maître d asked, solidifying my theory that Dex regularly brought women to Adore.

Dex gave a subtle nod as he moved his chair next to mine and settled in at my side. "You don't mind if I move a little closer, do you? It's cozier this way."

I smiled. "This is fine." Truth was, I liked the fact he

wouldn't be staring at my face while I ate. Just my luck, I'd spend the entire evening with spinach stuck in my teeth. I made a quick mental note to not order spinach or anything green and leafy.

"Do you need help with the menu? I can order for you if you like."

I glanced at the menu and saw that everything was in basic English and pretty clear. I didn't know what women he'd been bringing to Adore before me, but if he had to order for them, I definitely had brains in my favor. "I think I'll go with a steak," I said, perusing the menu and trying not to think of Rider's attempt to ruin my evening, or that wallop of a kiss he'd dropped on me. I'd eaten meat since turning, I could eat it again.

"Ah, the filet mignon or a real steak? You have to love a steak and potatoes kind of woman. It's depressing enjoying a full meal while your date nibbles on salad the whole evening."

I'd been planning on getting the smallest filet mignon on the menu just in case Rider wasn't completely bullshitting me, but if Dex liked women who ate well… "I love the taste of filet mignon, but they're just so small. I love to eat. Not, like, I love to eat so much I have a weight problem," I quickly added, realizing his other dates were probably supermodel material, "but I enjoy a good, full meal. I was blessed with a great metabolism, and I exercise."

"Ah, do you go to the gym?"

"I'm more of a runner," I answered, recalling my run back to my apartment the other day to avoid my skin sizzling off.

"Explains the great legs," he said as our server arrived with a bottle of champagne and asked if we were ready to order. Dex suggested the porterhouse for two with potatoes au gratin and asparagus and wanting to ensure our date went well, I agreed to what he wanted. "Wow. That's the first time I've gotten a date to share a porterhouse with me." I smiled and bit back my desire to inform him how rude it was to keep bringing up other dates on what was supposed to be *our* date.

The air shifted and the hair along the nape of my neck stood on end. I looked across the restaurant to see Selander Ryan walk in with Gina on his arm. Every man in the restaurant stared at her as she glided by in a long, golden gown that fit her like a glove and left little to the imagination thanks to the plunging neckline her breasts threatened to pop out of, and the women all stared at Selander with his long blond hair and angelic good looks that hid the evil inside him. I found myself drawn to him as well, pulled to him like a magnet despite the fear crawling up my spine, urging me to run.

"Danni?"

I snapped out of the trance to see Dex placing the champagne bottle back in the bucket of ice. He'd filled both our glasses, and I hadn't even noticed. Judging by the way he was looking at me in expectation, he'd been speaking to me too and expected a response. "I'm sorry. Can you say that again?"

"Wow. Something sure got your—" he looked over and saw Selander and Gina settling in at a small corner table diagonally from ours. Selander had moved the chairs, so they had their backs to the wall like we did, but I knew he hadn't done it to get cozy with Gina although she'd practically affixed herself to his side, but to keep me in his sights and to make sure I knew he was there and that he could get to me. "—attention. Is that Gina with Selander Ryan?"

"I believe so," I answered as the cold fear that had been climbing up my spine warmed into an angry flush I felt crawling up my neck. It was bad enough Selander had appeared to not only ruin my date, but threaten my life, but he'd brought Gina with him and of course she had to look a thousand times better than me with the perfect breasts I should have been getting in the morning but couldn't because the bastard with her had attacked me and turned me into a freak who couldn't get surgery. Seeing Gina's bouncy balls across the room mocking my mosquito bites reminded me I hadn't canceled my appointment, and it was less than twenty-four hours away, so I was going to be billed a no-show fee. I smacked myself in the head and groaned.

"Are you all right?"

I looked over to see Dex looking at me with what I hoped was concern for me and not worry he'd picked the wrong woman to ask out. "Yes, sorry. I'm fine. I just remembered I'd forgotten something. Don't you just hate when you do that?"

"Sure." He nodded and sipped his champagne. "Nothing important, I hope?"

"Oh no, nothing dire." Just something that was going to cost me a lot of money for absolutely nothing in return.

"That's good. I suppose it would be good manners to say hello to Ryan and Gina or invite them to our table, but I'm feeling a bit selfish tonight." He smiled at me and dropped his voice as he draped an arm around my shoulders. "I want you all to myself."

A nervous laugh escaped me as I struggled for something to say in response, something witty or flirtatious, but staring into Dex's baby blues while sitting close enough to soak in the scent of his warm, spicy cologne did a number on my verbal skills.

A slight commotion came from the front of the restaurant, just loud enough to grab our attention and break me loose of the spell Dex's eyes had put me under. "I wonder what that is."

"Probably someone upset they can't get in," Dex said, and took another sip of his drink. "I see it all the time. People think they can just arrive without reservation and get right in."

I took a long sip from my own glass as I weighed Dex's words. He'd asked me out that morning and gotten right in the same night. Maybe it was possible to do, but combined with the familiarity of the maître d, I was pretty sure I could safely presume he had a standing reservation and I was that week's plaything. I'd fantasized about being his plaything, but in my daydreams I went straight from plaything to wife. Also, in my fantasies, I was his only plaything, not a flavor of the week.

The commotion died down and the maître d, slightly rumpled, stepped through the dining room archway, a large black man in all black with closely shaven hair and a huge diamond gleaming in his ear and a leaner but powerfully built Hispanic man in nearly identical clothing and a tattoo peeking out over the collar of his shirt followed behind him, scouring the dining room. The Hispanic man zeroed in on Selander, who'd shifted his focus to them the moment they walked in, and the black man who I recognized as the guy who had removed Billie from Rider's room met my gaze and elbowed his friend, or associate, nodding toward me. "We'll take this table right here," I heard him tell the maître d as he pulled out a chair from a table near the front that gave them the perfect view of my table without sacrificing a view of Selander's. The maître d opened his mouth but seemed to think better of it and clamped it shut, reluctantly depositing menus on the table before going back to the front, head hung low.

A pale, thick-necked thuggish man also dressed in black sitting across from them on the other side of the room turned his chair to face them and glanced over at Selander. As I watched, they seemed to communicate with their eyes and barely noticeable nods. Rider had told me he'd have men watching me, and I knew the two who had apparently bullied their way past the maître d were my watchdogs, and apparently Selander had come with his own. I scanned the rest of the dining area, checking to see if there were more. A few burly men threw off a vibe, and I also caught some dark glances from a few women, whether it was because they were wondering how I'd landed a date with such an attractive man or they were on either Rider or Selander's payroll, I had no clue, but my gut twisted as I realized I was sitting in a den of wolves who could break out into a fight at any moment. I threw back the glass of champagne, chugging all the bubbly nectar inside.

"Thatta girl," Dex said, grinning as he refilled my glass, no doubt hoping I'd chug a few more and be a sure thing for him. I should have been offended, but at the moment, my nerves were too jittery. Unlike Dex and Gina, I didn't have the luxury of ignorance allowing me to enjoy my evening. I was being stalked by vipers and hoped like hell the hawks eying them would swoop in fast enough if they decided to strike.

Speaking of striking vipers, Selander Ryan rose from his table and crossed the room with Gina on his arm, his gaze locked on mine. I tried, but couldn't look away as he steadily closed in on our table, whether it was due to some sort of incubus mojo he'd thrown at me or pure fear of letting him out of my sight, I didn't know but our eyes stayed locked until he reached the table.

"Prince," Selander said, extending his hand. "I thought that was you and our talented account representative."

"Mr. Ryan," Dex greeted back, standing to shake Selander's hand and nod toward Gina. "Gina. Have the two of you ordered?"

"Yes, we just thought we'd stop over, say hello, and share a couple of drinks with you while you wait on your dinner," Selander answered, producing a champagne bottle and two stemmed glasses I hadn't even been aware of him holding.

"Oh, very thoughtful," Dex said, helping Selander to grab chairs from a nearby table so the couple could join us. They sat side by side across from us, Selander directly across from me, Gina and her huge breasts directly across from Dex. Of course. I downed my second glass of champagne.

"Pace yourself," Gina warned me, reaching across the

table to touch my wrist. "All the bubbles will go straight to your head." As she reached across the table, her upper body leaned forward, causing her breasts to practically sit on the tabletop. I could just see the pink hint of nipple pushing the limitations of the golden material she'd poured herself into and if a picture were taken of us at that moment I was pretty sure it would look just like that famous photo of Sophia Loren giving the perfect side eye to Jayne Mansfield as she dusted their dinner plates with her nipples. I, obviously, would be Sophia.

"Allow me to pour," Selander said, popping the champagne cork. He began filling glasses, his gaze locking onto mine as he got to my glass. He grinned and looked over at Dex, then back at me, grinning wider. I glanced over to see Dex sipping his champagne while staring into the abyss of Gina's cleavage. The glare I directed Selander's way as I quickly looked elsewhere only managed to put a sparkle of laughter into his eyes. He finished pouring and shrugged. I felt the message he delivered without needing the aid of words. I could make any man want me if I joined him. It was the same message he'd delivered in my dream before it twisted into him trying to kill me. Apparently he thought I'd overlook that part and fall for his promise of a sexy forever after as a demonic sex-kitten if he kept offering. He didn't want to turn me. He wanted to kill me. I knew it with every fiber of my being, even if I had no clue why he'd rather wipe me off the face of the earth than induct me into his harem. Maybe incubi had breast size requirements just like regular men.

I lifted my glass as Gina started telling a story and started to sip, then paused. I had no idea what Selander had poured into our glasses. I looked over at the bodyguards Rider had assigned to me and noticed both of them leaning forward, ready to pounce. Whether it was because they expected Selander to make a move or they knew something was off about the drink, I had no clue. I felt the heat of an intense stare and scanned the room until my gaze landed on a beautiful black woman with close-shaven hair in a scarlet red dress sitting near the back. I recognized her as the woman who'd been in my apartment and helped Rider get me into the bathtub. Nannette. She watched me with a wineglass held before her as if she'd paused mid-drink and once she saw I'd noticed her, she shook her head, a clear warning in her dark eyes. I set the newly poured glass of champagne down and watched with dread as Gina lifted hers.

"No!" I grabbed the glass out of her hand, sloshing some of the golden liquid over the edge and earning shocked looks from her and Dex. From Selander, I received a dark glare. "I'm sorry," I blurted as I scrambled for an explanation for my behavior.

"That's very expensive champagne, I'm sure," Gina said, fuming. A lightbulb went on in my head as she brought up the cost.

"Exactly," I said. "I'm so sorry, Mr. Ryan, but according to company policy, this would be considered a gift and we aren't allowed to accept such an expensive gift from a client. I'm sorry I didn't recall the rule until after you'd poured."

"I'm afraid Danni is correct," Dex said, setting his untouched glass away from him. "Such a nice offer though. I'll tell you what. You said you plan to be in the city for a while. How about we go golfing later this week and we can have drinks at my club? They're on the house for club members and guests, so I won't be getting into hot water with the human resources department."

"That would be great," Selander said with a tight smile as our server arrived with our food. "Well, we should get back to our table. Until we meet again," he said, looking at me with the promise our next meeting wouldn't be a good one in his eyes as he stood from the table and picked up the champagne bottle he'd brought over. He winked discreetly before turning away, jostling the bottle just the tiniest bit in his hand, just enough to let me know he still had it and he still had Gina.

I watched them move across the room as our food was placed before us, itching to walk over, clamp a hand around Gina's arm and pull her out of there. "Should she be dining with him?" I asked Dex, not wanting to get Gina in trouble for fraternizing with clients, but willing to do it if it saved her life.

"They aren't working together directly on any projects and I'll make sure they won't in the future to make sure there are no issues human resources wants to get their underwear in a bunch about, and I'd hate to bust up the guy's date after refusing his champagne. Besides," he said, leaning closer, "if I told her she had to pay for her own meal, the same would apply to you and I never let a lady pay for dinner. My mother would have a fit."

"You're close to your mother?" I asked, trying to quit worrying about Gina. She and Selander had settled back in at their table, and I noticed only one of Rider's men watched them while the others continued to watch me. If there was something in the champagne, Nannette didn't seem to care what effects it would have on Gina.

"We get along well," Dex answered and asked the server for another pair of glasses. A few minutes later, he'd filled two champagne flutes from the bottle we'd started with and we began to dine. He told me about his family home in New England and the time he'd spent in Paris while cutting the steak and filling a plate for me. A Texas Roadhouse kind of girl, I'd expected the porterhouse to simply be a large grilled steak, but Adore's version was covered in mushrooms, onions, herbs, spices, and some sort of dark sauce. The au gratin potatoes seemed cheesier than any I had ever seen and the asparagus was drenched in another sauce just a shade darker than what covered the steak. "If you enjoy this, you'll love my favorite restaurant in New York."

You'll? I scooped a piece of steak up with my fork, mushrooms and all, and gave it a try as I pondered his tense. He didn't say I would enjoy his favorite restaurant. He said you'll as in you will. Was he intending to take me to New York?

"Good?"

I nodded, smiling, as I swallowed and scooped a second bite. The meat went down easy as I'd suspected it would. Damn Rider and his immature antics. For someone constantly urging me to trust him, he'd not cared one bit about lying in order to get in my head and ruin my date. I didn't know why he bothered to send people to watch over me, unless maybe I was just a prize in a tug-of-war between him and his enemy. That must be it, I realized. I didn't mean anything to Rider. He just wanted to beat Selander Ryan, and screwing with me was a bit of fun on the side. All his supposed need to protect me was just him playing a game with Selander Ryan and winning. They'd both marked me and whichever side I went to fully determined who won. But I was pretty sure Selander wanted me dead, so I had to be missing something.

"A penny for your thoughts?"

I looked over at Dex and realized I'd spaced out again, my thoughts on Rider. I cursed him silently. All I'd dreamed of my entire time with Prince Advertising was a chance at love with Dex Prince and here I was, dining with him at the best restaurant in the city, and I had Rider on the brain. Unbelievable. "I'm just thinking of how good this is," I said, recalling how he'd mentioned liking healthy eaters earlier.

"Wait until dessert," he said with a look in his eye that made me wonder if he meant actual dessert or if I'd ended up on the menu. I felt a blush crawling up my neck and stabbed a piece of asparagus to save me from having to come up with a response. "If I haven't told you how stunning you are tonight, you are. You seem to have caught the attention of more than a few men in here tonight. I can't say I blame them."

I looked over at the table where Rider's two men sat. If

they were supposed to be covert, they weren't doing a great job. I grabbed my champagne flute to wash down my food as I changed direction to check on Nannette. Again, she shook her head at me. I paused with the flute half way to my mouth. "I'm pretty sure all eyes are on Gina."

"Gina is a very sexy woman," Dex said, igniting a flare of jealousy inside me, "but in an obvious way. Sometimes a less in-your-face beauty can have a much greater impact and hold one's interest longer. You certainly seem to be holding more than just my interest tonight. Is something wrong with the champagne?"

"No, I just think maybe I've had enough," I said, and lowered my glass, pondering his words. Hearing how sexy Gina was stung, especially after he'd been staring right into her cleavage earlier. But hell, I sometimes caught myself staring at it at work and I didn't even like women in that way. Her boobs just had a way of demanding attention. He was with me and seemed pleased to be there. "I wouldn't want to fill up on champagne and not finish this delicious dinner." I smiled and took another bite from my plate while checking to see what Selander and Gina were doing. They appeared to be drinking champagne, and it didn't look like she suffered any adverse effects. Now I was confused. Was there a reason I shouldn't drink champagne at all? Did vampires get drunk? I'd downed two full glasses and didn't feel the slightest buzz.

"We can always have more afterward," Dex said, winking. "I was thinking after dinner we could go back to—" He frowned as my stomach started twisting painfully. "Are you all right? You're looking a little green."

I clamped a hand over my mouth as bile rose in my throat and made a mad dash for the ladies' room.

ELEVEN

I'd barely reached the toilet before I was on my knees vomiting everything I'd eaten. I hadn't even had time to close the stall door, allowing those already in the bathroom to see my disgusting act of illness. As soon as I could pause my retching, I closed and locked the door, but I'd already done enough damage to ensure the three women who'd fled the bathroom after my stomach had erupted would not be enjoying the rest of their dinner. I didn't want to even think about the bathroom attendant.

"Are you all right, ma'am?" the young woman asked.

Just peachy, I thought as more bile burned its way up my throat and exploded from me in a manner I could only describe as violent. My stomach cramped as I continued to heave and vomit more food than I could have possibly eaten.

I heard the bathroom door open and heels clicked across the tiled floor. "Danni? It's Nannette. How are you doing?"

"I'm dying," I answered before heaving and this time producing blood. Whether I'd ruptured something and was bleeding internally, or the blood came from my "dinner" the night before, I didn't know. Either way, my stomach hurt like a bitch and I felt sicker than I'd ever felt in my life. Just when I thought it couldn't get any worse, a loud gurgling sound escaped my stomach and my bowels decided they wanted to let loose and join the torture party.

I sat on the toilet with the skirt of my beautiful dress pulled up, looking down at my sexy red panties around my ankles, and knew my date was over. If the sound effects my body was involuntarily making reached the dining room, my hopes of a relationship with Dex Prince were over. My life would be over. Surely I would die of embarrassment right there on the toilet as the poor bathroom attendant sprayed what sounded like five cans of air freshener in sheer desperation.

"I'm a nurse," I heard Nannette tell the woman. "You may want to stand outside the bathroom and keep others from entering. I'll take care of her."

"Oh thank goodness," the woman said, and I heard the bathroom door close behind her so fast I thought she might be part cheetah. I'd made the poor thing flee.

"You're probably going to be stuck on that toilet for about fifteen to twenty minutes," Nannette warned me. "Once you pass the first round of toxins from your body, you'll get a small reprieve. I'll get you home then, but you are in for a rough night."

"The first round?!" My stomach cramped again as more disgusting things I'd rather not go into great detail about happened and I realized Dex was sitting at our table, clueless about what was going on. "I'm here on a date. I can't just leave him. You have to tell him I'm sick and you're taking me home."

"No I don't. Girl, my name is not Iyanla and I'm not here to fix your damn life. What was your dumb ass thinking eating all that human food and drinking all that champagne anyway? You know alcohol thins blood, right? Do you really not know how stupid it is to drink something that thins blood when you have thin blood to begin with?"

"How was I supposed to know?" My stomach bubbled, and I belched. "You don't have to be so rude."

"It's my off night at the hospital and instead of having a good time of my own, I'm stuck watching you because Rider knew your foolish ass would get into a situation like this. Don't expect sympathy from me. I have no sympathy for the stupid."

"I'm not stupid!"

"There's no way in hell Rider didn't warn you this would happen if you ate, and yet you did. You know there is an incubus after you and you put yourself in a position of weakness, and for what? A date with a mere mortal man?"

"I didn't ask for any of this!" I snapped before getting sick again.

"And ungrateful, on top of everything else. Selander Ryan would have turned you into a rabid whore, using your body to ensnare and murder innocent men over and over again. Rider might have turned you into a vampire but it was the only way he could save you without killing you and you can blame him as much as you want but it doesn't change the fact you're the one who chose to leave the safety of his bar with Selander Ryan. That bartender you spoke with that night? He's lucky to be alive after Rider got through with him for allowing you to leave, but I don't expect you to care about anyone but yourself. You have no idea how good you have it."

"This is good?" I belched again and my stomach cramped.

"You have a sire who lets you live on your own. He directed you to a vampire to talk to through your transition and told you who to see if you were injured. He even set up a blood account for you. If you want to have a pity party for yourself, go ahead, but realize you're the cause of it. Rider is not to blame for your problems. You're damned lucky you got him for a sire."

"If he's so great, why'd he allow me to get this sick?

Where is he?"

"Do you really want him here with you now?"

I'd flushed the toilet too many times to count since entering the stall and was back on my knees, throwing up blood and belching up the foulest fumes from my body each time my stomach rolled. My body was cold with sweat and I wasn't sure if my continuing need to vomit was still due to eating food or if it was the smell I'd created in the bathroom causing the nausea. "No! I don't want him here!"

Nannette chuckled. "I didn't think so. Rider knew what would happen if you didn't listen, but he has given you free will, something a lot of new vampires don't get. He sent me to take care of you and spare you your humility. He's taking care of you, though. He's always taking care of you, even though he has a whole city to protect."

"You sound jealous."

The stall door banged open, the lock broken, and Nannette stood over me, looking like the angel of death, or at least the angel of ass-kicking. If I hadn't already voided my dinner from my body, I might have messed myself. "Are you done yet? I've grown tired of you and this conversation."

By the time I'd finished the first round of sickness Nannette had warned me about, Dex was no longer at Adore. Gina had attempted to enter the bathroom to check on me and Nannette had assured her she would get me home safely, which Gina had relayed to Dex. He hadn't bothered to wait for me, which was a good thing considering Nannette hadn't lied about me having a very rough night, but it still hurt that he would just leave me in the care of a strange woman claiming to be a nurse.

My reprieve lasted roughly long enough for Nannette to get me to my apartment, and I was back on my knees in the bathroom again, and that was the easy part. Let's just say that all the bagged blood Nannette fed me seemed to be fuel for more sickness. By the time day broke and pulled me under its sleeping spell, my throat was raw and scratchy, my ass was on fire, and I never wanted to eat food again.

The sickness must have worn me out because the next time I opened my eyes after my head hit the pillow, it was nightfall. I didn't recall any dreams, so Selander Ryan must have taken the night off, or he had satisfied himself with Gina, who I feared was dead or turned into something horrible. I turned my head, expecting a naked vampire to be lying next to me, but I was the only occupant in my bed. Rider had never joined me, which was a relief. The fumes coming out of my bathroom were horrendous despite all the hours since I'd been sick in there. I pinched my nose closed as I entered and opened the window to allow the room to air out. I also emptied half a can of air freshener to help so I wouldn't overdose on funkiness as I quickly brushed my teeth, showered, and washed my hair.

I donned a pair of sweatpants, a T-shirt, and thick, comfy socks, towel-dried my hair and stepped into my living room to find Eliza sitting on my couch. I looked around for Rider, but she was the only intruder in my apartment. "How did you get in here?"

"Nannette let me in when I relieved her," Eliza answered cheerily, placing the magazine she'd been reading on my coffee table. It was one of mine, a *Cosmopolitan*. "How are you feeling?"

"I don't think I'm sick anymore," I answered as I picked up the phone and dialed Gina's number. "Excuse me." Eliza nodded and walked across the living area into my kitchen space, where she removed a bag of blood from my refrigerator and went through the process of pouring it into a mug and warming it. I disconnected when Gina's voice came on her answering service. "I suppose you don't know what happened to the woman Selander Ryan was with last night?"

"You expelled a lot of energy last night fighting off the sickness," Eliza said as the microwave dinged and she removed the mug. "You need to drink this."

"The woman? Do you know what happened to her?"

"She's fine. You never had anything to worry about as far as she was concerned," Eliza assured me as she crossed the room and handed me the mug before settling on the couch, her back against the arm so she'd be facing me when I sat. She pulled her feet up beneath her and patted the cushion in front of her. I'd say something about her feet on my couch, but she'd kicked her shoes off, and I was too worried about Gina to care that much so I sat on the opposite end of the couch, facing her, and asked, "Are you sure? I don't know how much you know about what happened last night, but Selander Ryan was with her and she's very promiscuous, so it wouldn't be hard for him to seduce her."

"No harm came to your co-worker last night. I'm here for you, Danni. Rider gave you my contact information so you would contact me to explain this new way of life to you and you have yet to do that, so here I am making a house call."

Okay, this was sounding cultish. "My new way of life? I'm a vampire-succubus hybrid thing. I know that and I know I drink blood." I looked down into my Dollywood mug full of the dark red liquid and cringed. There was just something wrong about blood in a pink mug with Dolly Parton on the side of it. "Thanks to last night's fiasco, I know I shouldn't eat regular food. I'm good. I don't need the indoctrination or whatever this is. I get it."

"If you truly got it, you wouldn't still be such a target for Selander Ryan. He wouldn't be able to get into your dreams or track where you are in the city. You wouldn't have gotten sick last night because you would have never eaten that food, and you wouldn't have downed two whole glasses of champagne knowing it would thin your blood.

Do you have any idea how easy you make it to kill you and how hard you make it on Rider to keep you safe without completely controlling you?"

"Geez, is every vampire in the city stalking me and reporting my every movement to Rider?" I set the mug on the coffee table and rose from the couch. "What is he paying you people, anyway?"

"If Rider didn't have vampires watching over you last night, we wouldn't be having this conversation right now, because I'm sure you'd be dead. Selander Ryan was playing with his food last night. You're the food, Danni. He would have killed you once you left the restaurant if we didn't have vampires in place to keep that from happening, and as for what I'm being paid, I'm not. I'm repaying a debt."

"What kind of debt?"

"I'm not answering questions until you get that chip off your shoulder and really listen, and drink the blood. You need to keep your strength up. It's good to in general, but especially when you have someone like Selander Ryan after you."

"Why is he even after me?" I asked, plopping down on the couch and drinking the blood as I'd been told to, like a freshly scolded child. "And what's kept him from just breaking down my door and attacking me here? I've been alone here."

Eliza smiled. "Guards have been assigned to watch over this apartment since you were turned. If you would have come to me sooner and allowed me to teach you some things, you'd have known that."

I glanced around the room, checking the corners. No cameras. I couldn't recall seeing anyone lingering around my apartment. "Are these guards invisible or are y'all watching me via creepy candid camera?"

"One of the many talents of vampires is the ability to wrap oneself in shadow, even in daylight. I can teach you how to do this yourself, and how to spot others doing it." I scanned the apartment again, earning a chuckle. "No one is here with us now, Danni, and no one would dare enter your apartment. Rider wouldn't allow that. The guards stay in the hall or outside the apartment, out of direct sunlight, though most of the daytime guards aren't vampires. It's never just one guard. Rider keeps a team on the building and will do so as long as Selander Ryan is a threat."

"If a team has been watching me, why did they allow me to kill a man?" I asked. "I went out walking Sunday night, and I was so hungry I killed a man. Shouldn't they have stopped me? Shouldn't they have done something to keep Selander Ryan out of my office building?"

"Guards have been assigned to watch your building because it is where you are alone and it's an obvious place Selander Ryan may strike. He's already tried, but the team kept him from reaching you. The night you almost killed a man, the team had their hands full with Ryan."

"Why hasn't anyone just killed the guy if he's such a big, bad threat? You're vampires. Aren't you supposed to be lethal? Even I've killed a guy and that was by accident." The statement sounded light, but it wasn't. The guilt still sat on my chest like a five-ton block of cement, but I was making a point.

"Selander Ryan isn't some random drunk stumbling out of a bar, and he has guards too." Eliza looked down at her hands. "There are other factors you're not aware of. Selander Ryan and Rider have been battling each other a long time, and I predict they will for many decades."

"Maybe I should just kill the bastard and end everyone's trouble."

"I'm not sure it would," she murmured. "You can learn how to protect yourself though. You should be able to sense other vampires close to you and sense danger. You are now faster than a human and stronger. You've been fighting so hard against accepting what you are now, still clinging to your human life, that you aren't allowing yourself to fully harness your new gifts."

"Gifts?" I raised my mug. "I have to drink blood now.

I just slept like a corpse straight through the day because I couldn't fight off its pull after I spent the whole night puking and... you know... after eating. I finally got a date with the man I've been drooling over forever and that was just ruined..." I felt my eyes burning and took a deep breath, willing myself to not give in to the satisfaction of crying. I looked over at my answering machine and saw the red light blinking, and I hoped Dex had left me a message. "I'm sorry if Nannette thinks I'm an ungrateful bitch, but I'm not seeing where I got any gifts in this deal."

"Sleeping through the day isn't a bad thing, and it's very necessary to do so if you want to be at full strength, especially after newly turning. It's rather surprising that you've been able to function so well and perform your job. It normally takes many years to build up the endurance needed to fight the call of sleep when the sun rises. It must be because of the conflicting marks."

"Conflicting marks?"

"Rider thought Selander was attempting to kill you in the alley. He didn't just bite you, he tore at your neck like a rabid animal, but he had, in fact, tried to turn you. Rider then bit you and redirected your turn so that you would become a vampire instead of one of those demon-whores. You were marked by an incubus and a vampire that night and you haven't fully accepted either. You got the vampire teeth, but they secrete the succubus venom that seduces your victims when you bite into them. You're repulsed by the thought of drinking from a woman, aren't you?"

I thought about it and cringed. "It sickens me and I feel really cold if I'm very close to a woman. When around a man, I get a pull toward him, toward his heat. What do you mean I haven't fully accepted either?"

"An incubus and a vampire marked you. Rider was successful in redirecting your turn so you would get the vampire teeth instead of those hideous, curved succubus fangs. You still have the venom and the aversion to estrogen. Two masters marked you, and until you accept one of them as your true master, you will continue to have strengths and weaknesses of both."

"My true master? Are you serious?" I laughed. "It will be a cold day in hell before I declare any man as my master."

"Then continue running from Selander Ryan for the rest of your very long life. He is no longer interested in turning you. He wants you dead."

"Why?"

"Because Rider cared enough about you to save you from turning into one of those vile creatures, and he hates Rider. You're easier to kill than Rider, and killing you would make Rider suffer, maybe more than killing him outright. I told you they have a history, and it's an ugly one."

I thought about what she said. I was afraid of Selander Ryan and I didn't want to die, but I didn't want to be owned by someone, or devoted to a man, just because he'd saved me from one type of monster by turning me into another. The lesser of two evils concept never worked for me. "So if I accept Rider as my true master, Selander Ryan just goes away?"

"Once you accept Rider as your true master, Selander Ryan will not be able to track you as easily. He will not be able to gain entry to your dreams, and you will feel no pull whatsoever toward him. You will also be stronger, especially once you accept the vampire lifestyle, which includes sleeping during the day, at least the majority of it, and using the night hours when you are at your strongest to your advantage."

"I work during the majority of the day. The only reason I could sleep through today without losing my job is because I took a week off for a surgery I can't even have now."

"You won't need surgery now. You will stay young and healthy."

"It was an elective surgery, and I don't know how

healthy I feel considering eating asparagus had me in the bathroom all night."

"And now you know not to do that. You will not die of old age, Danni, and although you can be killed, it isn't as easy to kill a vampire as it is to kill a human, so you have the potential to live several decades, or centuries. Is your current job really that important in the grand scheme of things?"

"I can't think about a hundred years from now," I said as I tried to wrap my mind around the concept of living that long. "I've worked hard to get where I am in life, to be taken seriously at a job in a world dominated by men, and you want me to accept some man I barely know as my master? I don't know how long you've been a vampire or what generation you were actually still a human in, but my generation has come a long way where women's rights are concerned. You might have had no problem cowering under a man, but I'm not going to just declare my devotion to some man and start calling him Master."

"I was sired by a woman," Eliza informed me, "and I had no choice whether or not she would rule over me. I was automatically her property the moment she turned me because she was my sire. This is the way it is for all vampires except you, because you got bitten by two masters the same night. She didn't take me to the side and explain the changes I would go through or waste a moment of her time caring about my well-being. She enslaved me and her other fledglings, made us sleep with the men and women in her nest as well as herself, and those who showed a talent for killing became her thugs. I was deemed too weak in that area, so I was treated as a maid and a whore. This lasted for twenty years and there wasn't anything I could do about it because, as my sire, she owned me. She controlled me and could make me do things like a puppet on a string."

I thought about what she said, my heart going out to her, but anger brewed inside me at the same time. "So you're telling me this is what a sire does and I'm pretty much free now because I have conflicting bites… and you want me to claim Rider as my master so he can do all that to me? Being chased by Selander Ryan doesn't seem all that bad now."

"No, Danni. I'm telling you that my sire was evil and you're lucky because yours isn't. I'm not some weak-willed woman who let some man control me because I lack a backbone. I was controlled by a woman because I had no choice. You may have been marked by both Selander Ryan and Rider, but you're more vampire than succubus, and Rider could control you if he wanted to. You have freedom because he has allowed it and that won't change when you accept him as your true master. When it comes to you and Rider, master is just a word."

"How do you know this for a fact?"

"How do you think I'm here now if I was under my sire's control and couldn't act on my own? Rider found out about our nest and how horribly the fledglings were treated. Rider killed my sire and liberated all of us. Whether he is a human or a vampire, a good man is still a good man, and Rider is one of the best men I have ever known."

I sat there, blinking, as I tried to absorb the information I'd been given. I still had questions. If Rider had killed Eliza's sire, why hadn't he killed Selander Ryan the night he attacked me? Was Selander Ryan more powerful than an evil sire who could control an entire nest of fledglings? How powerful was Rider? Nannette had mentioned something about him protecting the city. The whole city, as in everyone in the whole entire city, or just his nest? What was a nest? I assumed it was like a pack. Werewolves had packs and vampires had nests. How many vampires had he sired? "Did Rider sire the vampires guarding my apartment?"

Eliza shook her head. "I've known Rider for a long time, but he's remained pretty mysterious even to those closest to him, not that anyone is considerably close to him. I don't know of anyone he's sired. To my knowledge, most vampires who work for him are ones he has liberated from abusive sires. He has also worked with shifters and just plain humans."

Shifters. There was that word again. "He didn't sire Nannette? She seemed very... upset with me last night, and she seemed very protective of Rider. She doesn't like me at all."

"Nannette was liberated by Rider and, like many of us, owes him a great deal. Some of us suffered worse than others, and some of us suffered far longer. All of us would do anything Rider asks of us, because he asks. Well, he orders some of his employees around, particularly when he's in a bad mood, and that bartender sure got his ass handed to him after you left the bar with Selander Ryan. Everyone working for him that night got their asses handed to them. He's a lot gentler with women, always has been."

I cringed. "I didn't mean to get anyone in trouble. Selander told me Rider had slipped something into my drink, a date rape drug, and I believed him. I was drunk too."

"Incubi are the kings of con artistry, so don't beat yourself up too hard over it. If he could slip past security, you didn't stand a chance."

"The same security watching my building?" My stomach sank. I'd actually felt a little safer when she'd told me I had guards watching my apartment.

"No, Rider has really good guys watching your building, and they are on high alert. On the night you were attacked, the only indication anything was up was the hunter scoping out the bar."

"The Barnaby guy? Rider told me he was a hunter, and he was there because of me."

"Yes. Barnaby comes from a long line of hunters and they're very good. He knows how to sniff out women considered incubus bait. It's an old trick. Find a woman with blood that attracts incubi and follow her to get to the incubus when it comes to get her. There'd been succubi attacks in the area and where there are succubi you'll always find at least one incubus. While patrolling the area, he picked up on you. Knowing Barnaby was there for a reason, Rider picked up on you too and tried to protect you."

"Why did he leave me alone to go talk to Barnaby when they were both aware an incubus was prowling the area and could get me? They're both on the same side."

"Barnaby is a hunter. He only leaves vampires in this area alone because of a family deal made long ago with Rider. However, when outside the city he will kill any vampire he comes across and whether he's in or out of the city limits, he will kill every other non-human he can, and he has no qualms about using an innocent woman for bait. He would have allowed you to be bitten and killed you, as well as the incubus who bit you. Rider was trying to protect you from him when the other enemy got past security."

"Lovely guy."

"Oh, he's a bastard. Of all the hunters in his family, Barnaby is the worst of them. Good hunter, not that I necessarily think that's a good thing. He gets some bad ones off the streets, but to him, the good or bad factor means nothing, except for when Rider says it does. He's a jerk, though, and he'd kill a shifter child without a pang of guilt."

"He made threatening calls to me at my job." I frowned. "How did he find out where I work? How does everyone seem to know how to get to me?"

"Barnaby is a good hunter, which means he's a good tracker, but this is the age of social media. All he had to do was Google search your image, which he probably got pretty easily without you being aware of it while you were drinking and end up on your Facebook or some other social media account. As for Selander Ryan, I've already explained that. He's tapped into you while you refrain from choosing a master. What you don't know yet is that he's getting some inside help. You really should consider finding a new job, Danni. There are snakes there smiling in your face while they set you up for danger. They don't even know it themselves."

A cold chill skirted up my spine, but then I remembered my last conversation with Rider and found myself warming right up, mostly from irritation. "Wow. I was starting to believe all this, but let me guess. Rider is still mad that I went out with Dex Prince last night, so he sent you over here to tell me some bullshit about him being my enemy now? He doesn't want to control me, but he still wants to tell me who I can and can't date. Go ahead. What story did he come up with for you to tell me about Dex?"

"Rider didn't tell me anything about the man you went out with. The guards watching you in the restaurant, however, told me about your co-worker. I told you no harm came to your friend Gina last night. There's a reason why. The harm already came to her. She's one of them, Danni. She's been one of them for a while now. That's why she sent you to The Midnight Rider that night and never showed up."

TWELVE

"You're lying!" I jumped up from the couch. "What the hell are you even saying, that she's a succubus?"

"I assure you I am no liar," Eliza spoke firmly, though her eyes didn't lose their gentleness. "Incubi can only turn those who have the specific blood type required to do so. For those who do not have the required blood type for turning into a succubus, they generally will kill or ensnare. Your co-worker has been ensnared. It's a common practice for incubi to mark women they can't turn and then do a sort of brainwashing on them. They visit the ensnared in dreams and make suggestions or spy on them through their connection. After Selander Ryan ensnared Gina, he more than likely spied on her through the connection and the moment she interacted with you at your place of work, he sensed your blood."

"How could he sense my blood by watching another person? Wouldn't he have to be close to me?"

"He wasn't spying on her through binoculars, Danni. He was using the link he created with her. It would allow him to sense what she sensed, to use her eyes, nose, and ears, if you will."

My heart felt as if it might beat right out of my chest

and my head swam as I plopped back down onto the couch and recalled every memory I could dredge up about Gina. I'd worked with her for so long and she'd always been promiscuous and extremely flirtatious, but she'd never been catty with me. She'd never seemed to have any hidden agenda with me either, and the recommendation to go to The Midnight Rider didn't seem odd either. I'd had a bad day and she recommended a bar for drinks like friends and co-workers all over the country routinely did. Sure, she hadn't shown up, but Gina was flighty and her top priority was always men, so her choosing a date with a guy over hanging out with an upset co-worker wasn't that odd for someone like her. "Wait. Gina recommended I go to The Midnight Rider. If Selander Ryan was controlling her and making her do this, why would he choose The Midnight Rider out of all the bars she could have suggested I go to? If he wanted to turn me at first, wouldn't it make more sense for him to do it in a bar not owned by a vampire who happens to also be his enemy?"

"You're thinking like a logical, sane person. Selander Ryan has not been a logical, sane person for a long time, if ever. He's very vengeful and snagging a woman out of Rider's bar and turning her in the alley behind it would be a slap in Rider's face."

"But he knew there was a chance Rider would know and stop him. Rider could have killed him."

"That's part of the game."

"The game? *The game*?" I stood again and paced the floor, flexing the fingers I wanted to wrap around Eliza's neck as she sat there so calmly telling me all this crap had happened to me because of some stupid game. No, I wanted to wrap them around Rider's throat, or tighten them into a fist and jab it right in his... chest. I couldn't even bring myself to think of hitting him in the face, not with those amazing sapphire blue eyes looking at me. Oh, brother. Maybe he was controlling me a little.

"I know it's upsetting."

"Upsetting? You think this is upsetting? Getting your period unexpectedly and bleeding through your pants at work is upsetting. Getting cat-called by some loser scratching his nuts on the street, then getting called a flat-chested bitch when you don't smile at him is upsetting. *Hindsight* getting canceled was upsetting! This is… I have no words! There are no words to describe what it's like to have nearly been killed, then turned into some freak because two grown men want to toy with each other like children and don't care if innocent people get hurt in the process. And why won't Rider say how old he is anyway? Why is he so cagey about it? He's such a child."

"Actually, that's something you would have already learned about if you'd arranged a counseling session with me. It is never a good idea for a vampire to confess his or her age. Even asking the wrong vampire how old he or she is could get you seriously injured or killed, as it is seen as a threat."

I stopped pacing as I considered how idiotic this new information was. "Seriously? You could be killed for asking a vampire how old he is? What, are vampires on vanity level one billion or something?"

"Generally speaking, the older a vampire is, the more powerful. Asking a vampire's age can be seen as measuring him or her up for battle. Knowing how old a vampire is can give an inclination to how truly powerful they are in comparison with oneself. For example, if I found out I was two decades older than another vampire, I would know I was that much more powerful. If it were my intention, I might consider trying to take that vampire out and take control of any vampires in his nest."

I pondered over this for a moment. As ridiculous as it was, it actually made sense. Gina being an enemy still didn't. "Okay, so Rider and Selander are both however many decades or eons old and they use people to play games with each other—"

"Rider doesn't use people to play games. That's all

Selander Ryan."

"Whatever. They play games with each other, and so you're telling me Gina is like this Trojan horse Selander Ryan snuck up in my life. If that's the case, why didn't she recognize him when he came to my office?"

"How do you know she didn't?"

"I know Gina. I've seen her spot a new hot guy and I know how she acts. The day he came to my office was the first time she'd seen him."

"Maybe it was, in the flesh. Some women are more susceptible to accepting incubi into their dreams. They can be marked without any physical contact. A woman who has been marked but not turned could dream about the same incubus every night for twenty years and not immediately recognize him after meeting him on the street. She could do hurtful things to people and not even realize she's doing it. There is no way it's a coincidence that you work with a woman marked by Selander Ryan, that same woman told you to go to Rider's bar, and you were attacked by him that very night after she mysteriously never showed up. Think logically, Danni."

"If I was thinking logically, I'd be thinking I was insane and checking myself into the psychiatric ward," I said, slumping back down on the couch in defeat. "I drink blood out of a Dollywood mug. That shouldn't be happening."

"You'll get used to it, and you can lead a very happy life once you embrace your vampirism and quit focusing on the negatives."

"I highly doubt that," I muttered. "The sun burns my flesh off, I can't eat food, I'm stuck with this body, a psycho sex fiend that can creep into my dreams is trying to kill me, I can't tell anyone normal because they'll lock me away in the nuthouse, I want to sleep all day which doesn't work well at all with my schedule, I accidentally freaking killed a guy, and my sire is an incredibly hot bastard that I want to punch in the face but I can't because did I mention the bastard is incredibly hot? Ugh!" I heaved out a frustrated groan. "Life sucks after you die."

"Clearly you are not dead." Eliza smiled. "Sunscreen protects you from the sun and you also have the choice of staying out of it, you will build up a tolerance for food over time although you only need blood to survive, you will never grow old and frail, you can always talk to me and there are other vampires in the community you may become friends with, you can find another job, killing a guy does suck, I'm sorry about that, and as for your sire… Rider has always been a bit prickly, but incredibly protective of women. Still, in all the time I've known him, I've never seen him look at anyone the way he looks at you."

"Like he wants to toss me off the roof?"

Eliza raised an eyebrow, and I remembered the way he'd kissed me after bringing me home from work. Yeah, maybe he didn't exactly want to toss me off a building but rather, on to something, like a bed. Maybe I didn't exactly want him not to, but he wasn't Dex, and he could control me if he wanted to. Was he even attracted to me or the fact he could make me do whatever he wanted? Just because he hadn't yet didn't mean he never would.

A knock sounded at my door and I started to get up. Eliza stretched her arm out and blocked me. "Can you tell who is at the door?"

I looked at it, then back at her. "Uh, surrrrre, because I can see through wood?"

Irritation flitted across her eyes and her nostrils flared just the slightest bit, but she quickly adopted her normal serene look again. "Close your eyes, open all your senses and feel who is at the door. As a vampire, this is one of your gifts."

I thought she was full of hooey, but I did as she instructed, closing my eyes and listening. I heard nothing.

"Feel who's at the door, Danni. Really open yourself up to what the universe is telling you."

Ooookay. I tried again and only heard another knock. I took a deep breath, prepared to tell Eliza whatever she was talking about wasn't working, when my heart sped up. Nervous excitement tingled up my arms and spine, lifting the fine little hairs on my body. "It's Mr. Wonderful," I said, as I felt a wave of what I could only describe as strength and familiarity. I walked across the room to open the door and let in the devil we'd just been talking about.

"How was dinner last night?" Rider asked, stepping inside my apartment uninvited. He quickly strode across the room and started checking locks on windows and closing curtains I'd opened after the last time he'd left.

"You know how dinner was," I snapped, closing the door, "and did you never learn manners? I guess you think as my sire you can just come in my apartment any time you please."

"I knocked," he said, closing the last curtain in the room as I walked back to the center of the living area. "Keep these closed."

"Is that an order?"

"Order, request, warning, I don't care what you call it as long as you do it," he said as he closed in on me, not stopping until he stood right in front of me, towering over me. "And I won't be coming in your apartment unless you come first," he murmured in a low voice before winking and stepping away.

"You wish, you disgusting, arrogant—" I caught a glimpse of Eliza grinning from ear to ear as she watched me. She waggled her eyebrows. Damn her and her vampire hearing. And how did I get mine to work? I made a mental note to ask her to teach me that next. I couldn't ask that very moment because Rider had disappeared into my bedroom.

"Hey!" I followed him in. "What are you doing?"

"Protecting you, the usual," he answered, frowning. "Why is there a draft?" He moved toward the bathroom. "Why is your bathroom window open?" he called out to me and I heard him shut it. "Oh." He stepped back out, barely suppressing a grin. "I guess it still smelled pretty bad when you woke up tonight, huh? All that vomit. I heard it was pretty bad, even scared some kids at the restaurant."

"There were no kids at the restaurant, you jerk." I folded my arms beneath my chest and glared at him as he checked the lock on my bedroom window and secured the curtains. "For such an old man, you sure are childish."

All the curtains closed, he turned toward me and raised an eyebrow. "Old man?"

"Yeah, Grandpa."

He chuckled. "Now who's childish?"

I glared at him as I tried to come up with a witty response and came up blank. I didn't even know why I seemed hell-bent on picking a fight with him. He just got under my skin and irritated the hell out of me.

"What's with my curtains?" I finally asked, conceding I wasn't quick enough to come up with a snappy comeback.

"If someone has a gun or crossbow, it's best they can't see into your apartment."

"A crossbow? Is Daryl Dixon hunting me now?"

"I don't know who that is," Rider answered, "but judging by your sarcastic tone, it's someone ridiculous, so I'm not going to worry about that. I will worry about Barnaby Quimby, though, and he has been known to use both guns and crossbows in addition to blades and whatever else he feels necessary to get the job done."

I swallowed hard past the ball of fear that had lodged in my throat. "You said Barnaby was the guy who made the threatening calls to me."

"He was."

"You said you were going to handle him."

"This is me handling him. He's a shifty little bastard when he wants to be. I can't find him right now, so I'm sticking to you until one of my people can get a bead on him."

"That's just great." I ran a hand through my hair,

exasperated. "I thought you said this guy was honoring some deal worked out between you and his great, great, great whatever. He's not supposed to touch vampires in this area without your permission."

"Word on the street is that Barnaby isn't honoring the deal because, as far as he's concerned, you're not a vampire. You're a hybrid and the prick thinks that means he can disregard the deal that was made, but you're safe in my care, Danni."

"He's a human, right?"

"Yes."

"You can't find a human? You can't find a simple human, but I'm supposed to be safe with you?"

"I said he was a human, but I never said he was a simple one," Rider growled. "Barnaby Quimby is the Dean Winchester of hunters."

"Honey, I've seen Barnaby Quimby and that fugly rodent is no Dean Winchester," I said, earning a grin. "I can't believe you know who Dean Winchester is, but you don't know about Daryl Dixon."

"Ah, so he's a television character."

"Hellooo… *The Walking Dead*. Very popular television show."

"Oh, that. Zombies are stupid. They make no sense. The dead can't eat people. They're rotting. How are they supposed to bite a person without their jaws just snapping right off, and no one ever explains how the whole zombie thing happens, but people just believe it?"

I sank down onto the foot of my bed and groaned. "I can't believe an incubus and a hunter want me dead and I'm in my bedroom with a vampire who's bitching about the absurdity of zombies. How is this my life?"

Rider sat next to me on the bed and squeezed my knee. "I'm not going to let either of them hurt you, Danni. You need to trust me."

"You don't even trust me."

He looked over at me, his brow furrowed. "What

makes you say that?"

"Eliza told me you have guards watching my every move, reporting to you. You had your people in the restaurant last night."

"I have guards on your building to protect you from Selander Ryan, and I had guards in the restaurant doing the same thing and he showed up. That's not a trust issue, Danni. I'm protecting you."

"Why didn't you tell me about them?"

"I told you I'd have men watching you at the restaurant."

"You didn't tell me about the ones here. This is my home. I should have known."

"Yes, you should have known." He nodded his head adamantly. "The fact you didn't frankly scares the hell out of me. The fact that you disregard everything I tell you terrifies me."

"Maybe if you'd quit ordering me around, I'd listen to you."

"Maybe if you'd quit being so damn stubborn and trust me, I wouldn't have to."

"Maybe you should remove your hand from my leg."

He looked down at where his hand had slid higher up my leg and now rested on my thigh, dangerously close to another part of my body. "Maybe I should."

He rose and crossed over to the window, where he stood with his back to me, his hands in his pockets. I already missed the warmth of his hand on my thigh and the tingle he took with him when he left. I shook my head and silently told myself to get a grip. Rider was eye candy, for sure. He was working the hell out of the tall, dark and mysterious thing, but he didn't say family man. He wouldn't give me a big house with a maid and sophisticated friends. He certainly wouldn't give me the kind of life that would show my mother I was just as good as my sister. I didn't need a Rider Knight in my life. I needed a Dexter Prince.

"I'm going to be the one throwing up all night if you continue along this train of thought," Rider grumbled, revealing to me that he'd heard my thoughts.

"Stay out of my head!"

"I'm not even trying to hear your thoughts," he said, turning toward me. "You're practically broadcasting them."

"A gentleman wouldn't listen."

"First of all, as I stated, you're practically broadcasting them. I don't have much of a choice. For another thing…" He stepped closer, his lips curled into a mischievous grin. "Who told you I was a gentleman?"

"Certainly no one who ever met you, I'm sure." I stood and made a shooing motion with my hand. "You've locked all my windows and closed my curtains. You can go now."

"If only protecting you were going to be that easy, but I'm afraid it's going to take more than securing your windows."

"You have guards in my building, yes?"

"They're not as good as I am."

"Cocky, much?"

"Wise. I know your two predators better than any of my men could ever dream of. I am the best choice for protecting you, so I won't be leaving unless, of course, you want to stay with me at the bar."

"No, thank you." I recalled his hideaway above the bar with its one bed and hooker takeout. "You don't have to stay here either. I've managed just fine so far, and you have guards on the building and Eliza is inside with me."

"Eliza isn't a fighter, and she has a busy schedule. She cleared time for you, but she has regular clients."

"For vampire counseling?"

"Yes."

I imagined a small office with a Count Chocula type vampire stretched out on a couch telling Eliza how lonely or perhaps *batty* he felt before going into his blood addiction issues and nearly laughed at the absurdity.

"You were getting vampire counseling when I arrived, so I don't know why the thought is so preposterous to you."

"I told you to stay out of my head," I snapped.

"If you want me to stay out of your head, you need to work on that broadcasting issue."

I growled. "You said I blocked you when I was at work. I know I've blocked you before. How am I broadcasting now?"

"It's harder to lock down your thoughts when your sire is near, or so I've been told. I usually detect anger before you block me out of your thoughts from a distance, so I think you've just been lucky when you've done it in the past. You get mad and accidentally form the wall. You need to learn how to do it when you're not mad. If you're not careful, you can broadcast to other vampires in your nest."

I frowned. "I have a nest?"

"You are part of my nest," he clarified. "I have mind-linked with other vampires, although the link you and I share is stronger because I sired you. You may be able to mind-link with those I have created links with, but right now, you are still two beasts fighting to see who will come out on top. The vampire in you is stronger, but as long as you hold on to that succubus part of you, you will mute your abilities. You can only serve one master."

"I will never bow down to you and call you my master, Rider. I will never do that for any man."

"I would never ask you to bow down to me. Unfortunately, I don't know of a better way to explain what is happening to you. It's not as if there is a manual for this sort of situation. Stopping one form of beast's attack and redirecting the change is rare. There was a chance it wouldn't have even worked. In fact, I know it wouldn't have had I not been old enough."

"And how old is that?" I asked him as I stood and walked a circle around him, studying him. He looked around my age, maybe a little older, but he *felt* older, if that made any sense at all.

He let out a frustrated sigh and pinched the bridge of his nose. "You must stop asking that. Asking a vampire's age will get you killed."

"Are you going to kill me now?" I poked his chest playfully, but felt a spark of something much stronger than electricity and decided it best I not touch him again unless I wanted to see what that spark led to and I didn't think that was a very good idea.

"If I wanted you dead, I'd just leave you on your own. I'm sure you'd be dead or worse in no time at all left to your own bad judgment and foolishness."

"Gee, thanks."

"You're welcome." He moved to cross the room, but I planted myself in front of him. "What?"

"One billion and ninety-two?"

"One billion and ninety-two what?" he asked, his brow furrowed.

"Years. You're like a billion years old and that's why you have such a stick up your butt."

"Wow. You got it."

My jaw dropped for a moment. "Seriously? You're a billion years old?"

"Yes, Danni, I'm a billion years old. I was just a young man out walking my dinosaur when a vampire jumped out of a bush and attacked me."

"Oh!" I attempted to smack him but he deftly grabbed my wrist and pulled me in close until we were chest to chest and I had to crane my head all the way back to look up at him. My wrist still in his hand, he rested it at the small of my back and wrapped his other hand around my neck with his fingers at the base of my skull and his thumb skimming my cheek as he made sure to keep me looking at him, giving him my undivided attention. I'd placed my free hand on his chest, planning to push away from him, but once my palm touched him, it wanted to stay there.

"This isn't a matter of trust, Danni, and all jokes aside, this is a serious matter. Deadly serious. Telling you my age would be like painting a target on you. There are some secrets I have to keep." His gaze slowly rolled down my face, his eyes dilating as his gaze locked onto my mouth. As his head lowered, his mouth seeking mine, my brain screamed to me I was in danger, but my hand, still on his chest, gripped his shirt tighter. He released my other hand, and I gripped another handful of his shirt as my eyes drifted closed…

He growled low in his throat the exact moment the doorbell rang, and stepped back, allowing breathing room. It felt like someone had thrown a bucket of ice water on us just as I was about to go up in flames and I was irked that I didn't get to burn with him, which only irked me more. This wasn't supposed to happen. Not with him. I stepped back and straightened my clothes, just then remembering I'd chosen sweatpants and a T-shirt. Ugh, how attractive. I mentally slapped myself for caring. I wasn't supposed to care what I looked like when Rider Knight stopped by.

The doorbell rang again, and I tried the trick Eliza had taught me. I closed my eyes and cast out my senses, picking up a hint of spicy cologne and an aura of wealth and sophistication that made my toes curl and a frenzy of butterflies kick up in my belly.

"Don't answer it."

I glared at Rider, now understanding why he'd growled when the doorbell rang. Apparently, he'd already been casting his senses out before Dex's finger had touched the buzzer. I was a bit miffed he'd not been one hundred percent focused on the kiss that had almost happened, and also miffed I wasn't as aware of my surroundings as he was. "You're not my master, you're just my sire, which I thought we'd established. Stay here and do not attempt to embarrass me or make an ass out of yourself." I grabbed my robe off my bed and pulled it on, wishing I'd chosen something better to wear when I'd finally crawled out of bed.

I made it out of my bedroom with Rider close on my heels. "I mean it," I said, turning to poke a finger into his chest. "You stay in there and don't interfere."

He looked down at my finger with a mix of irritation and amusement. "I don't think you understand how this sire-fledgling thing works. You don't tell me what to do."

"I don't think you understand how I work. *You* don't tell *me* what to do, and you don't do as you please in *my* home. Stay out of sight." I turned on my heel and marched toward the door, but not before I caught the grin on Rider's face or the surprised look Eliza cast his way as I passed her where she sat on the couch, nose deep in another issue of *Cosmopolitan*. I ran my hands through my hair and hoped I didn't look horrendous as I opened the door to find Dex standing in the hall with a bouquet of mixed flowers. "Dex, you shouldn't have. I'm so sorry about last night."

Dex stepped back and extended the flowers to me at arm's length. "I'm sorry you fell ill. I thought I'd check on you and bring you these to cheer you up. Still sick I see?"

I cast a glance back at Rider to find him grinning from ear to ear, the devil dancing in his eyes. He looked seconds away from a full barrel laugh and the glare I delivered his way seemed to be tipping him toward that point.

"I'm feeling much better," I said, stepping out into the hall and pulling the door closed behind me.

Dex frowned, trying to sneak a look inside before the door closed, but keeping a safe distance from me. "Is this a bad time? I didn't intend to stay long."

"No, you're fine. I just have a friend over who is a bit nosy. I love the flowers," I said, taking them from him. He made sure our fingers didn't touch.

"Well, I won't stay long. I just felt bad after the way our date went. That was not the night I had planned."

"Me either," I said, smelling the sweet blossoms. I could hear Rider chuckling in my head and would have been completely pissed, except I also picked up on his angry undertone. It seemed the hot and powerful Rider still got jealous of mortal men. I heard him growl and knew he was eavesdropping into my thoughts again.

"Maybe we can try again this weekend, after you've had time to recuperate. I saw you had taken the rest of this week off, so if you don't have weekend plans, I have family coming in and would love to have you as my dinner guest."

My whole body stilled except for the butterflies in my belly. They went into party mode. "Dinner with your family?"

"It's casual, in my penthouse, actually. You'll probably be a little bored, what with all the shop talk, but I plan on making that up to you once dinner is over and I can get rid of everyone." He winked at me and it sent a shiver of excitement down my spine, straight to my toes, which promptly curled... inside my socked feet. Ugh, could I look any worse?

"I would love to have dinner this weekend," I said, "and I took this week off before the Nocturnal, Inc. deal came through. If you need me to work, I can just cancel the rest of my paid time off."

"No, no, no. You should take this time off and make sure you're really well before the dinner this weekend. Maybe even treat yourself to a spa day. You came up with solid concepts and the degree of detail you notated in your files is really impressive. If there are any issues, we have your number, but don't worry about it. I want you rested and back in good health. I have plans for you."

I felt my cheeks warm and was pretty sure I was blushing from feet to hairline. "All right, but please don't hesitate to call me if I'm needed. I know this is a big contract."

Dex winked. "That's my girl, always giving her all. Get some rest and seriously consider that spa day. You deserve a little pampering. I'll talk to you soon."

And with that, he left. No kiss goodbye, which I didn't expect since he'd made it quite obvious he thought I had some sort of contagious illness, but he hadn't touched me at all. Still, I'd scored an invitation to dinner with his family, which was pretty huge, especially this early in a relationship, so I didn't let it get me down that he'd seemed more than ready to get away from me. I mean, he didn't have to visit me at all. He could have just sent the flowers by courier if he hadn't wanted to see me. Speaking of seeing… I scanned the hallway, searching for my mysterious guardians, and came up empty, but I knew better. Someone was there. Now that I was aware I was being watched over, I sensed someone there in the hall but I couldn't lay eyes on him, and I was sure it was a him.

My door opened and Rider stepped out. He gripped my shoulders from behind and turned me to face the corner at the end of the hallway before crouching down so he was at eye level with me. "Do you see the shadows there?"

I nodded, seeing a mass of shadow in the corner.

"Look deep in the shadow, using all your senses. You'll feel him out before your eyes reveal him."

I peered closer at the dark mass of shadow, my mind open. I sensed his power, not anywhere close to Rider's but far stronger than mine. I smelled him; he smelled like cinnamon and some other spice I couldn't quite place, and slowly, I started to see him. The shadow became a form and there he was, a thin Hispanic man dressed in black from head to toe. He winked at me, and my mouth fell open. "He's right freaking there. If he was a snake, he would have bitten me."

"Nah, I'd have had to kill him then, and he's a vampire, so the snake idiom isn't really needed." Rider ushered me inside. "Out of the hallway. It's not as safe out here."

"Well, those are lovely," Eliza said, eying the flowers Dex had given me as Rider locked the door behind us. "That was considerate."

"Yeah, I really liked the part where the jackass jumped

back from her like she was a leper," Rider said, crossing the room as he pushed a button on his cell phone and raised it to his ear. "I'll leave you two to continue your counseling session while I make some business calls because you know, I do have a business to run in addition to protecting you from killers while you preoccupy yourself with dates."

"Is he always such a prickly bastard?" I asked as Rider disappeared into my bedroom.

"Eh, well, he has his moods," Eliza said, "but never anything this entertaining."

"Entertaining?" I rolled my eyes as I set the flowers down on the coffee table and adjusted them until they sat perfectly in the center. "Yeah, he's a real riot. A thousand laughs a minute."

"You know how to spot someone hiding in the shadows now?"

"Yes. At least he took a moment from mocking me to show me something useful."

"Good, now let's continue. There are all kinds of vampire tricks you have at your disposal. Would you like to learn a few?"

"I'd like to learn them all," I said, plopping down on the couch, "starting with how to block that jerk out of my head."

"Not dating men he wants to split in half would help with the him being a jerk part," Eliza suggested, smiling impishly as I delivered a dark glance her way.

Vampires were such pains in my ass.

THIRTEEN

"Yikes!" I jumped back and glared at Rider. "That was too close!"

Eliza had taught me how to block him out of my mind last night, not that I was particularly proficient yet, but I at least knew how to do it, and now Rider was teaching me how to block punches and throw them as well.

"I'm not going to hit you. Now get back in position and this time, instead of jumping away from the punch, block it."

"Fine." I got back into position, which meant standing in the center of my living area with my legs apart and my feet grounded, whatever that meant. I really wasn't sure. I just imitated the stance Rider had taken when he'd showed me.

"OK, now I'm going to start slow. Just block me." He started throwing punches, and I blocked them. It was pretty simple until he started picking up speed, which meant I had to pick up speed, which meant we appeared to really be fighting and that scared the bejeebers out of me. The guy was a powerful vampire. One punch and I'm sure a broken jaw would be the least of my problems. Heck, one solid punch from him and he could probably knock me back into whatever century he'd came from.

"Now block and throw," he ordered, slowing down his punches.

"What's the point of this?" I asked as I blocked his punch and threw one of my own, only to be blocked. "You're not hitting me and I'm not hitting you, so I doubt this is like a real fight."

"Do you want me to hit you?"

"No, you'd kill me," I answered, making him laugh. "I wouldn't mind hitting you."

"I let you hit me earlier. Several times."

"Yeah, I liked that. Let's do that some more."

"That was when I was teaching you the proper way to throw a punch. Now I'm teaching you how to throw and block. How well you punch won't matter at all if your enemy knocks you on your ass before you can ball your hand into a fist."

"Wouldn't it be easier for me to just bite my enemy?"

"If you want to kill your enemy, and provided your enemy isn't beating the hell out of you so you actually can bite him or her. Then there's the possibility your enemy is a vampire. In which case, what's biting going to do?" He grabbed my fist, easily stopping my latest punch, and backed up a step. "You look a little pale. You need to feed."

"Ugh." I shivered. "Do you have to say it like that? You make me sound so ghoulish."

"Feed, drink, whatever. I haven't seen you feed at all since I've been here. I warned you about allowing yourself to get thirsty."

"I haven't seen you feed either since you've been here," I said as I crossed over to the kitchen and grabbed a bag of blood out of the refrigerator.

"You said you didn't want my donors in your apartment, and I don't want to leave you while Barnaby and Selander are hunting you." He pulled the coffee table back in place, signaling our fighting lesson was over for the day, or so I hoped.

"I said I didn't want your hookers in my apartment," I clarified. "Don't forget to put the flowers back on the coffee table, please." I watched him carefully as he picked up the vase of flowers Dex had given me and placed them on the coffee table. The way his lip curled in disgust amused me.

"I thought I already explained to you that my donors are former hookers. They don't need to sell their bodies anymore." Rider entered the kitchen area and leaned against a counter as I stirred my freshly nuked blood around in my Mickey Mouse mug. I made a mental note to buy mugs that didn't have people or characters on them. "You've gone from pale to green."

"This stuff is so gross." I grimaced. "You'd think putting my mouth on someone's neck and draining their blood straight from the tap would be more disgusting, but it isn't. Seeing it in a cup is just nasty, and the smell of it warming in the microwave is disgusting. Don't even get me started on when there are blood clots." The image of a blood clot I'd seen in a previous cup flashed before me and I gagged reflexively.

"Are you all right?" Rider asked, quickly moving to my side as I clapped a hand over my mouth. I nodded and waited a moment for my stomach to settle before speaking.

"I'm sorry. This is just really gross. I hate that I need this stuff, and that I have to have it this way."

Rider sighed heavily as he took the mug out of my hand and poured its contents down the sink. "You're right. This stuff is disgusting. I haven't drunk from a bag in years and you shouldn't have to when you have someone right here you can drink from."

"You?" My stomach flip-flopped as I watched him wash out the mug. "I thought you said that was a bad idea."

"I said it was a bad idea for you to drink from

167

humans," he said as he placed the mug in the drying rack and dried his hands off, then turned toward me. "Come on."

He took my hand and led me over to the couch where we sat side by side and he rolled up his sleeve. I gazed longingly at his throat, where the blood would flow more freely, but I understood why he offered his wrist instead. "What about my, uh, um…"

"Succubus bite?"

"Yeah, that." I felt the warmth of a blush fill my cheeks.

"I'm prepared for it, and I'm not a wild animal. I can control myself. I slept on the floor this morning, didn't I?"

Eliza had left around midnight, and Rider and I had watched a *NCIS* marathon on the TV until the sun came up. I went to sleep in my bed and he slept on the floor at the foot of it, until the alarm I'd set woke us up around noon, something he was still perturbed about, but I couldn't sleep the day away. I had to call the office, find out who was covering the Nocturnal, Inc. account while I was out and ensure no one was scheming to take the account from me, even though I was sure Selander Ryan would never agree to work with anyone else seeing as how he'd come to the agency as a way of getting to me to begin with. Still, I was getting too close to an actual relationship with Dex Prince to allow anyone to attempt to sabotage me, so I called Chatty Cathy, the queen of office gossip, and got all the fresh news she'd collected for the day. I would have called Gina, but according to Rider and Eliza, calling her would be equivalent to calling Selander Ryan. I found out that she'd showed up to work, so I no longer had to fear that Selander Ryan had killed her and left her body in a dumpster somewhere.

I was pretty sure the lesson in punching and blocking was Rider's way of punishing me for refusing to sleep through the day. I looked at his wrist and contemplated if I should drink from him. He had slept on the floor like a gentleman rather than sharing my bed, but the last time I'd drank from him things had gotten out of control within the space of a heartbeat, and it wasn't just him who'd lost control.

"Take my blood or go warm up another bag," he said. "I can't allow you to get too thirsty and do something you'll regret."

I nodded my head, knowing he was right. No matter what happened, drinking from him would be safer than drinking from someone else. I couldn't kill another person. I would be haunted by what I did to that man in the alley for the rest of my life, which might be a really long time if Selander Ryan or Barnaby didn't rob me of my immortality. "How much can you spare?"

"I'll cut you off if I need to," Rider assured me, "but as you age, you won't need to drink as often as you do now. I fed very well before I came here and I haven't exerted myself, so don't worry about me. I have enough to share. I'd have even more if you didn't insist on being awake during the day."

"Really?" I rolled my eyes. "Just being awake during the day makes you lose blood?"

"It makes us lose power, which makes us need to feed more. Eliza told you all of this, I'm sure. It's one of the first things she teaches a new vampire."

"Yeah, yeah," I muttered as I lowered my head, stopping just before I opened my mouth. "Don't watch me do this."

Rider sighed in frustration and rested his head along the back of the couch, eyes closed. The move exposed the length of his throat and I licked my lips, imagining sinking my teeth into that delicious column, but I knew if I did I'd be in his lap in a heartbeat and then we'd both probably be in my bed. Hell, if we even made it to my bed.

My fangs elongated, and I sank them into his wrist, knowing it was the safer option thanks to my cursed vampire hormones. Or maybe it was the succubus in me that desired him. Whichever part of me it was, I could only deny it. His warm, coppery blood spilled over my tongue and I nearly moaned as the rich flavor hit me. It was a thousand times better than what I had stored in my refrigerator and it packed a stronger punch. It flowed slower from the wrist, though, which was frustrating. I angled my head so I could glance up at Rider's throat again as I contemplated switching. His jaw was clenched tight enough I could see the indentation in his cheek and his breathing was extremely controlled. My succubus bite was working its magic on the poor bastard. His free hand gripped the arm of the couch for dear life and I recalled what Eliza had told me about her sire controlling her, making her do anything she commanded. I wondered how hard it was for Rider to know he could control me, yet choose not to. Of course, that was assuming everything they'd told me about the conflicting marks was true. Maybe the other mark prevented him from making me do anything, and that was the only reason I had my freedom. He may have freed Eliza and Nannette from their sires, but he hadn't created them. Maybe I was different.

I drank my fill and licked the puncture marks, healing Rider's flesh. He took a deep breath as he lowered his head back to its normal position and opened his eyes, eyes that now swam with desire. "You get enough?"

"Yeah, thanks." I slid over a little, putting distance between us on the couch as he appeared to gather himself. "Definitely better than out of the fridge."

"Yeah." He nodded and looked over at me. "You still have to drink it out of the bag, if not from me. It's important."

"I know."

"We can set up a regular feeding schedule if you want—"

"What the hell am I, your new puppy?"

He laughed. "That did sound bad, didn't it? Sorry. I just meant that if you wanted, we could arrange a time for you to drink from me so you won't get thirsty and you won't have to drink from the bagged blood if you're getting it regularly from me."

I stared back at him, pondering whether such an arrangement would be considered wise. Although the act seemed like such a simple one, he was merely offering the nourishment my body needed. There was an undeniable sexual charge between us when it happened. "Do you offer this service for all your fledglings?"

"I don't have any other fledglings."

Although something in my gut had told me as much, hearing him admit it still threw me for a bit of a loop. He wouldn't say how old he was, but I could easily deduce he wasn't freshly turned. He spoke of decades, and Eliza had been enslaved for twenty years before he freed her and even then he'd been powerful enough to kill her sire. He had to be at least fifty, maybe even up to a hundred years old? And in all that time, he hadn't sired anyone? "Your fledglings have died?"

"You are the first vampire I've created, Danni."

"Why?"

"I didn't want you to die." He looked at me, his face revealing nothing.

"Why?"

He leaned toward me and when his lips covered mine, I didn't protest. This kiss was soft and sweet, yet hungry at the same time and I melted right into his arms, not a care in the world about whether what we were doing was right or wrong.

I heard my grandmother's yapping ankle-biter before they knocked on my door, and I quickly detached myself from Rider to pull him up from the couch and push him toward my bedroom. "You have to get out of here."

"What?" He turned toward me and planted his feet firmly on the floor. "Why?"

"Shhh!" I pushed him, but he wouldn't budge. "Keep your voice down so they don't hear you. My mother and grandmother and perfect sister are out there and you can not be in here when they come in."

He arched an eyebrow. "Why?"

"Because how the hell am I supposed to explain my vampire bodyguard? Just get in my room and be quiet. Please," I added in desperation when he continued to stand there like a statue after they knocked a second time. He looked down at me a moment longer, seeming put out by the fact I'd asked him to leave, but finally did as I asked and hid himself away in my bedroom.

I opened the door to find my mother with her fist raised, ready to knock a third time. "Finally," she said as my grandmother's dog leaped from her arms and took off through the living room. My mother, grandmother, and sister barreled in as the ankle-biter raced straight into my bedroom, yapping away.

"Terry!" my grandmother called after it before looking at me. "What have you got in there that he seems to want?" She plopped down on the couch, setting the bag she normally carried the rat-dog in on the floor next to her feet.

Just a vampire, I thought to myself, hoping the annoying dog didn't bark at Rider the entire visit. It didn't seem I had anything to worry about as a second later the dog yelped and ran back into the room, quickly jumping into my grandmother's purse and burying itself inside. The entire bag shook before the little scoundrel let out a particularly foul fart.

"Oh, dear." My grandmother fanned the air beside her. My mother and sister sat on the other end of the couch, doing the same. "What happened, my precious little angel?" she asked the dog. "What upset you?"

"Probably a rat," my mother said, scanning the apartment with disdain. "Really, Danni, if you're going to insist on working for a living, you could find a job that would afford you better accommodations. This place is a dump. I'm sure I saw a roach outside, not that I know for sure what one of those disgusting things would look like, but this is probably the type of place that would have them."

"My building is very clean," I defended myself. "You probably saw a beetle."

"Well, something upset my precious angel," my grandmother said, worrying over the dog.

"He probably saw himself in the full-length mirror," I suggested, although I knew damn well what had terrified the dog. The tiny tormentor farted again, and I stepped back, fanning the air. My new vampire senses made the awful smell a hundred times worse. "Why are you here?"

"Well, isn't that a fine welcome?" my mother asked, patting her hair. It appeared to have been freshly dyed blonde and set in bold waves. "As you know, your sister has found an acceptable mate and secured an engagement. We have an appointment at the dress shop for fittings. You'll need to come with us. Lord knows your dress will need to be tailored so it doesn't slide right off you." She turned toward my grandmother. "I swear I don't know why she doesn't have any breasts. Even on her father's side, they had breasts. I don't know what happened to her."

My grandmother chuckled with her. "I think what should have gone on top went to her backside. Still eating too many sweets, dear?"

I was the only woman in my family who didn't have a flat pancake-butt and, according to them, that made me fat. Fat and flat-chested. I was a huge disappointment and would never find a man due to my hideous disfigurement. My sister Shana, who had yet to speak, simply eyed me, grinning.

"The appointment is today?"

"Yes. Get dressed, dear," my mother answered. "We'll probably dine afterward and you can't go into a respectable restaurant dressed like that. Is that what you wore to work?"

I looked down at my T-shirt and leggings and sighed. "No, Mom. I, uh, changed into this after I got home." The last thing I wanted to do was let her know I had the week off. She'd find a way to make me run errands for Shana's wedding and I'd rather run nails through my eyes than help my spoiled sister out. "You didn't tell me about the fitting. I didn't plan on going anywhere."

"Of course you didn't," she said, laughing as she cut me off. "Where would you go? A date?" This brought laughter from the other two. "Go get dressed. With luck, we'll be able to set you up with someone at the wedding. Have you been wearing your gel bras? You must wear your gel bras if you want to attract a man or, better yet, get the surgery. There's nothing wrong with fixing the mistakes nature made. I gave you the information for that wonderful plastic surgeon. Have you at least looked at the information on his website?"

"I can't get the surgery," I said, knowing that if I didn't, they would ask me why I hadn't had the surgery every single time they spoke with me.

"Why?" my mother asked as all three of them looked at me as if I'd just told them I had a life-threatening disease.

"Something about my blood," I told them. "It turns out if I have the surgery, I would most likely bleed to death."

"Have you gotten a second opinion?" My mother asked. "What odds did they give you? Doesn't the doctor have a way of making your blood clot or—"

"Mom." Shana grabbed my mother's arm, squeezing it. "You don't really want Danni to risk dying just to get bigger boobs, do you?"

"Of course not," my mother said quickly, her face turning red. "I just think it's such a shame and it certainly wouldn't hurt to get a second opinion just in case there's something that could be done."

"Boy, Mother Nature sure screwed up on that one," my grandmother said, shaking her head. Terry farted from where he continued to shake inside her bag.

"Ugh." Shana stood and walked toward my room. "Come on, Danni. I'll help you pick something out."

"Oh, that's not necessary!" I said, moving toward her, but she'd already entered the room. I rushed in, expecting to find her surprised, face to face with Rider, but the room appeared empty.

"I had to get out of there," she said, turning toward me as I entered. "I've spent all day with that mangy mutt and I've had all I can take of its gas. I really wish she'd just put the rodent to sleep already."

I scanned the room, knowing Rider was there. I found him in the corner, wrapped in shadows and wearing a scowl to beat all scowls. My sister continued on, unaware of his presence, missing the ability to see what I saw. "Don't worry about what Mom and Grandma said in there. It's not the end of the world that you can't have the surgery. There are some guys out there who don't mind flat-chested women. I mean, hello, if fat women can get husbands, surely you can too." She walked over to my closet and started going through my clothes. "We should go shopping. We really need to update your wardrobe. You don't have nearly enough dresses. I can show you where to get the cutest dresses at."

Yes, because I wanted to go clothes shopping with my perfect sister, as if she would have a clue what would flatter me. "We're trying on dresses. I'll just wear something easy to slip in and out of," I said.

"You have to look nice at all times, Danni. You never know when you're going to run into an attractive man."

"I already have a man," I blurted.

"Who?" Shana asked, whirling around. "What does he do? What kind of car does he drive?"

"He's my boss. His family owns the entire company, and he drives an Audi R8."

Rider growled and Shana looked in the direction where he stood. "What was that?" she asked.

"My belly!" I grabbed her by her arms and moved her toward the door. "I'm hungry, so I should get dressed so we can go."

"Oh, I haven't picked out a dress for you yet."

"I'm a big girl. I've been dressing myself for years." I pushed her out the door and closed it with a smile that quickly withered as I locked myself in and turned to see Rider step out of the shadows. "Was it necessary to draw attention to yourself?" I asked. "And what did you do to my grandmother's dog?"

"It growled at me, so I growled back. Where do you think you're going?" he asked, stopping right in front of me. Fortunately, he was being considerate enough to keep his voice low as I'd asked.

"My family is very pushy. They made the appointment for the dress fitting and I have to go. Trust me, they won't take no for an answer."

"Forgive me if it's ill-mannered to say this, but your family is a pack of bitches. I don't like them."

I laughed. "Yeah, that's not a bad description of them."

"There's two predators after you. You shouldn't be dress shopping or dining out. Your life is more important than pleasing them."

"It's not just pleasing them," I said. "They won't take no for an answer and I don't want to hear all the complaining. Plus, weddings are pretty big deals. I have to be fitted for the dress."

"Now?"

"There's kind of a deadline for these things, Rider."

He sighed and ran a hand through his hair. "Fine. I'll stay close and call in some extra security. You really make protecting you hard."

I grabbed a pair of black dress slacks and a lacy white top from my closet and tossed them onto my bed. "I need to change. Would you mind going into the bathroom?"

"I've seen you naked before."

"Reminding me of that does nothing to endear you to

me," I advised him.

"What can I say? I really liked the view."

I felt myself blush, but maintained a glare. "Bathroom. Now."

"Can't blame a guy for trying," he muttered as he turned and walked into the bathroom.

"Close the door!" I hissed as low as I could so my nosy family wouldn't hear me.

Rider shook his head and did as ordered, grumbling under his breath. I dressed quickly, oddly not worried too much about being hunted. I felt safe with Rider close by and, honestly, there was nothing like dress shopping and dinner with my family to make me almost want a hunter to shoot an arrow through me.

FOURTEEN

"Can you do something to minimize her butt without making her chest any flatter, if such a thing is even possible?" My mother asked, circling me like a vulture as I stood before the triple-paneled mirror outside the dressing room, wishing I could be anywhere else. I'd tried on so many dresses I'd lost count and my lovely family had criticized each one, but not after wasting time brainstorming what alterations could be made to make me presentable before just giving up because apparently I was a lost cause.

"If we go tighter, it will draw more attention to her rear," the dressmaker said. "We could add a bow or drape some fabric to hide it."

"Oh no, she'd look like a Thanksgiving Day parade float." My mother heaved out a frustrated sigh and shook her head. "I just don't know what to do with you, Danni. You have absolutely the worst shape."

"A shapely rear is quite fashionable," the dressmaker said, straightening. Her mouth pinched as she narrowed her eyes at my mother. "Look at Jennifer Lopez and Beyoncé."

"I'd rather not. We're going for classy, not trashy." My

mother waved her hand dismissively. "We'll just have to make do. Fortunately, Shana will look so gorgeous all eyes will be glued to her. We'll just have to take the least ridiculous looking dress to use for the bridesmaids. I think the A-line gown with the V-neck, sleeveless wraparound top will hide her flaws the best without looking horrible on the bridesmaids who have breasts. What do you think, Shana?"

I scurried away to the dressing room and removed the current dress, a form-fitting lacy torture device that did nothing for my figure, and slid back into my black dress pants and white blouse, all the while wishing I was back in my apartment in my T-shirt and leggings.

I walked out of the dressing area, past my mother and grandmother who were going over details with the dressmaker, past Shana, who was busy ogling herself in the mirror, and out onto the sales floor. I walked toward the front and looked out the glass window, immediately spotting Rider just outside, across the street, sitting on his black motorcycle. Dressed head to toe, or helmet to boot, in all black himself, I knew he had to be attracting a lot of sunlight, but he'd chosen to stick close to me anyway. At least his skin was covered, but I knew the sun had to be zapping his power. He had to feel pretty miserable. I was pretty tired myself.

Try not to stand in front of glass windows, babe. Not safe while you're being hunted.

I heard his warning in my head and stepped back, touched by his concern. It sure beat the attitude of my shopping mates.

By the time we reached the restaurant, we'd hit four other stores, and I'd accumulated over a thousand dollars on my credit card because, according to my family, I didn't have good enough clothes. I'd been picked apart and criticized for hours, and now I would be sitting down to dine with my critics. The good news was the sun had gone down, which made me feel a little less guilty about Rider following us around for the day. If not for the special sunscreen we wore, we both would have fried and for what? Dresses? I'd felt a boost of energy the moment the sun left the sky, but even that wasn't enough to refresh the foul mood I found myself in. I prayed the restaurant service would be quick so I could hurry back home. There was only so much of my family I could take.

Since my grandmother was with us and refused to go anywhere without her mutant rat, we were dining at Café Crystal, one of the fewer upscale restaurants that allowed dogs, or what passed for dogs for uppity types. Don't get me wrong, I love animals, but when it comes to dogs, I preferred a German Shepherd or a Labrador to the tiny, cute little fur balls women toted around in their purses. My grandmother preferred her tiny precious and since he was small and trained well enough to stay in her purse next to her chair, he got to come into the restaurant with us.

I wondered what kind of dog Dex would allow me to get for the family after we married, provided my dream worked out, as I perused the menu, also wondering what I could eat without getting hellishly sick again. I tried to picture him with a big dog, and it just didn't seem to fit. I kept picturing a cocker spaniel instead.

I felt a warm shift in the air and looked up to see Rider and two other men being shown to a table across the room. The two men were almost as tall as him, one about his build, the other much thicker, but neither carried the air of power and authority as he did. You could tell with just a glance that Rider was the big dog in that pack. Now Rider, I could see with a big guard dog, maybe a Doberman or a Rottweiler.

Our server came to our table, greeted us cheerily and did the expected bit of flirtation with Shana. I swear the girl could make a monk give up his beliefs for just one kiss. I ordered water to drink and went back to worrying about what in the world I could eat, or how I could play off not eating.

I'd recommend a salad without dressing, or a fruit bowl. Rider spoke in my mind. *Stay away from anything with spices or herbs.*

I glanced across the room to see him set his menu aside and start scanning the room for threats. His gaze met mine, and he winked. The men with him looked over at me, studying me, which made me feel awkward, so I went back to looking at my menu. When the server came back, I ordered a salad with strawberries, no dressing.

"That's a good choice," my mother said. "You don't need to add any more pounds to that backside. You should go to yoga class with your sister. Look how svelte she is."

The rest of our dining experience went the same. My weight was a major issue with my mother, who was actually a very chubby woman who projected her weight insecurity onto me. My grandmother's constant ridicule of her weight mixed with her bragging about how she simply never had any weight issues exacerbated the problem. My grandmother ragged on my mother, my mother ragged on me, and my grandmother joined in while Shana picked at her salad and did who-knew-what on her iPhone in-between posting pics of her food and selfies to her social media platforms. At some point, a female jazz singer with a sultry voice took the small stage and couples took to the small dancefloor. I watched them, tuning out my mother and grandmother's commentary on my lack of breasts and lack of relationship.

"Danni is dating someone," I heard Shana say and wished I hadn't told her anything. "He drives a really nice car and has money. Tell them, Danni."

I turned my attention back toward my mother and grandmother to find them staring at me, wide-eyed and slack-jawed. That lasted exactly a split second before they moved in with the rapid-fire questions. Who was he? What was his name? Where did we meet? How much money did he make? How old was he? Had he ever been married?

Did he have any money grubbing leftover children from previous marriages? Had I slept with him? Was he satisfied with my lack of breasts? Had I met his mother? Sometimes men liked women who favored their mothers and if his mother was flat-chested I had a good shot at marriage because anyone born without breasts would have bought some by my age.

"I'm dating my boss," I said, jumping in when they stopped to take a breath, "and it's still pretty new, but he took me to Adore the other night and this weekend I will be meeting his family. The company is family-owned. They are very successful."

"Meeting his family?" The three of them spoke at once before turning to each other to confer.

"Well, that's a sign, isn't it?" My grandmother asked.

"Possibly, but a sign of what? It's rather soon to meet the family if they just started dating," my mother said.

"He took her to Adore. Could he possibly be smitten? Maybe he finds small-breasted women a novelty. Most everyone else would have fixed the problem, so I doubt there's many to choose from."

"Maybe he's gay and needs a cover," my mother suggested.

"Well, that's not the end of the world as long as she gets to spend his money," Shana chimed in. "She still wouldn't die unmarried."

"Have you slept with him?" my mother asked me again.

"No, I haven't slept with him," I said, keeping my voice low, suddenly feeling as if every ear in the restaurant was tuned in to this humiliating conversation. I already knew Rider and his men had to hear everything thanks to their cursed vampire hearing. I contemplated hiding under the table and never coming out. "I told you we just started dating."

"You're too old for virtue," my mother said. "Your best baby-making years are flashing by."

"Are you on the pill?" my grandmother asked. "If so,

throw them away. What you need is to get pregnant. Men from good families always marry the women they knock up to preserve the family image."

"Yes!" My mother snapped her fingers, her face alight with excitement. "A pregnancy is just what is needed. You could be married before the year is out."

"Excuse me."

I glanced up to see Rider standing over me. As he kneeled by my side, Terry the Tiny Terror growled. Rider shot the dog a dark look, and it ducked back down into my grandmother's bag, where I heard what sounded like a lot of liquid spilling. "You are the most beautiful woman I've ever seen, and if I don't get to dance with you before this evening is over, I'll just impale myself." He held his hand out to me as the women at my table gasped. He might not be the owner of a huge company, but Rider Knight was a gorgeous man, not the type they'd expect to walk across the room and ask me to dance, especially when my equally gorgeous sister who I'd caught ogling him a few times was seated right next to me.

I took his hand and allowed him to lead me onto the dancefloor, aware we were under the disbelieving eyes of my family, and the watchful ones of the men at his table. "You would impale yourself?" I asked after I finally found my voice through the humiliation of knowing he'd heard everything my family had said to me and thought he needed to come rescue me. I could only imagine what the men at his table thought about me. Poor little flat-chested me, the woman whose own family thought she had to get knocked up just to get a husband. "Laying the vampire shtick on kind of thick, huh?"

"It amuses me," he said as he pulled me close and we began to sway together along with the music. "I need some amusement after all I've had to endure today. How have you not stabbed one of them with a fork already?"

I grinned despite my discomfort. "Not a bad idea. You made my grandmother's dog piss inside her purse. I kind of hope I'm there when she figures it out, but then again, she'll find a way to blame me for it."

"Have they always treated you this way?"

I looked down at our feet as we continued to move. "I was a daddy's girl, and he adored me, but he died. Cancer. My mother became very bitter afterwards, upset he didn't leave us with much money, and my grandmother harped on her about how she should have married someone rich and if she'd lost weight, she might have. My mother turned to us for her retirement plan, I guess. My sister is the blue-eyed busty blonde supermodel type and then you have me. She always doted on my sister, figuring she'd be the one to marry rich and move them in with her. Turns out, she was right. I'm the wasted child that Mother Nature played a horrible joke on."

Rider lifted my chin up, forcing me to look into his eyes before placing his hand back around my waist. "I don't want to hear you say anything like that again. You are a beautiful woman, Danni Keller."

"Just stop." I ducked my head again as I felt heat flooding my face.

"Stop what?"

"Stop the pity party. I know you asked me to dance to try to make me look good in front of them. I appreciate the thought, but I'm not in the mood for the pep talks. It's been a long day."

"I don't pity you. You annoy the hell out of me, and I'm pissed that you allow your family to talk to you the way you do, but I understand why. You're a peacekeeper. I once was a peacekeeper too, and it didn't do me any favors." He nudged my chin so I'd look at him again. "I've never lied to you about anything. You are a beautiful woman and despite the lies I've heard from them, you have a great body. I asked you to dance because I care about you and thought you needed a break, and clearly you're not going to tell them to shut the hell up or point out the fact you're the most beautiful member of the family."

"Now I know you're just trying to make me feel better, and I wish you wouldn't while your friends over there listen to us. It's embarrassing."

"No, I'm just hoping you wake up and see what I can see before you make a bad mistake. As for my men, they know better than to listen in on my private conversations. They value their limbs too much to intrude upon my privacy."

"That doesn't sound very peacekeepery of you, and too late for me to avoid mistakes. I'm the big dummy who went to a bar by myself to get drunk and got attacked by an incubus."

"I said I once was a peacekeeper. You have to partake in some violence to last as long as I have as a vampire. Being attacked wasn't exactly a good thing, but it's not as bad as being the woman who marries a man for money just to please a family she doesn't even like."

My back stiffened. "You may have turned me into a vampire, but you didn't create me. You don't know who I like or don't like, or why I make the choices I make."

"I know you better than you think, Danni, and I know you don't believe in the things your family has said. I know you've been miserable the entire time you've been in your family's company and still you continue to crave a relationship with that douchewad boss of yours because you think it will impress them. Why do you care so much about impressing people who should be happy with you, just as you are? Tell them to go to Hell and live your life the way you want to live it. You're going to be around a lot longer than them anyway. That is, if I can get you to stay out of trouble until Barnaby and Selander Ryan are dealt with."

"I can't tell my family to go to hell. They're my family. They love me."

"Do you even understand what love is?"

"Yes." I bristled. "Do you?"

"I gave my life for it."

I stopped moving. "Is that how you became a vampire?"

He looked down at me, mouth firmly closed, until the song ended and he led me back to my table, where my family sat glued to our every move.

"Thank you for the dance," he said, kissing my hand. "If you change your mind about that drink tonight…"

"Drinks?" My mother leaned forward. "Excuse me. I'm Danni's mother, and you are?"

"Rider Knight, ma'am." He bowed his head. "It's nice to meet you lovely ladies."

My mother blushed straight into her hairline. "Well, Mr. Knight, might I ask what it is that an attractive man such as yourself does?"

"I own a security company," he answered, "among a few other properties."

"Oh, you own your own company? That's nice. You do good business?"

"Well, I was raised not to brag, but I do very well."

My mother and grandmother shared a look as Shana pouted, clearly put out that Rider hadn't hit on her. I honestly couldn't even get mad at her or take her reaction as a dig. She wasn't used to being the overlooked one, regardless of who she was with. "Danni, don't stay on account of us," my mother said, making a shooing action. "We'll drop off all your shopping bags later. You and this gentleman should enjoy the rest of the evening."

"But—"

"I *insist*," she said sternly, before looking up at Rider and batting her eyelashes. "Have a wonderful night."

"Wow. I could be a serial killer, but your mother just pushed you off on me because she thought I was loaded," Rider muttered, escorting me out of the restaurant.

"Do you really own a security company?" I asked, looking back at the two men he'd sat with at the restaurant. "Is that why you have so many men available to watch me and my building?"

"Yes."

"You never told me that."

"You never asked." He handed his ticket to the valet, and we waited for his motorcycle.

"You're taking me home on a motorcycle?"

"I have an extra helmet. You'll be fine." He scanned the perimeter, looking for threats.

"Are helmets necessary for... people like us?" I asked, lowering my voice as another couple approached the valet stand.

"Thin-blooded people who could die from blood loss alone if severely injured?" He raised an eyebrow and looked down at me with amusement.

"Okay. I see your point. I just thought we'd be more invincible."

"We can't catch disease and can survive almost every wound imaginable as long as we have access to blood and healing sleep. That's nothing to turn your nose up at."

"I suppose." The valet returned with Rider's Harley and I was handed a black helmet. No design. I didn't expect any. Rider didn't seem the type to go for frills. Other than naming his bar *Midnight Rider*, he didn't seem to do anything to draw attention to himself or shout "This is mine!" like most other people did. I hadn't even been able to find a Facebook page or Twitter account for him, not even an Instagram. I climbed on and wrapped my arms around his waist, and away we went.

I knew we were heading for the bar when we should have taken a right, but took a left instead. I seethed in silence rather than shouting at him over the roar of the bike and strong wind that whipped past us as he sped through the night. He routed us down a dark alley behind the bar and pressed an entry code on a keypad that opened the door to a garage I hadn't known was there. The lights above us came on as he drove inside and parked between a black Ferrari and a black SUV.

"This isn't my apartment," I said as I removed my helmet and handed it to him.

"Powerful deduction skills you have there," he replied, hanging the helmet over a handlebar opposite the one he'd worn. "After being out in the sun all day after feeding you, I need to replenish. So do you. I'll feed and you can feed. It wouldn't hurt for me to shower and get a change of clothes while I'm here. I wouldn't dare take my eyes off you long enough to do that at your apartment. It's not as secure as the bar."

"These are your vehicles?" I asked as he led me through a door that opened into the hallway at the back of the bar, just to the side of the staircase which led to his apartment over it.

"Yeah. I'll take you home in the Ferrari. I know how you love expensive cars."

"Clearly, you do as well."

He grinned. "I like cars that just happen to be expensive." He led me up the stairs and pushed through the door to his living quarters.

I walked in and stopped before the large bed, remembering my last visit as he walked over to the bar and reached for the box he'd used the last time to call on someone to remove the hooker he'd drank from that night.

"Are you going to just slurp on some hooker with me here in the room?"

He paused with his hand just over the box and turned toward me. "It's not a sexual act, Danni."

"Could have fooled me," I mumbled, looking around. There was absolutely nowhere I could sit in the small living space where I wouldn't have full view of him suckling some hooker's neck.

He grinned as he walked toward me, stopping just a

breath before me. "For someone who spends so much time fantasizing about her arrogant boss, you sure seem upset about the thought of me putting my mouth on another woman's body. Why is that?"

"Because it's gross," I replied, not going to give him the satisfaction of thinking I was jealous of him feeding off of hookers. They were hookers, for crying out loud. "And it's awkward. No one would want to watch that."

"You feed from me."

"We don't have an audience."

"I'll feed from the wrist, Danni. It won't be so bad and I promise you I have no desire for my donors other than a source of fresh blood."

"Good thing we can't catch disease," I grumbled, folding my arms beneath my chest as I plopped down on the foot of the bed. "Oh, I'm sorry. Will you be using the bed for this feeding?"

Rider shook his head and muttered under his breath before turning to push a button on the bar. A large flat screen TV monitor rose from inside the bar and he turned it to face me. He passed me a small remote. "Here. This should keep you entertained while I go downstairs and feed there."

"You're leaving me alone up here?"

"You're secure."

"There's not even a lock on the door!"

"Yes, there is. I've had my living quarters spelled. No one can enter or leave this space unless I desire it. This is the safest place in the world for you right now."

I looked at him for a moment, blinking, before looking at the door. Well, if I could be a vampire I supposed there could be witches or whoever did the bespelling. "Oooohkay, but where are you going to feed?"

"Right downstairs in the bar. I'll use the office. Don't worry about anything. I'll stay close and no one can get up here anyway. I'll be right back." He left through the apparently magical door and I was left alone in his home to watch *Supernatural* and try not to think about him suckling on a hooker. Normally, Jensen Ackles could take my mind off any man, but I couldn't quit wondering who Rider was slurping on and if he liked it. I also couldn't help but wonder who the dark-haired woman in the painting over the bar was. If he were any other man, the painting of a woman in a dated dress wouldn't bother me at all, but for all I knew, Rider was old enough to know the woman. Hell, he could have painted the portrait himself. The woman could be the love of his life. Why did that bother me?

He came back upstairs forty minutes later. "I would have been quicker, but drinking from the wrist is slower and I wanted to take in a lot so I could share with you, plus I had some bar business to attend to."

"What are you doing?" I asked as he pulled his shirt over his head and tossed it to the floor.

"I'm going to take a shower and change after I feed you." He grabbed a change of clothes and disappeared into the bathroom with them, coming back out shortly. He sat next to me on the bed and tilted his head, offering his neck. "Drink up."

I gazed longingly at the throat I'd wanted to drink from so badly earlier that day and licked my lips. "You, uh, don't think drinking from your neck will be a bad idea?"

"I think just about everything with you is a bad idea," he answered as he pulled me onto his lap, positioning me so I straddled him. "Do it anyway."

FIFTEEN

The moment my lips touched Rider's flesh, I knew I was a goner. Shirtless, there was nowhere I could place my hands and not feel a spark of electricity shoot from my fingertips to my core. The temperature seemed to increase by several degrees and the warm, powerful blood gliding over my tongue may as well have been a drug. I greedily lapped it up, my hips grinding against him as his hands slid under the back of my shirt and unhooked my bra. A moment later, it and my shirt had been discarded and my small breasts filled Rider's hands.

"Rider," I gasped, the feel of his hands caressing a part of my body I never allowed anyone near bringing me out of the haze his blood had pulled me under.

"I can't keep fighting what you do to me," he said, flipping me onto my back. "I want you, Danni Keller, and tonight you're mine." He stretched my arms over my head, exposing me fully as he kissed me deeper than I'd ever been kissed before, then moved from my lips to my chin, my throat, and down my chest until he took one nipple in his very talented mouth, and used his strong yet gentle fingers to tease the other. I gasped and arched against him, desperate to have him inside me even as my brain screamed no. He wasn't Dex, but he was there and he was gorgeous, and he wanted me even if it was because of some succubus mojo, and he was doing things to my body that made it harder and harder to think.

He kissed me again, long and hard, as he unzipped my pants and slid his hand under my panties to cup the most intimate part of me and I decided then that I was going to sleep with Rider Knight and face the consequences later, no matter how awkward. He'd already seen me naked anyway, and if I had second thoughts about being with him, I still had the date set up with Dex. It wasn't like I didn't need practice in case things went well with him.

Rider's entire body went still. He raised his head and glared down at me, his eyes dark with anger. I trembled beneath him and it had nothing to do with the air hitting my exposed skin. If looks could kill, I'd be six feet under. "I'm practice for no man," he growled before rolling off me and entering the bathroom, slamming the door behind him.

I pulled a sheet over myself and bit my lip, cursing myself for not blocking my thoughts.

I'd found my clothes, redressed, and even made Rider's bed nice and neat by the time he came out of the bathroom, freshly showered, hair still damp, dressed in a gray T-shirt and black jeans. He didn't speak to me as he sat at the foot of the bed and pulled on his boots. I sat at the bar, not sure where in the room was safest for me, but I felt the bed was probably the last place I should be. If he noticed I'd made the bed in an effort to be nice, he didn't comment on it. He didn't comment at all as he slid into a black leather jacket, turned the TV off, sending the monitor back down into the bar, and headed for the door.

"Rider…"

"Let's go." He opened the door and stepped out, taking for granted I'd follow him as he made his way down the stairs. Of course I would. Even if he was pissed at me, he was still my sire and I assumed he'd still be guarding me, if only to beat Selander Ryan. I didn't think he was a big fan of mine at the moment, maybe ever again.

I felt the anger rolling off him as I followed him down the stairs, down the hall, and through the door leading to the garage. He reached into his jacket pocket as we neared the Ferrari, and stilled. The fine hairs along the nape of my neck stood on end a split-second before Rider grabbed me and spun me around to the front of the car, shoving me down to the floor. Something whistled past us and I turned to see an arrow hit the brick wall and bounce off.

"What the hell was that?"

"Barnaby," Rider answered, his eyes starting to glow a pale yellow. "Stay down."

He grabbed the arrow and sped toward the front of the garage, a blur of movement. I heard grunting and peeked around the car to see Rider and Barnaby fighting. Barnaby was dressed in thick leather from neck to toe and some sort of bulky, spiked rings adorned his knuckles. He'd come prepared to fight and was smart enough to not allow wide expanses of skin to show, clever when you knew your opponent was a vampire. Also clever, his leather got its sheen from some sort of oil. I heard Rider hiss each time his fist connected with it, and I could see his skin growing redder with each contact.

"You made a deal with my family," Barnaby huffed out, the fighting wearing him down. "Are you proving yourself a lying vampire?"

"You didn't hold up your part of the deal," Rider shot back at him, delivering a blow to his face that sent Barnaby sprawling, blood pouring from his nose, but the hunter bounced up pretty quick for a man of his size.

"She's a succubus!"

"She's mine!" Rider growled, plunging the arrow Barnaby had shot at me through the man's eye. He pulled back on it as Barnaby screamed and used his other hand to rip the neck of the man's leather jacket off before sinking his fangs into his throat. He jerked his head side to side, growling, reminding me of the time I'd seen a dog tear into a cat and wring its poor body to death. Rider didn't need to wring the life out of Barnaby Quimby. The hunter's knees hit the floor and Rider drew back, the majority of Barnaby's throat in his mouth. He spit the fleshy meat out of his mouth and dropped down to drain the man.

I turned away, one hand clasped over my mouth, the other over my stomach. I was a vampire. I'd just drank blood not an hour earlier, and I'd once killed a man in an alley similar to what I'd just seen Rider do, but I couldn't bear to watch him drain the hunter dry. The man had tried to kill me, and I wasn't sorry he'd been killed, but the way he'd been killed was too much to handle. Rider hadn't just bit the man and drank him. He'd plunged an arrow through his eye socket and ripped his throat out with his bare teeth. It was animalistic, monstrous… It was a side of Rider I'd never seen, not even when he'd fought Selander Ryan in the alley. He'd been bloody then, and I'd heard the growling and seen the strange glow in his eyes, but I hadn't witnessed the viciousness he'd just displayed. I imagine it had been there, but I'd been out of it.

Garage. NOW.

His voice boomed through my mind, but it was different from when he'd spoken to me that way before. More powerful. Stronger. Louder. He wasn't just talking to me. In fact, he wasn't talking to me at all. He was calling his people to him.

They started pouring through the door shortly after, five in all, including the big black man who'd removed the hooker from Rider's apartment the first time I'd been in it, and the bartender I'd spoken to the night I'd been attacked. Surprise, curiosity, and confusion passed over their faces as they filed in to find their boss standing over the hunter's bloody, dead body. Blood drenched the front of Rider's T-shirt and his hands were red from whatever he'd connected with on Barnaby's clothes, but he was otherwise unmarred. Barnaby had never been able to connect his spiked rings to Rider's flesh. For a human, he'd put up a damned good fight, but he was no match for the vampire.

"I called you here because of all my employees, you are the ones I trusted with the access code. Which of you betrayed me?"

In addition to the bartender and the man who'd removed the hooker from Rider's room, the employees consisted of a tall Hispanic man with corn-rowed hair, a short but powerfully built Asian man, and a woman. She was of average height and build, brunette with olive skin and dark eyes. All of them appeared to be in their twenties, but for all I knew, they were senior citizens. They glanced at each other, but no one said a word. I studied their faces, looking for a hint of fear at having been found out, but if any of them had let Barnaby in or given him the access code, he or she wore a damn good mask. If I'd screwed over Rider, I'd be pissing myself. His eyes had dimmed, but he still radiated a truckload of anger.

"No one wants to confess?" His voice rivaled thunder as he paced before them like a caged animal. The bartender and woman shared a quick glance that sent my Spidey senses in a tizzy. The large black man stood straight, shoulders back, his hands flexing as if he were itching for a fight. The other two men kept their eyes on Rider, expressionless. "Do you think I even need to ask?" He shook his head. "Your first mistake, obviously, was betraying me to begin with. Your second mistake was thinking you could get away with it. You clearly have no concept of who the hell you are fucking with. I've been more than generous to all of you. Apparently, some of you have mistaken my generosity, my lack of abuse as weakness, a mistake you will pay for with your life. I SHOW NO MERCY TO TRAITORS!" His voice bounced off the walls, rattling everything in the garage that wasn't nailed down, including me.

The bartender turned to run. A split-second later, his body hit the wall to my right hard enough to send up a puff of dust as the brick outlining him crumbled. His body was partially *in* the wall and it was stuck there... and Rider hadn't even touched him. I wasn't the only one to gasp. The rest of Rider's staff stood slack-jawed. Well, except for the stoic Asian man who gave off the impression nothing much fazed him, but his eyes had grown wider.

When Rider turned toward the bartender, his eyes were fully aglow. The bartender struggled to break free as Rider slowly walked toward him, but couldn't. The entire garage was thick with the weight of Rider's power pressing the man into the wall. All I could think was... If Rider could do that to a vampire he hadn't sired, what could he do to me?

"James... I was good to you."

"I'm so sorry, Rider," the bartender apologized, tears wetting his eyes. "We felt we had to do it. The woman is a danger to everything."

What woman? Me? This jerk was blaming me for... what exactly? I stepped out from behind the shield of the cars and stood, hands on hips, waiting for an explanation.

"I am the master. What I say goes, and I am not in the habit of making rash or foolish decisions. I have freed many and protected more, and you think within a week of meeting a woman she can... what? Destroy me?"

"She's not even a full vampire," the bartender, James, said. "We all know she's a hybrid and she hasn't devoted herself to you, yet you put us in harm's way protecting her. Beating my ass for not seeing Selander Ryan come into the club and walk out with her was one thing, but we've lost ten men in a week's time, all because of her. When does it stop?"

Ten men? Ten men's lives had been lost because of me? I knew Rider's men had been guarding me, but I had no idea some had given their lives. I had no idea so much was going on around me, because of me. Was I that wrapped up inside my own selfish longing for a relationship and success that I'd been completely blind to just what all Rider had made his men do to protect me while I insisted on going to work and out on a date? Had men been killed fighting Selander's people while I was shopping with my family, or had they lost their lives to the sun exposure I'd forced them to endure while I insisted on maintaining as close to a normal lifestyle as I could?

"It stops for you tonight," Rider said, his voice lower, but no less threatening as he took the final steps toward the trembling man and pulled him free of the wall only to sink his fangs into his neck and drain him before effortlessly snapping his neck and tossing the traitor's body toward the Asian man so that it fell at his feet. "Remove his head and place it in the employee quarters, so anyone who thinks I've gone soft knows better. This is my one and only warning for all who dare betray me." He stepped toward the woman as the Asian man removed a long blade from a shelving unit in the corner and sliced the bartender's head clear of his body.

"You have never hurt a woman," the female vampire said to him, her chin held high.

"This is true, and why your betrayal cuts me far deeper than his. I saved you from a life of whoring just to survive, Marie. You were treated as less than an animal before I killed your sire and freed you and your fledgling sisters."

"Yes, I was. I paid my dues. We all did, all except for her." She jutted her stubborn chin in my direction and spit on the ground. "What makes her so special that she deserves such devotion and protection? Why does she get the gift of immortality without the sacrifice of her dignity?"

"I have protected every single one of you and I had no control over who sired you or how you were treated, but I have freed many from abusive masters and will continue to do so. I've never asked for a thank you, but I did expect your loyalty. I sired Danni and I will not treat her or any woman, for that matter, the way you were treated after you were turned. The fact that you resent her for not being abused in that way speaks to an evil inside you that sickens me to my core."

"We're vampires, Rider. We all have a bloodthirsty beast inside us, including your precious dark angel over there who killed an innocent man not long after turning. If it had been any of us, we would have been dealt with, but you coddled her, gave her more security. You spilled our blood in order to keep her safe despite her grave sin. Where we've been punished, she's been rewarded. Don't speak to me about loyalty. Go ahead. Take my head. Hang it for all to see. Show your new girlfriend what you really are."

Rider grabbed the woman by the throat and held her high above him, her legs dangling limp in the air. She glared down at him, her eyes bulging as he squeezed her throat. Her nostrils flared, her top lip curled, twisting her attractive face into an ugly mask of animosity.

The air in the garage seemed to thicken even more, humming with the surge of Rider's power, and then it snapped, nearly knocking me off my feet. I grabbed the car for support to remain standing as Rider lowered the woman to the floor and pushed her toward the front of the garage. Her hand rose to her throat, her eyes wide with fear. "What did you do?"

"You are no longer a part of this nest," Rider answered, his tone even. "You have been shunned, and as a result, are no longer under my protection. You will no longer be supplied with blood or sunscreen from my sources, and are no longer welcome in any establishment owned by myself or anyone under my protection. You are right that I have never hurt a woman and refuse to. You were foolish to think that meant you could betray me and walk away unscathed. I don't need to lay a hand on you to hurt you, Marie. All I need to do is stop protecting you from others who will." He nodded toward the large black man and the garage door was opened, revealing a moonlit night. "You'd better take advantage of the night to find shelter. I'll allow an hour before I send a team to the apartment I arranged for you. If you intend to live, you'd better have grabbed whatever you hold dear from there and be gone by the time they arrive. The women I have in mind for the team are excellent fighters and knowing I won't step in to save you, their bloodlust may get away from them. I'm only warning you because I'd rather not have to clean your blood off the walls before turning the apartment over to someone who will appreciate it more."

The woman's eyes watered, but she bit her trembling lip and straightened her shoulders. "I'll see you in hell, Rider Knight, you and your precious girlfriend." She turned and fled into the night as if the hounds of hell were on her heels.

"If she comes within a hundred feet of Danni, I want her destroyed," Rider advised the muscular man who now fiddled with the security panel at the side of the garage door.

"Understood, Boss."

"Has there been any talk of unhappiness with my leadership?"

"None, Boss, unless you're counting the women upset you aren't bedding them, but there's always been grumbling by any who felt overlooked. I haven't heard anything more than normal jealousy. Those two were close and smart enough to keep their dissatisfaction to themselves. I and a few trusted others will do some digging, see if we hear anything else you should know about. I'm changing the security access code now."

The Asian man re-entered the garage. "The warning has been delivered." He nodded his head and set to work cleaning up what was left of the bartender.

Rider turned toward me, his eyes no longer glowing, but still not what I would call friendly. He used the bottom of his T-shirt to wipe the bartender's blood off his chin and I noticed his skin was no longer red. The healing possibly sped by the blood he'd drained from the man he'd just killed. "Let's go," he said as he walked past me to the driver's side of the Ferrari.

I got in, knowing better than to argue or ask questions. It wasn't that I didn't have questions; I had plenty, but after seeing Rider put a man through a wall without lifting a finger, I didn't know how to take him. I'd always had a feeling he was powerful, but I'd had no clue it was to such a degree. Even in his bedroom, when I'd trembled under his dark glare, I hadn't imagined him capable of what I'd just witnessed. I recalled the night I'd been attacked, the fight between him and Selander Ryan and wondered… was Selander Ryan an equal match for him or had he pulled back? I shivered, hoping for the latter, even if it didn't make sense. The only thing worse than knowing you were sired by someone powerful enough to hurt you without lifting a finger was knowing there was someone else out there just as powerful who *wanted* to hurt you.

SIXTEEN

Rider didn't say a word as he drove to my apartment, and I didn't attempt to coax any bits of conversation out of him. I opened my own door when we pulled into the parking lot and he didn't say anything. As usual, he held my door open for me when we entered the building and we shared an awkward silence as we climbed the stairs to my floor. I was bubbling over with curiosity, a hundred questions bouncing around my cranium, and he had to feel it.

I could tell the guard outside my apartment had been briefed on what had happened in the garage. He stood straight as a rail and respectfully nodded his head in greeting as we reached my door. I almost expected him to salute, but he stopped short of that. Rider said nothing to him, or to me, as I unlocked the door and entered my home.

Rider made sure the door was locked behind us and did his usual sweep of the apartment before standing before my living room window, staring at the closed curtains with his hands in his pockets. As far as I knew, he didn't have x-ray vision, so I had no idea what he was looking at so intently and figured he just didn't want to deal with me, yet there he was in my apartment playing bodyguard. He was a very complex man.

I knew I was in for the night, and for all I knew, the entire next day as I had no plans, so I entered my bedroom and changed into lounge pants and a plain T-shirt. I grabbed the largest T-shirt I owned, a black one devoid of any sort of design or logo, and took it into the living room.

"Here." I held the garment out to Rider. Without even a glancing my way, he shrugged out of his leather jacket, dropping it over the back of a chair before pulling the bloody gray T-shirt over his head and wiping excess blood off his chest with the unsoiled part. He started to drop it to the floor, but I caught it. "The blood is fresh enough. I think it'll come out in the wash," I said, passing him the clean shirt I'd taken from my closet.

"Thanks," he muttered, pulling on the clean shirt. Despite it being my biggest, it fit him like a glove, but still looked good on him. A burlap sack would look good on him. I remembered the anger in his eyes when he'd read my mind earlier, remnants of which I could still feel, and shook my head. What I'd thought might have sounded horrible, but how he could think he was runner-up to another man was insane. I wanted to tell him what I'd meant by the thought, how Dex was simply more attainable compared to him, but I lacked the guts.

Maybe it was for the best, I thought a moment later as I tossed his bloody T-shirt into the washing machine with the rest of my dirty clothes. Ten people working for him had lost their lives protecting me. Maybe if I kept him angry with me, he would leave me alone once Selander Ryan had been dealt with, and no more of his people would die because of me. The thought of finding Selander Ryan myself crossed my mind. With my death, multiple lives could be saved, but despite his anger with me, I knew my death would hurt Rider. And why should I have to die? I never asked to be attacked and fought over by two supernatural men. I definitely didn't ask for ten strangers to die over me, eleven counting the bartender who had seemed so nice my first time at the bar.

"I didn't ask to be saved in that alley just so I could lead a long, undead life feeling like hell because of it," I muttered to myself before starting the wash cycle and stepping out of the tiny laundry room off my kitchenette. Rider still stood at the window, staring at nothing and seeing who-knew-what play in his mind. I walked past him, feeling a myriad of emotions, and fought not to touch him, to give him a reassuring squeeze. I felt safe yet afraid with him all at the same time, so I gave him the same silence he'd been giving me since we left the garage, and I went to bed well ahead of the dawn. I knew I was too wide awake to sleep, but I couldn't stay in the same room with him getting frost burn from his cold shoulder. So I lay in bed counting vampire bats until the sun broke through the darkness and pulled me under.

I stood in a great big bunch of nothing. Pitch black, quiet, never-ending nothing. Unlike my previous dreams since becoming a vampire, I couldn't see myself. That's how I knew I was in control.

"Selander!" I yelled into the vastness. "You marked me! I know you can hear me!"

"You needn't shout," his voice echoed around me as the darkness faded away and I found myself in an elegant dining room. Selander Ryan sat at the head of a long dining table, dressed in an all-white suit, his golden hair cascading around his shoulders. He looked like what I imagined a fallen angel would look like as he poured wine into two jeweled chalices. "Of course I can hear you. You are mine."

I opened my mouth to tell him I was Rider's, but paused, suspecting the moment those words left my lips I would fully belong to Rider and he would be my master. After seeing what he'd done to James the bartender, I was more wary than ever about giving myself to either of them completely.

"Cat got your tongue?" Selander swirled the wine around in his chalice. "You're the one who sought me out this time, not that I'm surprised. It was just a matter of time."

"What was?"

"I marked you. Rider can watch over you day and night, but you'll always find a way to me. Sit. Drink." He nodded toward the wine he'd poured for me.

"No thank you," I said, gripping the back of the chair at the opposite end of the table across from him. "I don't accept drinks from those who wish me dead."

"But I no longer wish you dead."

"Oh?" I studied his face, and he looked as devious as ever as he gazed back at me with his cunning eyes. "Whatever changed your mind?"

"Sometimes strategy has to be changed in order to win the game."

"Does anyone actually win this game?"

"Yes. I will destroy Rider and come out the victor."

"What if I don't want to be a part of your game?"

"You are the game, Danni Keller."

I pondered that. "So you hurt me, or kill me, in order to hurt Rider. What if you kill me and it doesn't destroy him?"

"Then we play another game, just as we have been doing for centuries, and I already told you I no longer want you dead. I don't want to wound the man, I want to destroy him."

"Why?"

He looked down into his chalice, watching the liquid move before taking a drink. "It is what we do, what we have always done."

"For centuries."

"Yes." He looked at me, a wicked gleam in his eye. "He hasn't shared his age with you, or anything personal, has he? Interesting."

"What's so interesting about that?" I asked defensively, wondering what info I could get out of Selander. He clearly knew a lot about Rider, and he wasn't a vampire. Maybe incubi didn't play by the same rules and refuse to give basic details like a person's age.

"The besotted fool is so in love with you he fears how you will react when you learn his dark truth, if you learn it."

"What dark truth would that be? He's been very kind to me."

"Oh, you wish I would tell you." Selander laughed. "I'm no fool, girl, and you forget I marked you too. Rider hasn't been the only one in your head."

A cold shiver snaked down my spine at the thought of Selander Ryan crawling around inside my hidden thoughts. "What do you intend to do with me if not kill me?"

"Make you mine, of course."

I frowned. "That's your master plan? Make me give my loyalty to you? That's how you intend to *destroy* Rider? Even he isn't that jealous."

"No, but he is that protective, and that self-loathing." Selander's grin widened. "You will eventually give yourself to me and you will become everything you've wanted to be but dared not say. The more you give in to your dark desires, the more he will suffer because he'll go to his long overdue final resting place, blaming himself for failing you."

"I'll never give in to you," I stated firmly. "I'm a very stubborn woman when it suits me, sometimes even when it bites me in the ass. I can't help it. I was born stubborn."

"I've noticed." His eyes darkened. "I've never seen a newly turned vampire so determined to hold on to every dismal part of her human life. Tell me, what is so great about your job, or just working during the day anyway?"

"Getting a paycheck and using it to pay bills."

Selander laughed. "Any job can give you a paycheck.

Your sire could cover your bills. My harem never pays for anything."

"I'm sure they pay every moment of their lives, and at a price far too steep for me."

"How valuable is a soul when there is no heaven or hell for you?" Selander sipped from his drink. "That is the most excruciatingly annoying thing about my... about Rider. You'd think the man would have loosened up after becoming immortal, yet he still has the same self-righteous stick lodged up his ass. Don't prey on the innocent, don't take life unnecessarily, treat women with respect, never use your powers to take advantage, blah, blah, blah. What a waste of power that bloodsucker is, still caring about morals and sin when he's escaped judgment day."

"You knew him before he turned."

Selander smiled, exposing a tip of curved fang. "Our game began long before either of us received our teeth."

"And has lasted this long?" I studied the incubus, taking in the power I sensed radiating from him and the storm of dark emotion beneath the surface, the product of ugly darkness masked by his golden good looks. "What connection do the two of you have that you haven't just killed each other and been done with this nonsense?"

"Vengeance is not nonsense!" Selander shouted, his eyes flashing red before he closed them and visibly calmed himself. He chuckled as he opened them once more, and they were back to their normal color. "Do you think you can get more out of me by making me angry? It won't work. You see, part of the fun in playing the game is knowing more than your opponent, keeping them in the dark and watching them go mad, trying to figure out your next move. Do you feel the madness sinking in, Danni?"

"I thought I was the game. Now I'm your opponent?"

"You're both."

"Because you're playing me." I shook my head, disgusted. "Has anything you've ever said to me been the truth?"

"Has it?" He shrugged, laughing. "You sought me out for answers, and I have given you answers. Whether they are right or wrong answers is for you to figure out."

"I didn't ask for any part of this!" I yelled at him, the strength of my voice causing the chandelier over the table to shake.

"I don't care." He leered at me over the rim of his glass. "A very special woman put her mark on Rider and me many, many centuries ago, and we both loved her, albeit in different ways. I would have given her everything, but Rider killed her to ensure I never could. Now we have both put our marks on the same woman, and I will use you to make him suffer as he made me suffer, but I will do it slowly. Rider's torment has just begun, and so has yours. It doesn't matter whether you asked for this or not. It is the price that is paid for being the object of his affection, and everything I do to you will be the price he pays for destroying the object of mine."

"Hurt me and he'll kill you."

"Perhaps he finally will." He leaned forward, a murderous gleam in his eyes as his smile took over his face, somehow becoming the most terrorizing thing I'd ever seen. "And when he does, I'll still win." He made a shooing motion with his hand and I flung backward, right out of my sleep.

I opened my eyes to see Rider standing at the foot of my bed, head bowed, hands clenched at his sides, jaw popped. "You went to him."

"Eavesdropping on my dreams now too?" I sat up, pressing my back against the headboard, which was as far as I could go from him and the angry energy he gave off.

"I felt his presence, and from what else I could feel, he did not seek you this time. You went to him. After everything I've told you about him, after all I've done to protect you, you went to him."

"You haven't really told me anything."

"I told you he was dangerous, that he will kill you.

What more do I need to say?"

"You could have told me ten people have died protecting me."

"News that obviously distresses you. What good would knowing that have done? Would it have kept you from him?"

"Maybe. If I got answers from you, I wouldn't need them from him."

"I've always given you answers. You merely need to ask the questions."

"Fine. Who was the woman you and Selander Ryan loved? The one you killed?"

"He did not love her," Rider said slowly, his voice vibrating with barely controlled rage. His nostrils flared, his eyes burned with fury. "You can't trust a word that devil says. He lies to all, even himself. He has one goal, and that is to destroy the good in everything he touches, to break down the hearts and souls of anyone who dares to live with honor."

"You killed a woman."

"I've killed many. You saw me kill a man last night. It is not something I do lightly or brag about."

"Did you love the woman Selander Ryan told me about?"

"Yes."

I swallowed. Hard. "How could you kill her?"

"I had to."

"She would have killed you?"

"That is not why I killed her."

"Then why did you kill her?"

"It was the only way to save her." His eyes grew wet, and he looked away. I felt a pang in my chest and it took all my willpower not to reach out to him, to comfort him while simultaneously dealing with my own jealousy. I was jealous of a mystery woman he'd killed because he still felt the pain of it. I didn't like that someone else could make him feel that way. Seeing him kill a man without touching him, knowing he had it in him to put that man's head on display scared me to the point I didn't think I could ever be with him, but I still didn't like him mourning the loss of another woman. For once, I wanted to be the love of a man's life.

I could give you the power to make men beg at your feet.

I focused within, building a mental wall to keep Selander Ryan out of my head, just as Eliza had taught me to do with Rider, hoping it worked. He'd been able to get inside my head all along and I'd been too focused on Rider getting in there to put up any resistance. No wonder he hadn't just swooped in and tried to grab me. He already had access to my mind. He was playing with me, using me to toy with Rider, all for some sick game. I was being used to settle a feud over another woman, just as I'd been used by guys throughout my school years to get to my sister or my better looking friends. He said Rider loved me, but I couldn't picture Rider's eyes wetting with tears over me. He might feel a responsibility to me since he'd turned me, but nothing he wouldn't feel for any other woman he'd turned in order to save a life. Selander Ryan hoped he would fall in love with me though. That's why he was giving us time before attacking me straight on. That's why I escaped the dream with no damage. Rider was fond of me, but he didn't love me. As long as he didn't love me, Selander Ryan wasn't a threat to me.

"You need to leave me alone," I said. "Enough men have died because of your need to protect me."

"You blame me for their deaths?" He asked, a wounded look in his eyes.

"I blame Selander Ryan, but that doesn't change the fact those men wouldn't have died if they weren't protecting me. He's killing your men for amusement. He has no intent to harm me, not right now. It's all just a game."

"Everything is a game with him, Danni, but his games are deadly. As long as he lives, you are not safe."

"He doesn't care about me, but he thinks you do. As long as you stand guard over me, giving him that impression, he will continue to taunt you with this illusion that he wants me. Forget about me and he will too."

Rider opened his mouth to respond, his eyes full of incredulity, but stilled as the doorbell rang. We both sighed as I sensed my sister.

"I didn't think you'd bought so much," Shana said, stepping inside with her arms weighed down with designer shopping bags. I took some from her, marveling how there were actually so few considering how much I'd spent. I cringed just thinking about the credit card bill I had coming.

"Thanks for bringing these." I set the bags down on the floor. "Are you just dropping these off?" I asked as I closed the door, only to have the doorbell ring again once it had shut. I jumped a little, surprised, my nerves already on edge after everything that had transpired since the previous night. "Mom came too?"

Shana shook her head, settling in on my couch. "I'm alone today. I've had all I can take of mom, Grandma, and that dreadful dog this week."

Yeah, I didn't feel sorry for the golden girl. If all my time spent with the women in my family involved being constantly flattered, I wouldn't mind so much. I could even take the dog's gas. I tried to sense who was on the other side of the door but came up empty. I hadn't heard any scuffling between the person and my guard on duty in the hall, and Rider remained tucked away in the bedroom, not sending me any warnings, so I opened the door, pretty sure I'd be safe.

"Good evening. Ms. Keller?" a small man with thinning hair and bifocals, dressed in a nice suit, asked. He carried a dress bag and a small envelope.

"Yes, I'm Danni Keller."

"This is from Mr. Prince," he said, handing me the envelope and the dress. "He requests your presence at his penthouse tomorrow night for dinner. You are to wear this dress and the envelope includes an appointment card with a stylist and some extra money in case you need shoes or anything extra. A car will be sent for you at seven." The man nodded his head and left me standing with the door open, perplexed, as I stared down at the envelope and dress bag in my hands.

"Oooh, Danni!" Shana stood, clapping her hands as she walked toward me and took the dress bag out of my hand. "He sent you a dress and wants you at his penthouse. This is like *Pretty Woman,* but you don't even have to be a hooker."

I closed the door and rolled my eyes. Of course, my sister would think it was great that a man sent me a dress and money. I, however, looked at the appointment card I'd pulled free of the wad of money inside the envelope and felt nauseous. "Have you ever had a man send you to a stylist before showing you off to his friends and family?" I asked as she unzipped the dress bag to reveal a gorgeous black gown.

"No, but I've had some take me shopping. What's the matter? Why do you look so down? This is awesome."

I shook my head. She wouldn't get it. She was beautiful, and fashionable, and perfect. A man wouldn't send her off to someone to make her presentable. If she received a dress from a man, it would be because she wanted it, or the man was trying to impress her. With me, I knew that wasn't the case.

"So this is from your boss, right? Or did things go well with that guy from the restaurant? Mom's been calling you for details. Have you checked your messages?"

I shook my head, remembering I'd turned my ringer off. "I'll check them later."

"Okay, but tell me now. He was really hot. What's he drive? What kind of place does he have? Did you sleep with him?" I couldn't miss the jealousy in her tone. It shocked me hearing that from her.

"Is that really an appropriate question?"

"Oh, come on. We're not kids anymore. Fess up."

"We left the restaurant on a motorcycle," I answered truthfully, "and we had drinks like he said. That's about all there is to share."

"Will you see him again?" She studied me, her nose slightly tipped, and I couldn't help but feel that she was trying to understand what he'd seen in me to make him choose to ask me to dance instead of her. I won't lie. It hurt like a bitch, and tears burned the back of my eyes, but I refused to let her see them fall, especially since she wasn't even trying to make me feel bad. She genuinely couldn't understand why Rider would want me over her.

"Thanks for dropping the clothes off for me. I'm not feeling that good, so I'm going to put everything up and rest to make sure I can still go to dinner tomorrow night."

"Say no more." Shana walked to the door. "Drink plenty of ginger ale and just rest. Sleep is great. You don't want bags under your eyes, and I wouldn't eat anything. You want to make sure you can fit in to the dress he sent you and don't be late to the stylist. Give them all the time they need!"

I ushered Shana out the door, locked it, and scooped up everything that had been delivered to me. I carried it all to my bedroom, where I dropped the bags and hung the dress on the back of my closet door. A glance at the price tag told me Dex had invested a lot of money in making sure I was a suitable dinner date. Rider sat on my bed, quietly watching me.

"Go ahead and say it."

"Say what?"

"Make a joke about how the man I'm dating sent me a dress and took it upon himself to arrange an appointment with a stylist because he thinks he needs to dress me and someone else needs to beautify me."

"Jokes are supposed to be funny. I don't think that's funny at all."

"Fine. Tell me how sad it is."

"I don't need to, and rubbing your nose in it is just mean. I will tell you that what he thinks doesn't matter."

"Yes, it does, and it's not just him. My family, my friends, guys from high school, and after. A lot of people think I need improvement."

"The only thing you need to improve is your confidence." He stood and stretched. "Are you thirsty?"

I shook my head. After what I'd seen the night before, I didn't think I'd ever be able to drink from Rider again. "I'm fine, thank you."

"I had to kill them last night. You know that, right?"

"The hunter tried to kill me. I understand why you killed him."

"And James?"

I studied the dress, unable to look Rider in the eye.

"Danni, I'm responsible for a lot of people in this city, including people who've never met me and have no clue vampires exist. If I can't control my own nest, if I have a traitor within my inner circle, and anyone found out I didn't kill him, that would be seen as weakness. With everything going on right now, I can't afford an attack."

"By everything you mean me. I'm the reason you had traitors to begin with."

"If they were so bothered by doing their damn jobs, then you weren't the problem. They were always traitors. If anything, you helped flush them out and not a moment too soon. You heard Marie. She was angry I didn't treat you as her sire had treated her. She was angry you weren't enslaved. Does a person like that deserve mercy?"

"You gave her mercy. You could have killed her like you killed the bartender."

"I've only killed one woman in my long life. It left a hole in me that will never heal. I wasn't merciful. I spared myself the pain of killing a woman by allowing my people to do it for me. She didn't make it to dawn. The members of my nest who are loyal to me are very loyal to me, especially the women who were forced to do things against their nature before I freed them. I didn't even have to order the hit and no, I won't punish them for taking her out. I won't apologize for killing James. I didn't want to do it. I've never wanted to kill anyone, but I do it when it needs to be done. I do it to protect my people. I will never apologize for that."

"Why *aren't* you like the vampires who sired your people? The two you killed last night suggested you were weak for not controlling me. You put that man through a wall without touching him and he wasn't even sired by you. You could make me do anything you want, couldn't you?"

"Yes."

"Why haven't you?"

"I came from a time when women weren't allowed much freedom. I never cared for that. I've seen women forced to do things against their nature, forced to soil their souls. There's nothing worse than that and I could never do that to another being. Flinging a traitor into a wall in battle, using my power in combat, is one thing. Controlling someone's every action?" He shook his head. "It is a depravity."

"But if your enemies see it as weakness?"

"Anyone who sees my respect as weakness lacks morality and deserves the death I will give them. James and Marie chose to turn on me after I saved them both from vampires who forced them to act against their wills. I protected them from harm and they schemed to hurt me, to take away someone I care for. There are many things I regret, but their deaths will never be on that list, and they shouldn't be on yours. The ten men I've lost this past week signed up for the job, just like soldiers. I regret their deaths, but that's my guilt to suffer, not yours."

"But it is. They died because they were protecting me."

"Danni—"

"They died because they were protecting me! The worst part about it? I didn't even know. Ten people lost their lives guarding me and I don't even know their names to thank them. I can't even visualize them to keep them alive in my memory. They were strangers to me and I was a stranger to them, but they died to protect me from some psycho playing a game. It has to end now, Rider. You have to stop the guard duty."

"What? Selander—"

"Selander Ryan isn't going to kill me. He wants to destroy you by killing off the woman you love, to get even with you for the woman you killed centuries ago. But you don't love me. You sired me, and you feel responsible for protecting me, and he's using that against you. He wants us to get closer, hoping you'll fall in love with me or just fill yourself with guilt over not letting me die in that alley. He marked me too, Rider. He can get in my head just like you. He can track me just like you. Why hasn't he come straight for me? Why did he hire my company to sell his product, sit right across from me and not harm me in any way? I've felt his power. No one in that building could have stopped him if he'd wanted me dead. He's playing a game. That's all it is, just a game the two of you have been playing for centuries. He made the mistake of showing me his hand this time. I know how to beat him. Take the guards off me. Leave me alone. That's how you beat him. If I'm nothing to you, then I'm nothing to him. I'm not worth the time it would take for him to kill me."

"I can't leave you—"

"I thought you didn't control women, Rider."

His eyes darkened. "I don't."

"Keeping me under guard, monitoring me, invading my mind, telling me where I should or shouldn't go is all a form of control. I want my freedom, Rider. Are you going to give me my freedom or keep me bound to you?"

SEVENTEEN

I pressed the button for the penthouse and stared at myself in the mirrored doors as the elevator ascended to the top floor, trying to recognize the woman staring back at me. The woman in the reflection had glossy, smooth hair that fell to her shoulders, wore a dress that cost more than a month's salary and heels that cost almost as much. She had spent the day being pampered and fawned over by a stylist who shaped and painted her nails, used an expensive array of products to give her hair a glossy sheen, applied makeup to make her look her absolute most beautiful, and tailored her obscenely expensive dress to make the most of her figure before being picked up and delivered to the apartment building by a chauffeur escorting her via luxury sedan. The woman staring back at me was on her way to meet the man who'd requested her presence at his home, a home she'd fantasized about sharing for a long time.

The woman staring back at me wasn't me at all. I wasn't the beautiful socialite whose only concern was landing the rich man in the penthouse. I surprised myself by feeling nothing as I rode the elevator to the top floor. I hadn't felt much of anything since Rider had left the night before. He'd actually left me. Sure, I'd told him to, made him feel as if he were denying me my freedom by staying so close, and I'd done it for his own good and the good of his people, but it still chafed that he'd gone so easily. I'd gotten used to him digging his heels in and protecting me, no matter what. As much as it grated on my nerves, I realized after he left that I'd actually liked it in a way. I'd felt safe, secure. Cared about. But Selander Ryan had mistaken Rider's protection as love, and so had Rider's people. Twelve had died in a week's time and more would die if Selander Ryan continued to think I was important to Rider. I had to let them all know I really wasn't, that I was just a newb the big bad vampire sire thought he had to protect from every perceived threat. As long as I allowed it, he would continue treating me like a damsel in distress. I wasn't. Eliza had given me the Vampire 101 to know what was up, and Rider had taught me some fighting moves. If it came down to it, I had the succubus bite to turn my attackers into lovers. Ew. Disappointed lovers, at least, because I would not get down and dirty with one just to save my life. I'd killed before, albeit by accident, but I'd done it. I could do it again if I absolutely had to.

The elevator dinged, and the doors opened to a beautiful foyer with marbled floors and mirror paneled walls. Dex must really love looking at himself, I thought as I stepped out to be greeted by the doorman who checked my name on a list, nodded, and opened the door, ushering me inside Dex's home. I'd wanted to see the inside of his home for so long, but as I stepped inside the living area to a party in full swing, it just didn't do anything for me. Everything was black, gray, and white. And mirror. A large mirror lined one wall and would have lined the rest if some of them weren't glass from floor to ceiling.

Not recognizing any of the elegantly dressed guests and not spotting Dex, I walked over to the far wall and looked out. From thirteen stories up, I had a clear view of downtown and it was quite breathtaking from so high above. People moved about, looking like shadowy little dots as the headlights from cars made the street below appear like a little star-filled sky. There was no star-filled sky above me. Even up so close, the pollution robbed me of what would have been a gorgeous view. I looked toward The Midnight Rider but couldn't see it. I wondered if Rider was there, what he was doing. I'd strengthened the mental wall inside my head, attempting to keep both him and Selander Ryan out. Reminding myself why I'd done it to begin with, I looked in the opposite direction of Rider's bar. I couldn't afford any emotional slip that might weaken my wall. I couldn't let Selander Ryan know how Rider affected me, that I actually missed him. I couldn't give him any reason to think I could be used to hurt him.

"Danni, there you are!"

I turned to see Dex approaching me with two champagne glasses in hand, a warm smile on his face. I did not return it because flanking his side was Selander Ryan with Gina on his arm. I didn't recognize the man on his other side and didn't care. I was too busy pushing back against the pressure in my frontal lobe as Selander Ryan tried to break through my mental wall.

"You look lovely as always," Dex said, handing me a glass. "This is my younger brother, Chad," he introduced the other man with him who kissed my hand, "and you, of course, know Mr. Ryan and Gina."

"I wasn't aware this was a business function," I replied, fighting to keep my voice normal as I continued to push back against Selander Ryan's attempt to invade my mind.

"It's not, really, but our best clients are always welcome." Dex offered me his arm and I accepted, gladly letting him walk me away from the group. I glanced back over my shoulder to see Gina playing up to Dex's brother as Selander Ryan grinned at me, a mischievous gleam in his eye. Dex guided me out of the room and the pressure in my head eased. I knew it was only a reprieve. Selander Ryan wouldn't give up that easily, but for the moment I was winning.

"How did you like the stylist? I can set you up on a regular schedule."

"If you think I need the extra help," I said curtly, unable to keep the barb out of my voice. I didn't know what kind of twits he normally dated, but I liked to think despite my general self-esteem issues, I had enough pride to be miffed that my date had decided I needed a makeover.

"You are a beautiful woman," he said. "Even the most beautiful of roses benefit from a little pruning, of course?"

I glanced at him sideways, unsure if he was attempting to deliver a veiled insult inside what he thought was a compliment or suggesting I needed a bikini wax. Considering he'd never been anywhere near my bikini area, I opted for the first.

"Dex, darling, is this your special friend?" an older woman asked as we entered the dining room. She stood next to a tall, attractive man with gray, thinning hair and a spray-on tan. I placed him in his sixties. I couldn't place the woman's age. Her voice suggested she wasn't a spring chicken, but her face was tight with Botox and who knew what was under the seven layers of makeup? I imagined she had been a knockout in her youth. Now she looked like an aging trophy wife trying desperately to hold on to the title.

"Yes, Mother, Father." Dex greeted the couple. "This is Danni Keller. Danni landed the Nocturnal Inc. deal with an extremely impressive campaign."

"Yes." Daddy Prince gave me a slow once-over, giving me the skeevies as his gaze held on to my body, or lack of, a little too long. "I got the email. I was rather impressed myself with such... talent. Pleased to meet you, Danni." He held his hand out and I forced myself to take it. I forced myself even harder not to yank my hand back when, instead of shaking it, he kissed it. Mrs. Prince smiled at me, or gave me the closest thing she had to a smile. It looked painful, and not just because of the Botox. I could see the fear in her eyes, the fear her husband had found someone younger to give his attention to. Was this what it was like to marry a man in the Prince family?

Forty minutes later, I was all small-talked out and feeling completely out of my element. My feet hurt from standing so long in the tight heels and dinner still hadn't been served. Dex had shown me off to his family and close friends, giving off the impression I was more than his employee he'd just started dating. At one time, I would have been thrilled and bursting at the seams with barely contained excitement over the possibility I could actually be in a real relationship with him. Maybe it was the events I'd seen over the past week, the knowledge I now had of how dark the world could be, but there was an uneasy feeling in the pit of my stomach and it wasn't just because Selander Ryan was still at the party. Something odd was going on. I found myself alone in the library, watching fish swim around a large tank and wishing I was anywhere else… with Rider.

The door opened and in stepped Gina, stunning in a form-fitting ivory gown that fell to her ankles but provided plenty of leg courtesy of the long slit in the side. Not that many cared to look at the leg, I figured, since they had so much cleavage to see. The neckline was cut low, but stopped just short of indecent. In fact, the dress would have been very sophisticated on me. With a body like Gina's, there wasn't much she could wear that didn't come across as uber-sexy.

"Hey, Danni." She smiled at me as she crossed over to one of the brown leather sofas and plopped down. "My feet are killing me." She propped her stiletto-clad feet on one of the ottomans and reclined. "I had to take a little break from all the socialization. I don't know why women get so angry with me when their husbands and boyfriends flirt. It's not like I'm asking for it. I'm here with my own date. Sheesh. They can buy their own boobs if they're so jealous of mine. They have the money."

I raised my eyebrow but didn't say anything about her seeking attention. I mean, it might be hard to not look ridiculously sexy with that body, but she did flaunt it. If fake complaining about the attention she got made her feel better, more power to her. Besides, I knew she wasn't there to get a little peace and quiet, and gripe. She was there as a spy because Selander Ryan couldn't get past the wall I'd put up. I couldn't even be mad at Gina. She had no idea she was being used to get information, and my knowledge that she was only made me sad for her. No one should be used.

"So, how are things with Dex?" she asked. "I thought you were with that Rider guy." Wow. Right on cue.

"Rider was just a guy who brought me home from the bar and took care of me while I was sick," I answered, sitting on the sofa opposite her, careful to keep emotion out of my voice, and my thoughts which proved harder. Just hearing Rider's name brought up his image, and I again wondered what he was doing, and if he missed watching over me. "Things with Dex are fine. We went to the restaurant that night and now I'm here as his date. It's a nice place."

"Penthouses are always nice," Gina said. "What type of place does Rider have?"

I could just picture Selander hidden away in a dark corner somewhere, puppeteering Gina with his mind. I took a breath, allowing myself time to think about how to respond to the questions. It was important I give the impression there weren't any deep feelings between Rider and me but I also had to make sure I didn't get caught in a lie. If I did, Ryan would know I was playing him. Did he know I'd been to Rider's apartment over the bar? Ugh. "Nothing much, I think," I finally said. "I don't know all that much about him, really. He owns that bar I was supposed to meet you at that night. He's a nice guy, pretty protective of women. I see why you like that bar. Have you been since that night we were supposed to meet up?"

"No," she answered, frowning. "I actually haven't been inside. Someone told me about it, but I can't recall who."

"Maybe Selander?"

She frowned. "No, it couldn't have been. I hadn't met him yet."

I nodded and said nothing, not wanting to overplay my hand. Judging by the way Ryan was using Gina to get information out of me, I didn't think he knew I was aware that he could.

"We should go to the bar tonight after the party is over."

"Nah, not feeling it," I answered. "I haven't really been wanting to drink anything lately."

"There's more to do at a bar than just drink."

"Not really."

"You can meet guys there."

"Aren't you dating Selander Ryan?"

She shrugged. "It's casual. I'd love to meet a guy like Rider."

"Then you should go to the bar. He owns it, so he's bound to be there."

"Don't you want to go with me?"

I kept my mind as blank as possible as I shook my head. "As far as bars go, it's probably where I'd feel the safest. Good security. I just don't really have any interest in the bar scene. I'm with Dex, and who knows if I'm going home tonight?" I was so going home. I was bored to tears with all the schmoozing and I swear if one more woman there told me what her husband or boyfriend had bought her or where he'd taken her that weekend, I was going to puncture my eardrums to make it stop. Every woman there seemed to think the party was a competition of who was sleeping with and being adored by the most successful man.

"So, you wouldn't mind if I went to the bar and asked Rider out?"

"Why would I?" I laughed, the knowledge that it was really Selander Ryan asking and not Gina, the only thing keeping my emotions at bay. I would absolutely die if I thought Rider would go out with Gina. I'd curl up into a ball and just die. "He's a decent guy. You'd be safe with him."

"Oh. I thought it would bother you."

"We don't have that kind of relationship."

"Oh." She perked up. "Okay, then. I'll ask him out. He seems just yummy."

"Whatever floats your boat," I said, straightening as I heard a bell ringing. "Is that a dinner bell?"

"Sounds like it. About time. I'm starved."

I wasn't hungry at all. I'd started the evening with a lack of appetite and what little I'd had had just plummeted after picturing Gina cuddling up to Rider. I doubted Rider would give her the time of day since he knew she was under Ryan's influence, but then again, with that body… Rider was a smart, powerful vampire, but he was still a man.

I squared my shoulders and followed Gina to the formal dining room, and took my place next to Dex at the long dining table. Gina found her spot next to Selander… at the other end of the table. Selander Ryan was definitely not amused that he was placed so far away from where I sat amongst family and the most important of friends and colleagues, which gave me a little joy, but the joy quickly soured as the dinner began and I sat through course after course of food I mostly could not eat and conversation I had just as much trouble stomaching.

I lay on the bed in Dex's bedroom and stared up at the ceiling. After dinner, I'd feigned a headache and sought out a quiet place where I could just rest. It had felt as if Dex's family was sizing me up the entire dinner and I could feel the frustration rolling off of Selander Ryan. He couldn't get past my wall, and his Trojan horse had given him nothing to use against me or Rider. I didn't even fear him, and he knew it. It was driving him crazy, especially since the first time I'd found myself in proximity to him after the attack, I'd immediately called upon Rider. This time, I simply acted as if he were beneath me, unworthy of a moment of my concern. I had been marked by both, but I leaned toward Rider, rendering Selander Ryan's mark no more than a tracking device. He couldn't even get inside my head unless I allowed it. I smiled, thinking how impotent the incubus must have felt. Poor little demon.

A little over an hour had passed and I could hear the penthouse growing quieter as the front door opened and closed, allowing people to exit. Vampire hearing was pretty cool, definitely one of my favorite tricks Eliza had taught me how to use to my benefit. My sense of smell was another. I'd been able to track Selander and Gina using it, and breathed a little easier once they'd left. I'd half expected them to stick around until they were told to go, but maybe Ryan had had enough disappointment for the night. He was nowhere near the last to leave. People continued to trickle out slowly until it was just Dex and his brother. Even the staff had left.

"Mom and Dad seem pleased with the match," I heard Chad say from where they stood just before the front door. "Are you sure you can seal the deal? She's not your usual type."

My ears perked up at this. Were they discussing me?

"That's exactly why I chose her. You know the agreement is that I find a wife suitable to present to society, a real Mary Tyler Moore type, not a Marilyn Monroe. My usual type wouldn't do."

"Speaking of Marilyn Monroe, did you check out the blonde with that Ryan guy? There's a notch I'd like to have on my bedpost."

"I've carved a few out with her already. Great body, and keeps her mouth shut if you compensate her well. I'll give you her number for when Caroline and the kids are out of town."

I sat straight up, my mouth hanging open in shock. Not because Dex had revealed he'd slept with Gina. That wasn't much of a shocker, but the fact he would offer her phone number to his married brother was.

"Thanks, bro. So when are you going to pop the question to Danni? I imagine you'll want to have as much fun as you can before tying yourself down with her. She fits what Mom and Dad want the family image to be, but she doesn't seem like she'd be a wild ride in the sack. I can tell you from experience once they start popping the little heirs out and know they have you by the bank account, they turn real cold."

"The sooner I get her down the aisle, the sooner I get the money and the new branch office, and I don't expect much to change. She's not like the other women I've dated. I don't think she'd care what I was off doing as long as she got my name. A girl like that? She'd be thrilled just to have the ring. I don't know about the wild ride part, though. There's something about her. That presentation she gave to Nocturnal Inc. nearly had me busting in the office. I don't know, maybe the less they're endowed with, the harder they work to please."

"Yeah, you'll have to let me know how that turns out."

"I will. Expect a call tomorrow morning."

They laughed, exchanged a few more crude remarks, and then Chad was gone, and only Dex and I remained in the penthouse. I'd wiped the tears from my eyes and slipped back into my heels by the time he came through the door, his tie undone and his shirt half unbuttoned.

"Hey there. I thought you were lying down."

"I feel better," I said, standing tall. "I'll be heading home now."

He'd just unworked the last button on his shirt and pulled it free of his pants. He stood there, partially undressed, and narrowed his eyes. "Don't be silly. You're welcome to stay here."

"I'd rather not." I felt tears burn the back of my eyes and I willed them not to fall. I'd just taken a major hit to my pride and what tiny little ego I'd had to begin with, but the only thing worse would be to let him know that.

"Stay," he said. His tone was firm, a direct order. He removed his shirt, flinging it and the tie onto the carpet before stepping out of his shoes and unbuttoning his fly.

"I'm not the type of woman to sleep with a man on the second date," I said, my tone just as firm. "Especially when there's not going to be a third."

He sucked in a breath, blew it out slow. "Do you know who the hell I am?"

"A spoiled bastard who thought he could buy me? I'm not impressed by your car or your home or the money you just throw around. I'm not interested in you, Dex, and I'm leaving."

"The hell you are." He took a step toward me and I started to back away until I remembered I was a vampire-succubus hybrid. Why the hell would I back down from a mere man? "That dress isn't cheap. That stylist charges by the hour, and I'm sure she took her time with you."

"What exactly are you saying?" I asked, knowing what he was saying, but struggling to wrap my mind around the reality of the fact the man I'd been daydreaming about for two years was such a lowlife.

"I'm saying I paid good money for you and you had no problem accepting my gifts. You knew what the payout was. You're a big girl, Danni. You know the game."

I ran my tongue over my teeth, felt the tips of my fangs as they started to press down. "You know what? I'm getting real sick of getting caught up in games I never asked to play."

He frowned. "I don't know what you're talking about or what the hell is going on in that head right now. I'm going to chalk it up to too much champagne and give you another chance. It's time for bed, Danni."

"I'll just be on my way then." I moved to walk past him, but he grabbed me by my arm and flung me backward onto his bed.

"I didn't take you for the kind that likes it rough."

"Trust me, I'm not. Let me out of this room or you will regret it."

He laughed. "Hard to get, huh? It's kind of turning me on."

I looked down as he stepped out of his pants and saw just how turned on he was. "I will kill you if you touch me."

He paused, one knee on the foot of the bed, his thumbs inside the waistband of his silk boxers, and I could see the wheel turning in his head. His eyes switched from confused to angry, to downright predatory as he moved forward and I kicked out, connecting my foot with his chest before he could get his boxers down.

I kicked him hard enough to ram the heel of my shoe through his chest. He fell back, crying out in pain as he clutched at the shoe now penetrating his body. I kicked the other shoe off and made a run for the door, but again he caught me by my arm and this time hurled me against his dresser, breaking the mirror over it.

"You bitch!" He growled as he yanked the heel out of his chest and came toward me with it raised over his head, ready to strike.

I raised my arm to block him and threw a punch just as Rider had taught me, sending him across the room, where he slammed into the wall hard enough to leave a crack. Fueled by rage, it wasn't enough to stop him. He lunged for me, wrapping his hands around my throat as he fell with me onto the bed. He reared back and slapped me hard enough I tasted blood in my mouth. I wondered if he'd done this before, if he'd done this to Gina or any other woman foolish enough to fall for his good looks and charm, or if this was the first time, brought on by the fact a woman had dared refuse him.

As he ripped my gown, determined he would have me, it didn't matter. All that mattered was that he never had the chance to do it again. I sank my fangs into his throat and greedily slurped the life-giving liquid that rushed out of him. As Rider had predicted, the succubus venom in my teeth turned him on, and he started humping against me even as I drank him to death. Disgusted, I snapped his neck and the sound of the bone splintering brought me out of the panic-fueled haze I'd been under.

I shoved his body off of mine and sat up. I was covered in blood. Dex's blood. I looked down at where his body had landed on the floor, his blood seeping into the cream-colored carpet. His neck was grossly contorted and his eyes stared back at me, wide and frozen in death. The blood I'd just drank rose in my throat and I ran to the bathroom, reaching the toilet just in time to throw up what I'd drained out of Dex's body as I'd killed him. I'd killed him, the man who only a week ago I wanted to marry and have children with.

I pulled myself up to the sink, washed my bloody face with water and took a good look in the mirror. It was a mistake. I was dreaming. I couldn't have killed Dex and he couldn't have attacked me. Not Dex. He was charming, good-looking, and rich. He could have any woman he wanted. There was no reason for any of this to have happened. It made no sense. I straightened my shoulders, took a deep breath, and stepped out of the bathroom.

The wall he'd hit after I punched him was still cracked, the mirror over the dresser he'd thrown me into was still shattered, the bed was a mess, and Dex's blood still stained the carpet around his body, his dead eyes still looked at me, accusing me. I was still covered in his blood and the last person in the penthouse with him. Security was still in the building, still able to tell the police I'd been the last to see Dex alive. Still able to tell the police I'd killed him. I was a murderer and this time, it wasn't some sleazy guy no one would miss. I'd just killed Dex Prince and I didn't see any way I wasn't going to prison.

More afraid than I'd ever been in my life, and with no idea what to do next, I dropped my mental wall, fell to my knees, and screamed for Rider.

EIGHTEEN

As soon as I'd realized I'd let my guard down, I'd thrown my wall back up and wasn't sure he'd heard me, but clearly he had. I was still on my knees in the same spot when Rider lifted the bedroom window and crawled in fifteen minutes later.

"This penthouse is thirteen floors up."

"Good thing I'm not afraid of heights." Rider looked around the room. His nostrils flared. "Damn it, Danni. I told you about this guy. You just had to keep chasing your damn fantasy with the human and the white picket fence, didn't you?"

I looked up at Rider. "What exactly do you think happened here?"

"You bit him and what I said would happen, happened, or you let yourself get too hungry again. I knew I shouldn't have taken the guard off you. I should have stayed right by your side instead of letting you talk me into thinking I was controlling you. Is this the freedom you wanted?"

I studied Rider as hot tears fell from my eyes. His blue eyes burned with barely contained anger, his nostrils flared, his upper lip curved as he took in the mess, no doubt calculating just how screwed I was and trying to figure out how to get me out of this catastrophe. It wasn't going to be as easy as dumping a random drunk's body into a dumpster. He wouldn't have come through the window had he not known about the security in the building. "You're mad at me."

"You killed a man, Danni. Yeah, I thought he was a prick, but damn. When you make a mess, you really make a damn mess."

"I'm sorry!" I shouted, standing. "I'm sorry I came to the party, and that I spent the whole time keeping a wall up against Selander Ryan and projecting the illusion that I didn't care at all about you and that I'd rather be at a snorefest of a party than with you. I'm sorry I told you to stop guarding me, trying to save you and your men from Selander Ryan's twisted games. I'm sorry I heard this bastard tell his brother he was going to call him with details after he bedded me and I'm sorry that after he forced himself on me I fought back instead of just laying down and taking it like a good little—"

Rider crossed the room in a flash of speed and wrapped me in his arms. "I'm sorry, Danni. I didn't know. I didn't—" He pulled away just enough to allow himself room to look down into my eyes. His own were dark with fury. "Did he manage to…?"

"No." I shook my head as I wiped my eyes with the back of my hand. "That crack in the wall is from where he landed after I punched him. I fought him the best I could, but he was so determined. I had to bite him when he got me on the bed and pinned me down. I just reacted. I bit him, tried to drain him, but he reacted like you thought a man would. I broke his neck, and that's when I realized what I was doing. I didn't really want to kill him, I just defended myself."

"That's my girl." Rider pulled me in close and kissed my forehead, letting his lips linger there as he held me tight. "You didn't do anything wrong. He asked to die. He deserved it. I have half a mind to have him brought back to life just so I get a chance to kill him too."

"Is that even possible?"

"If you know the right people."

"Can you have him brought back to life so I don't go to prison for his murder?"

"I'm afraid not." Rider kissed the top of my head and whispered, "I'll take care of everything." He stepped away and walked over to Dex, squatting next to his body. "If you'd just bit him, the bite marks would heal and medical examiners wouldn't know what the hell happened. They'd most likely rule his death a heart attack. The broken neck is a problem though. There's no way we can heal that." He stood, looked down at Dex's body for a moment, and kicked him.

"Rider."

"Sorry. I had to." He reached into his pants pocket and pulled out his cell phone. "This is more than my normal crew can handle given this happened at a party and I assume there were a lot of witnesses to you being here, not to mention the building security. I'm going to have to bring in a witch for this one."

"A real witch?"

He nodded as he raised the phone to his ear and waited a moment. "Yeah, it's Rider. I have a real mess here I need cleaned up. I need it now. This has the potential to be very bad for the community. Can you flash on over? That's fine. Yeah, yeah… yes. Thanks, Rihanna."

"Rihanna?" I asked, as he placed the phone back in his pocket.

"Not that Rihanna."

"Oh." I folded my arms. "It would explain all the record sales. How long will it take for her to—" I yelped as green lightning struck the center of the room and a short, curvy, brown-skinned woman dressed in black leather stepped out of the billowy smoke.

"Was the lightning necessary?" Rider asked, shaking his head.

"You asked for me to flash on over. This is how I flash," she replied, full of sass as she stood hands on hips and craned her neck to look over at Dex's body. She scrunched her nose. "You know I love you all to pieces, Rider, baby, but you also know I don't just be cleaning up bodies all willy-nilly." She gave me a good once-over before turning her attention back to Rider. "Was this legit?"

"He attempted to rape her. She stopped him."

"Aw, well, that's as legit as it gets. Good for you, honey," she said to me before stepping over to Dex's body. She raised her hands and paused, looking at me. "Do you want the penis?"

"The what?"

"The penis." She blinked at me like I was stupid. "The dick? The wang, the chub, the Mr. Happy…"

"I know what a penis is," I said. "Why would I want his?" Obviously, had I wanted it to begin with, I wouldn't have killed the guy.

"Lots of women I help in these situations keep the penis," she explained. "I don't always ask what for, but I know they do different things with them. Chop them up and put them in stew, tack them to a dartboard, mail them to the wives, keep it as a trophy…"

"She doesn't want the penis," Rider said, pinching the bridge of his nose. "Can you just get rid of the evidence?"

"That's what you're paying me for," Rihanna answered and closed her eyes. Green light poured out of her hands and enveloped Dex's body. She seemed to vibrate as the green light grew in size and brightness. Beads of sweat popped out on her forehead, and I looked over at Rider. He reached out and squeezed my hand, reassuring me this would work. We continued watching the witch as the light grew, eventually filling the whole room. I gripped Rider's hand, and he pulled me close, holding me snug against his side as the witch worked her magic. I gasped as the green magic started to spiral up my body.

"She's just getting the blood off you and mending the dress," Rider explained softly against my ear. "She's thorough."

The room seemed to pop with static electricity as everything was bathed in green and then there was a snap and the green light was sucked back into Rihanna's hands. She rocked back on her heels but caught herself. "It is done," she said, standing where Dex's body had been. The carpet was cream-colored again and even my heels had been repaired. I walked over to scoop them up off the floor at the foot of Dex's bed. "Where is Dex?"

"Hell, I imagine," Rihanna replied. "I don't think they take too kindly to men who use their willies as assault weapons upstairs."

"I meant his body," I clarified as I slipped into the shoes.

"Oh, girl, you do not want to know that." She shook her head, her lips pressed together, and wiped the sweat from her brow.

"How are you feeling?" Rider asked her.

"I'm feeling like I need some money." She held her hand out and rubbed her fingers together. Rider grinned and withdrew several large bills from the wallet in his back pocket. "Thanks, Rihanna."

"As long as the money flows, so does my magic," she said, winking. "And you know I'll always come through for a friend. Speaking of which, there are security cameras all over the halls and lobby, even the elevator. I don't know the specifics of what happened, but I imagine your girl was seen coming up in here. Tell me what you need done and we can talk price."

"It was a party," Rider said. "Can you make it look like she left long before the last guests did?"

"Sure thing, honey. How about you?"

"I came in through the window, and we'll be going out it."

"What?" I walked over to the window and looked

down. Way down. "I don't even know how you got up here in the first place. I'm not going out that window."

"We're vampires. We jump. We land on our feet."

I looked at him, blinking, trying to determine if he was serious or if he'd lost his mind.

"I'm with you, honey," Rihanna told me. "Men are always trying to jump out windows and scale buildings and stuff. Rider, walk this woman out of the building like a gentleman and I'll just erase it off the surveillance. I'll make it look like she left alone well ahead of the last to leave, and I'll erase you altogether... for only about twenty more of those bills."

Rider shook his head and passed the money over.

"For a little more, I could just flash you out."

"We'll walk, thanks." He smiled. "I have bills to pay too."

Rihanna winked. "Always a pleasure."

"I'm sure it is."

"I'm sorry this cost you so much," I said as we stepped out onto the street a little while later. I'd held my breath the entire time, sure security would stop us, especially since the doorman frowned upon seeing Rider step out of the penthouse. "Are you sure Rihanna will do as she said?"

"Rihanna is a pro, and a damn good one," he said. "She's expensive, but worth every penny. Don't worry about it."

"Dex is still dead, isn't he?" I asked, my voice low even though we'd already stepped out of earshot of the security and were rounding the corner.

"Yeah, he's not coming back. His body won't be found. No body, no crime."

"So I just go to work and act like I don't know anything when he doesn't show up?"

"That'd be less suspicious than just not showing up yourself, unless you disappeared completely too." He looked down at me as we strolled down the alley. "I can help you if that's what you want to do. I can run a business from anywhere."

"I thought this was kind of your city."

"Yeah, it is. I can leave someone in charge here and take over another territory."

"Sounds like something that would require a lot of fighting."

"It usually does."

"And you'd do that for me?"

"Of course I would."

I looked down, realized he was holding my hand. It had felt so natural I hadn't even paid any attention. I withdrew my hand, missing the warmth of his instantaneously. "Thanks for helping me out tonight, but nothing has changed. I shouldn't have called on you. I'm sorry I did."

"You can always call on me, Danni."

"No," I snapped, then took a deep breath. "No, Rider. I can't, and you can't keep helping me. It's best that we not see each other."

"What are you saying?" He reached for me, but I stepped away. "Danni. What's going on?"

"She's trying to win the game," a voice that sent chills up my spine said, its owner stepping out of the shadows. "Nice try with the whole pretending the two of you don't feel anything for each other scheme, sweetheart, but I couldn't help but notice the second you were in trouble you called for him and of course he came running."

"Ryan," Rider growled, stepping forward to shield me with his body. "Leave her alone. This is between you and me."

Selander Ryan laughed as more shapes separated from the shadows. He'd brought his people to battle. I felt power emanate from Rider and knew he was sending out the bat signal, no pun intended, calling for his own backup. "I have waited far too long to be able to witness you finally truly suffer."

"I suffered worse than you that night, Ryan. My love was pure."

"She was everything to me!" Selander Ryan yelled, his eyes flashing red. "She was to be my queen, and you killed her!"

"You'd turned her into everything she hated! What you felt for her was unnatural!"

"It was the most natural thing in the world! You are the unnatural one, forcing people to live by your ideas of morality, yet you kill, don't you? You pretend to protect people and to value life, but you took hers!"

"I freed her of the hell you'd caged her in!"

Ryan lunged, his face a mottled red as anger took over his body. Rider pushed me out of the way and turned just in time to deflect the blow and deliver one of his own. The two of them fought hard and dirty, moving in a blur as they pummeled each other. Meanwhile, Ryan's people moved in on me. He'd brought a group of incubi and a few burly men I assumed to be some sort of shifters. They were all dressed in T-shirts and slacks, whereas I was in a long evening gown and high heels. As if the odds weren't already stacked against me. I risked a quick glance at Rider, saw he was still busy with Ryan, and sent up a quick prayer as the first man lunged for me.

I raised my arm as Rider had shown me, blocked his punch, and threw one of my own. His head snapped back, but he didn't fall. I shook my hand out as pain ran the length of my arm and ducked when he threw another punch at me. Once his fist went over my head, I rose, connecting my head with his stomach, and this time knocked him back on his ass just as I was grabbed from behind.

I heard a roar and looked to see Rider jump free of his tussle with Ryan quick enough to grab my attacker's head and effortlessly twist it, breaking his neck. Ryan surged toward me, only to be knocked back by Rider as he jumped in front of me and then the two were back to exchanging blows.

"Danni, duck!" I heard a familiar voice order, and I dutifully followed the command, luckily, right before a silver dagger flew over my head and embedded itself in the chest of the shifter that had been about to attack me from behind. Nannette pulled the dagger free and flung it into another shifter, this time planting it in the center of his face. "Here," she said, passing me a silver dagger she'd had strapped to her leg. "Use it on the shifters. Leave the incubi to us."

The cavalry had arrived, thank goodness. I recognized some of the other vampires from Rider's bar, and the Asian man from the garage, who apparently was also a shifter, I realized as he turned into a tiger midair and clamped his jaws onto an incubus's head before twisting his body, slamming the incubus on the ground and proceeding to eat him. I was so entranced by what I was seeing I didn't notice Ryan's man lunging for me from behind until he'd grabbed my clavicle. Acting purely on reflex, I turned and rammed the dagger in the man's stomach. I jerked the blade up, gutting him like a fish, and as more blood poured onto my dress, I hoped Rider hadn't paid Rihanna extra to clean the blood off of it earlier because it would have been a waste of money. I glanced around, looking for the witch as my gutted attacker fell to the ground, but she wasn't there. I guessed she just cleaned up messes, leaving the actual battle to others without magic.

All around me, bodies fell as both parties continued to fight. Some Ryan's, some Rider's. I helped where I could, using the dagger to slice as many of Ryan's men as I could, but I was nowhere near as elite a fighter as the others Rider had called on. I made a mental note to take more lessons if I survived the night. Each body that fell to the ground left a cut in me. Rider wouldn't blame me for their deaths, but I knew that once again, he had lost people because of me. Bodies continued to drop until I was lifted in the air.

Everyone stopped and watched as my body was yanked over to where Selander Ryan stood, smiling like the devil himself. Covered in blood, Rider watched in horror as Selander used his power to suspend me in the air. "Why such surprise?" Selander Ryan asked. "We both marked her. She is as much mine as yours. You tried to save her from what you claim to be a completely immoral existence, but so full of self-loathing for what you yourself are, you never forced her will. You never broke her. I don't have such issues."

"Let her go," Rider ordered him, his voice a growl. "I swear I will rip your heart out if you hurt her."

"Will you?" Ryan laughed. "We've been fighting for centuries. You would have killed me by now if you could, but you're too soft. After all this time, you still value family and can't bring yourself to break the promise you made to her, even though it eats you alive every time I draw a breath. Your own guilt for taking her life is what guarantees I will never die. You are the only one powerful enough to kill me, and you can't even do it."

"Just kill me!" Rider screamed. "You hate me so much, you evil bastard, take my life! She's nothing to you!"

"But she's everything to you," Ryan said, turning his finger in the air, and my neck moved similarly. He was puppeteering me, twisting my neck at an angle that brought tears to my eyes.

"Kill her and you'll have nothing on me," Rider said, projecting strength into his voice, but I was sure I wasn't the only one who heard the fear beneath it.

"I don't want to kill her," Ryan told him. "You took my queen. I'm taking yours. I won't enjoy her as much, but I'll enjoy what it does to you to see her follow my every command."

You can only serve one master.

The words popped into my head, and I cursed myself for being so stubborn before. This was exactly what Rider and Eliza had warned me about. I'd been so afraid of being controlled by the man who never would have hurt me, I'd allowed the one who would the access he needed. Hopefully, it wasn't too late.

"You can't make me do anything," I growled from behind teeth gritted against pain. "You are not my master!" I said, my voice growing stronger as Ryan's hold weakened. "I am not a succubus."

"No!" Ryan cried in rage as he tried to tighten his mental hold on me.

"I am a vampire," I declared, my voice even stronger, "and I serve Rider. Rider is my master! I belong to only him!"

Selander Ryan's hold over me snapped, and I fell to the ground as indescribable energy surged through my body. I'd denied Ryan, voiding his mark on me completely. I belonged to Rider, a full vampire, and the first in his line.

"Now I'll kill the bitch!" Ryan screeched, furious I'd bested him, as he grabbed me by the throat. I heard a guttural cry of pure rage and dropped to the ground as Rider collided with Ryan. I watched in complete shock as he reached into Ryan's chest, his whole body glowing with yellow power, and pulled the incubus's heart out of his chest just as he'd said he would do.

Selander Ryan clutched at the hole in his chest and fell backward, his mouth open in surprise as he hit the ground and stared up at the man he'd just said could never kill him. Tears streamed down Rider's face as he fell to his knees, his enemy's heart in his hand. "Forgive me, Mother," he said, his voice a rough whisper as he crushed the organ.

He threw his head back and let out a roar so full of pain and agony it was as if part of him were dying with the incubus. The yellow glow around him pulsated and suddenly my mind was filled with images.

Two young boys ran through a field. One was dark headed with eyes the color of sapphire, the other had white hair with dark eyes. A beautiful woman ran behind them, laughing. I had seen her before. Many more images followed of the boys playing together, the woman always nearby, watching them with smiling eyes, but then the images changed as the boys grew older. They no longer played. They fought. The woman didn't smile. She worried.

Images flew by so fast I could barely latch on to any of them, and what I did see didn't make sense, or was just so disturbing I didn't want to find any sense in it. The images flashed by faster and I saw Rider end the woman's life as he'd just ended Ryan's. Then I saw the two fighting over and over, breaking bones and drawing blood, their apparel changing with each passing decade, but every time they stopped just short of death as Rider heard the last words the woman said before he crushed her heart.

The images disappeared as Selander Ryan died on the ground next to me, and I looked into Rider's eyes, knowing he'd just killed his own brother to save my life..

NINETEEN

Two weeks after Dex had vanished, his scummy brother, Chad, stepped in to run the office and was a complete jerk. He'd immediately zeroed in on Gina, who'd actually filed a sexual harassment suit against him. Gina might be a bit loose, but she was no home-wrecker. She barely remembered Selander Ryan and didn't seem to have been harmed by whatever he had done to her. Chad remembered him. He was angry as hell that Nocturnal Inc. had shut down operations before we even ran the ads and tried to take that anger out on me, who he remembered being the last person at Dex's penthouse the night he'd gone missing, but there was video proof that I'd left before he had. He didn't understand it, but you couldn't very well argue with proof like that. When he'd attempted to release his frustration by yelling at me right on the floor in front of everyone, I'd taken the resignation letter I'd just grabbed off the printer and shoved it into his mouth before scooping up my things and making my exit to the sound of applause. As far as walking out on jobs went, it wasn't a bad way to go.

I didn't know what I would do for money, but I had enough in my savings account to last a couple months and

I had two weeks of unused vacation pay coming my way, so I wasn't that worried. If things got bad, I could always clear out my 401K instead of rolling it over into another account. Money wasn't my concern.

I missed him.

I hadn't seen Rider since the night he'd saved my life by killing his own flesh and blood, something he'd had to do twice. When I looked into his eyes that night, I'd seen pure pain. He knew I'd seen it. As many times as I'd accused him of invading my mind, I didn't think he'd ever done anything like I'd done that night. I'd seen his memories, relived them with him as if they were my own. I hadn't meant to, but I had and I couldn't unsee what I'd seen. I didn't know if he'd ever forgive me for that. He certainly hadn't contacted me since, but I felt him. Our bond was stronger now that I was his and his alone.

My vampire abilities were stronger now too, which could explain why I hadn't seen anyone guarding my building since the night before Dex's party. He knew I could take care of myself if I had to. I had a standing weekly session with Eliza and was back on the bagged blood. It was disgusting, but it did the job. I was pretty sure the succubus bite was completely gone, but I couldn't bring myself to find a person to feed off of. It just didn't feel right drinking from anyone other than Rider.

Two weeks after I'd quit Prince Advertising, I found myself out walking in Rider's neck of the woods. It was late, an hour away from dawn, and I should have headed for home, but I couldn't fight the pull. I felt him so much deeper now. He was so tired, growing more tired with each night that passed. He was in pain, and not the kind that needed medical attention. He was suffering worse than that. I found myself in front of the bar not long before closing time. His pain overwhelmed me, drawing me like a moth to a flame, but what if he didn't want to see me? He hadn't reached out to me.

Danni.

I smiled, just a little, the mere sound of his voice in my head warming my soul. My eyes grew wet. I'd missed it so much.

You are always welcome here.

I entered the bar, immediately drawing the attention of the bartender who happened to be the Asian shifter, and a waitress collecting glasses off abandoned tables. She eyed me curiously, and I sensed she knew who I was and was checking me out. The bartender looked up from wiping the bar down and nodded at me, stoic as usual. I recalled him eating the incubus and looked away, wondering if I'd ever get that image out of my head. I think what bothered me the most about it was that it really didn't bother me anymore.

I went through the door at the back of the room and climbed the stairs to Rider's private quarters above the bar. I took a deep breath and pushed the magically locked door open. It gave for me and I stepped inside to find Rider in bed, shirtless, the silk sheets covering him from his waist down. If not for how tired he looked, and the lingering heartache in his eyes, he would have looked like an appetizer lying there.

The apartment was just as it had been the last time I'd visited, except the portrait over the bar was down. "She was your mother."

"Yes."

"I'm sorry." He didn't respond and I looked his way to see him looking back at me, studying me. "I'll leave if you want me to."

He shook his head. "I will never want you to."

I frowned, confused. "You've stayed away since that night. I thought you were mad at me."

It was his turn to frown. "Why would I be mad at you?"

I shrugged. "I made you do something that hurt you."

He patted the bed next to him. "Come here, Danni."

I crossed over to the bed and sat on the edge, kicking my shoes off before swinging my legs over to lie next to him. I kept my clothes on, not sure where this was going or how long I'd be staying. He wrapped his arm around my shoulders, pulling me against him. "Why do you think that?"

"You killed... your brother... to save me."

"He was my half-brother, actually, but yes, I did, and I'd do it again."

"But I saw you. I saw the two of you fighting over and over and you never killed him. You could have, but you didn't. You always stopped yourself, honoring your mother's last request to save him."

His arm tightened around me and I feared I'd said too much, opened a wound best left alone. "My mother was a good woman," he finally said. "She had the purest heart and an innocent soul. I noticed the darkness in Ryan as he grew older, but she tried to look past it."

"Ryan wasn't his last name?"

"His middle. At least it was then."

"I'm sorry. I didn't mean to interrupt."

He kissed my temple. "You can always ask me questions, just not my age or anything else that could be dangerous for you to know." I felt him smile, though it wasn't filled with much joy. "Ryan got involved with a witch, a very dark witch. In time, his associates grew even darker. I'm not even sure how it happened, but he was turned into an incubus. I think he actually sought them out, wanting the dark power of being such an evil thing. Finally, he was the more powerful brother, or so he thought. He was immortal and strong, but I fought him with everything I had when he came for my mother. I kept him at bay for a while, but I was only a man then, and my mother loved him still. He was her son, even if another woman had given birth to him. He was my blood and her husband's blood, and that was enough for her. She loved him as if he came from her own womb. Despite my best efforts to protect her, he eventually succeeded in turning her. She was the most virtuous woman I knew, and so modest. It killed me knowing the things she was doing as a succubus, the things he made her do, and the things he eventually did with her. He'd taken the pure love of a mother and son and turned it into something more evil than the hell his kind had originally come from."

"I'm so sorry," I whispered, unable to speak in a full voice. My stomach was so full of nausea as I realized what he was telling me. Had his mother actually bore Ryan, I would have been sick.

He took a deep breath and continued. "I never quit hunting him or others like him. Incubi, vampires, werewolves. They plagued the country then. I and a team of hunters went after every one of them. I got good at it, though I could never get him. I got close, close enough to scare him, so he thought to make me join him, but not as an incubus. My brother resented me long before he became that vile creature. He befriended a particularly nasty nest of vampires and set a trap for me. He was there, laughing, watching as I was turned."

"He set up his own brother?"

"His heart had gone black long before that. The hunters I'd traveled with wiped out the nest shortly after, but spared me because I did not fight them. I actually helped them. The change had turned me into a vampire, but I did not lose my conscience or morality. Maybe I would have had my sire stuck around long enough to control me, but he'd been one of the first to die when the hunters struck. Elias Quimby spared me, and made a pact with me that as long as I didn't hurt his kind, he would spare any vampire I vouched for. I held that pact with him and his family line until Barnaby chose to break it."

"Because of me."

"No, that was all him. He always did have a streak of something bad in him. The man lacked honor."

"You went after Ryan after you were turned?"

"I heard he had announced he was taking a queen. My mother. *Our mother.* It was the vilest thing I could imagine, and I knew the woman my mother had been would rather die than be part of such a union. I tracked them down, and I spared her the vulgarity the only way I could, freeing her from his sick, twisted relationship with her, and from the profanity of what she had become. I had every intention of killing him too, but she begged me with her dying breath to spare him, to find a way to save him. Even after what he'd done to her, she loved him that much. Her heart was so big, so genuine, even that evil thrust upon it couldn't blacken it completely. I honored her request until I could honor it no more."

"I'm sorry." Tears fell from my eyes. Rider tipped my chin and looked deeply at me.

"Why do you cry for him?"

"I don't," I answered. "I cry for you. I hate being the reason you had to kill him. You made a promise to the woman you loved so much and kept it for so long. Then I came along and ruined everything. I saw how much it hurt you. I feel how it hurts you now. It's all my fault. He thought he could use me to make you suffer, and he did."

"None of that is your fault."

"I could have rejected his mark, given myself over to you when you first told me about the two marks."

"It doesn't matter. He still would have sought you out. It might have been harder, but the end result would have been the same. We were always going to have a final faceoff. He was always looking for a way to destroy me, and he nearly did, but I won, Danni. I won. Not him."

I wiped my tears and studied Rider, noting the pain and tiredness in his eyes. "You broke your promise to your mother and killed your brother. You still hurt, you haven't even slept since that night. I can feel it. How did you win?"

"My mother wanted me to save him. I couldn't save him the way she wanted me to. There was no way to make him stop being what he was," he explained. "Killing him saved him as it saved my mother, or maybe it didn't but it stopped him from hurting others, which I know would make her happy. And I promised you I wouldn't let him hurt you."

"I know."

"And the promise I made to you was just as important as the promise I made to her, because I love you too."

I opened my mouth and just let it hang there as I stared into his face, searching for traces of humor. He had to be joking.

"You know it's true," he said, tipping my chin up to close my gaping mouth.

I shook my head. "You've been so quiet. You haven't checked on me, reached out to me…"

"I haven't slept in weeks, slowly going out of my mind because I need you near me." He brushed my hair away from my face and kissed my forehead. "I killed my brother in front of you and you saw me kill my mother. I never wanted you to see anything like that, to know that part of me. I didn't want you to know I shared blood with someone as evil as Ryan. I didn't know how you would feel, if you would be frightened by me, disgusted… so I gave you space. I've told you over and over I am always a call away, no matter what."

"I thought you were angry I invaded your mind and saw those memories."

"You didn't do that intentionally, and even if you did, I wouldn't be mad. I don't think I could ever truly be mad at you. Irritated, maybe. Frustrated, especially when you don't listen to me when I'm trying to protect you or when…" He laughed a little. "All these centuries I've been alive and I don't think anyone has ever made me so jealous. I know I'm not the man you wanted—"

I remembered the fiasco that had occurred the last time I was in his bed and groaned. "Rider, I never thought you were second runner-up to anyone, and what you heard in my head that night was just what I do when I'm scared. The truth is, you were taking my clothes off and I was terrified you wouldn't like what you saw and I wouldn't please you because shocker, I've only had sex with one guy and he made fun of me to all his friends afterwards. That was just nerves and stupidity rambling around in my head. And yeah, I was excited Dex asked me out, and I'd daydreamed about it, but I would have fantasized about any guy that had that office. He was rich, good-looking and successful, everything my mother, grandmother, and sister act like I could never have and I'm just pathetic enough to have cared, but I don't care about that anymore. Honestly, the more time I spent with him the less I liked him, and I spent every moment at that party wishing I was with you and hoping like hell Selander Ryan didn't find out because the thought of something happening to you—" I choked on a sob and shed a fresh batch of silent tears. Rider wiped them away with his fingers.

"I need to know the name of this man you slept with."

"Why?"

"He saw you naked and therefore has to die." His mouth turned up into a grin.

"I never took my shirt off."

Rider laughed and rested his forehead against mine. "I don't know why any man would not be pleased by you or what they could even make fun of. I highly suspect you project your insecurities so strongly, you attract such bastards. Your insecurity is the only flaw I can find in you. Even your damn stubbornness is somehow endearing to me, and I aim to fix that one flaw."

"Oh really?"

"When I'm through with you, Danni Keller, you're going to know how beautiful and incredibly sexy you are." He kissed me, long, deep and with enough intensity to curl my toes. He broke away, sighing as I felt the sun rise. My eyelids grew heavy. His looked about to snap shut. "But first, you're going to lie here next to me and allow me to hold you in my arms while I finally get some sleep, knowing you're safe right here with me."

I shimmied out of my jeans and slid under the covers, allowing him to spoon me from behind. "You're naked."

"Yep," he said, kissing the curve of my ear. "Don't worry about it. You will be too once the sun goes back down. Now get some rest."

My insecurity reared its ugly head once more. "I don't think I have the succubus venom anymore. My bite might not—"

His throaty chuckle cut me off. "Sweetheart, you don't need venom to send a current of ecstasy through me. Just putting your lips on me has always done the trick. Now sleep."

I smiled and settled in. I still had a ton of questions for him, and for myself as well. I had no idea where I was going to work or how I was going to handle my family, let alone the rest of my long life as a vampire. I knew I was safe, and that I loved the vampire holding me in his arms. Maybe I'd eventually find the nerve to tell him that one day. After all, I had a century or more to work up to it.

ABOUT THE AUTHOR

Crystal-Rain Love is a romance author specializing in paranormal, suspense, and contemporary subgenres. Her author career began by winning a contest to be one of Sapphire Blue Publishing's debut authors in 2008. She snagged a multi-book contract with Imajinn Books that same year, going on to be published by The Wild Rose Press and eventually venturing out into indie publishing. She resides in the South with her three children and enough pets to host a petting zoo. When she's not writing she can usually be found creating unique 3D cakes, hiking, reading, or spending way too much time on FaceBook.

Find out more about her at www.crystalrainlove.com

Printed in Great Britain
by Amazon

28929293R00146